A SERIES OF MOMENTS

From the Moment We Met

M.L. BROOME

TERRACOTTA DRAGON ARTS

A Series of Moments
From the Moment We Met
Copyright © J. E. Soper 2019
All rights reserved.

Digital Edition MARCH 2019 ISBN: 978-1-7338964-0-5
Print Edition ISBN: 978-1-7338964-1-2

Publishing by:
TerraCotta Dragon Arts
Cover Art by:
Suzana Stankovic, LSDdesign
Editing by:
Emily Tamayo Maher
Interior Design & Formatting by:
Suzana Stankovic, LSDdesign

"The best motivators are ones that equally inspire and awaken you. Trouble is, many of us never realize we're asleep."

~ J.E. Soper

TO THOSE WHO TAUGHT ME TO NEVER STOP
SEARCHING FOR THE MAGIC

TO LILLY & JACOB,
WHO BROUGHT THE MAGIC TO LIFE

"You have to keep breaking your heart until it opens."

*~ **Rumi***

CONTENTS

TITLE PAGE.. I
DEDICATION.. V
EPIGRAPH.. VII
ACKNOWLEDGEMENTS.. XI

CHAPTER 1.. 1
CHAPTER 2.. 11
CHAPTER 3.. 22
CHAPTER 4.. 35
CHAPTER 5.. 45
CHAPTER 6.. 54
CHAPTER 7.. 64
CHAPTER 8.. 77
CHAPTER 9.. 84
CHAPTER 10.. 93
CHAPTER 11.. 101
CHAPTER 12.. 116
CHAPTER 13.. 136
CHAPTER 14.. 155
CHAPTER 15.. 168
CHAPTER 16.. 180
CHAPTER 17.. 190
CHAPTER 18.. 199

ABOUT THE AUTHOR.. 217

ACKNOWLEDGEMENTS

My love of writing extends back as far as my memory, along with my fear of releasing any of my work into the world. It took a small army to get to this point, and I'm forever grateful for each and every one of these amazing souls in my life.

Adam, you've been my rock for the last seven years. You never questioned my choices, you simply held my hand and reassured me that success was imminent if I would only try. Above all, you never stopped loving me… and I can be pretty difficult to love sometimes.

Mom, you wanted me to pursue my writing since I was a child. Sorry

it took so long to follow your wisdom.

Emily, you began as my writing coach and editor—now you're one of my truest and dearest friends. Thanks for having my back throughout this journey and forcing this 'baby bird' to test her wings.

Sarita, you've always believed in me, even when I didn't believe in myself. Especially when I didn't believe in myself. I'm forever grateful for your guidance and camaraderie. To the moon and back.

Joel, you and I have weathered the decades together. We have celebrated our successes and cried over our losses. There has been one constant in these 25 years—our friendship.

Eliza, you are my Anam Cara. I need not say more than that.

To Terry, Lianne and Elizabeth, thank you for dealing with my endless barrage of questions. You took the time to read my story and give me honest feedback—but that is the kind of friends you are—beyond amazing.

To Suzana, your design work is superb, but it is your kind heart and endless patience that is truly award-winning.

To my ever-present cheerleading squad, who along with the others mentioned above, kept my head above water when I was drowning in my insecurity and doubt. Much love Scott, Traci, Jason and Jenny.

To Poppo—I did it—just like your buddy Jack. I know it's your spirit that flows through my veins and helped me reach the finish line. Meet you on the other side.

CHAPTER ONE

Jacob

I f one more person walked past him and said, "better luck next time" or "you should have won," he'd punch them in the throat. Externally, Jacob fit the picture of a dignified, gracious actor. But internally, he was seething.

He wheeled his suitcase towards the airline gate, returning to London defeated instead of a celebrated victor. Granted, most folks wouldn't see it that way.

Jacob was the definition of a Hollywood success story—lead roles in blockbuster films, million-dollar endorsement deals and adoring fans who would endure a hailstorm for an autograph. Despite these accolades, he felt like an utter failure.

He was snapped from his reverie by a squeaky voice at his side. "Excuse me, Mr. Edmonton, may I have your autograph?" Gazing down, he saw a girl of about six with a wide toothless grin; she reminded him of his niece, Elizabeth.

For the first time in the last twelve hours, his smile was genuine as he knelt by the little girl. "I'm honored. What's your name?"

"Susan."

Jacob chuckled as it came out "Thuthan", skewed by a lack of front teeth. His gaze drifted to Susan's mother, ogling him like an alligator eyeballing a ribeye. He always enjoyed a good romp, and she looked like a willing participant, but Jacob was in no mood, even for sex. Ignoring her carnal stare, he signed Susan's paper, adding a smiley face below his signature.

The little girl beamed, first at the autograph and then at him. "My mommy says you're the most handsome actor ever and she wouldn't have dumped you for that Latin singer."

Jacob glanced back to the mother, her face paling at her daughter's candor. "Come Susan, let's leave this nice man alone." With a nod, the duo departed down the airport corridor.

Jacob arrived at his gate and slumped into a seat, pulling his hat over his dark blonde curls. He hoped the beard and long hair would disguise him from the public eye, but his attempt was moot. His reputation in the last few months preceded him, thanks to the relentless media tracking his every move.

His life wasn't always media fodder. Jacob spent years training to be a serious actor whose primary—and only—focus was his craft. Then he met Victoria, and life as he knew it unraveled.

Victoria—one of the biggest names in show business—was a larger-than-life singer both on and off the stage. It didn't matter that her talent was mediocre; Victoria was a marketing legend. Her entourage tailed her everywhere, with assistants fulfilling every whim from applying makeup to walking her teacup chihuahua.

Her personality was exhausting and demands relentless, but Victoria epitomized beauty. She was an Amazon at six feet, with platinum waves cascading over her silicone implants. But it was her eyes, emerald green too bright to be natural that stopped you dead in your tracks. And Jacob should know, she hooked him the moment their eyes connected at a charity event.

Jacob's friends bombarded him with warnings when he returned from the bar with Victoria by his side. Her reputation as a femme fatale was well deserved. She possessed an extensive line of past lovers, and once they outlived their usefulness, were swept into a black hole beyond moral and critical reprieve. God help anyone who angered her; she had a legion of fans serving as ruthless foot soldiers, defending her honor at all costs. It was her very own teenage, hormonally-charged Mafioso.

But it didn't matter. Warnings from friends fell on deaf ears once Jacob tasted her forbidden fruit. Her sexual prowess should have been a red flag for Jacob, she had more tricks than a prostitute. It was a relationship built on pure lust, as fiery and superficial as the town in which they worked.

Their romance burned out within months, and the media buzzed around the dying carcass before Jacob knew the cause of death. It turned out monogamy was only a requirement on his end of the deal. Victoria had screwed at least six other men during their courtship.

He swore he would never fall prey to the wiles of a woman again, his life would be filled with unforgettable films and nameless fucks, a rotating lineup of starlets and models. The rotating lineup was easy enough. He never wanted for company, but after a couple weeks in bed with a different woman every night, the thrill was gone. To get even with Victoria, he behaved exactly as she had, but it left him cold and empty. Hell, he couldn't even be bothered with the last woman; he sent her packing from his hotel room only fifteen minutes after her arrival. She was as stimulating as a post-it note.

Time to refocus on what was important, his acting career. But he soon realized the awful truth; the world now considered him a media darling instead of a serious thespian.

Jacob was the shoo-in for the Best Actor award. His latest movie was box office gold; a fast-paced adventure about a doctor working in Africa amongst the toils of revolution. The movie grossed 150 million dollars the first week, while critics and fans alike raved about the film and its leading man.

However, his breakup with Victoria surfaced in the tabloids, along with eyewitness accounts of Jacob pleading for a second chance. It didn't matter that he never begged Victoria to return; the media concocted their version of events and the public ate it up. His reputation, carefully sculpted through the years, was ruined.

Jacob's buzzing phone interrupted his mental pity party, but he shut it off without looking at the screen. He wasn't in the mood for a pep talk with his agent. A few seconds later, it buzzed again, and once again Jacob shut it off without a glance. Only after the phone vibrated a third time, with palpable urgency, did he look at the screen.

It was Audrey, his sister-in-law. Why in hell was she calling? She made no secret of her contempt for Jacob and his egoist lifestyle. They were close once, in fact, he convinced his parents that his sister could still be the quintessential daughter with the white picket fence and 2.5 kids, even with a wife instead of a husband.

Sighing, Jacob answered the phone. "Yeah?"

"Jakey? It's Janie. I misplaced my phone, and I wanted to check on you." His baby sister, Janie—the kindest soul he'd ever known—choked out her words.

Sitting straighter, he adjusted the phone. "Janie, are you okay? You sound out of breath."

"I'm hiding from Audrey. If she sees who I called when I borrowed her phone—" Janie broke off in a flurry of coughing.

Jacob chuckled at an image of Audrey chasing Janie down a London street, yelling about contemptible siblings. Janie's innocuous cough cut his laughter short, bringing him back to the conversation. "Are you sick?"

"Who knows? I've had this awful cold for the last couple weeks. I can't seem to shake it. Mum made me her famous ginger concoction. Remember when she used to feed us that mess? I swore the virus would run away screaming at one whiff of that glop."

"Mum was never renowned for her culinary skills, or her nursing ones. Have you been to a doctor? You might need an antibiotic."

Jacob could see Janie shaking her head in disgust; her opinion of Western medicine hovered on an even par with the flu virus. "I'll be fine. Enough about me, how are you? I can't believe they chose Howard Banks over you. That movie was atrocious. Who cares about a colony of mutated humans on Mars, anyway?"

"The Academy Board, apparently." Jacob smiled in spite of himself;

Janie always cheered him up, even in his bleakest moments. "It's fine, Janie. I'll be in London for the next month; get to spend time with family."

"I would love that Jakey, Elizabeth misses you so much. You haven't seen her in two months, since Boxing Day. I miss you too, so does Audrey."

"Like hell I do." Audrey's voice cut into the conversation, her tone biting.

"Audrey!" Janie hissed, but once Audrey opened her mouth, there was no closing it.

The line jostled, and Audrey's voice boomed in Jacob's ear. "Sorry to hear about your loss; perhaps now that you're one of us commoners again, Elizabeth might finally get to see her uncle? Or will you be too busy flitting around the globe with another silicone-filled floozy?"

Jacob's jaw gritted, but his tone remained even. "No floozy globe flitting for the next several weeks, Audrey. You're in luck, I'll be only a few kilometers from you."

"I can hardly wait." Her sarcasm was unmistakable. "You'll have to explain to Elizabeth who you are since she so rarely sees you."

Jacob had a biting retort at the tip of his tongue when his sister wrestled the phone from her wife's hands. "Jakey I'm sorry; Audrey is so tired with the business and Elizabeth, and now me being sick...she doesn't mean what she says."

"Yes, she does, Little Bit, she means every word. I'm about to board. I'll call you when I land at Heathrow."

"Sure Jakey, I love you, big brother—"

Jacob stared at the phone. He ended the call before he could return the sentiment. He adored his sister, but he wasn't demonstrative. Victoria had been an exception to the rule and look where that landed him. His public affections toward her had cost him his career; a mistake he wouldn't make again. It was far safer to keep his feelings buttoned up with his head down, nose to the grindstone.

The ticket agent's voice boomed through the seating area. "Our first-class passengers are now welcome to board, first-class passengers only."

Sighing, Jacob grabbed his bag and headed to the plane.

Lilly

"I assume that's nursing related?" Lilly smirked at her co-worker behind the nurses station.

Sabina shoved the newspaper into a drawer, her hands fluttering to her face in mock surprise. "Of course, Ms. Staver, what else would I be reading during my shift?"

Lilly chuckled, pulling the paper from the drawer. "Hmm, the stock market crashed again, bombing in Iran, Jacob Edmonton loses acting award to Howard Banks—you're catching up on your market analysis, aren't you?"

Sabina snatched the newspaper, smoothing it in front of her. "I don't understand how he lost. Aces High was one of the highest grossing movies last year, and Jacob is so sexy, it ought to be illegal."

"Which movie was this again?"

"Which movie?" Sabina gasped. "He's a handsome doctor fighting a jewel cartel in Africa; he even learned Krio. Did I say how sexy he looked?"

"You might have mentioned it," Lilly chuckled as she perused a patient chart. "I can't keep those movies straight; they're all the same to me. Same plot, same premise, same tired sex scenes."

"Hmm. Jacob Edmonton is a fine piece of ass, even if he is a little too skinny for my taste. But damn, that mouth; he could kiss me anytime…and anywhere." Sabina cooed, fluffing her mane of tight curls.

Lilly burst out laughing, hiding it behind her hand. "Good to know."

"Do you even know what he looks like?"

Lilly shrugged, flipping through the patient chart. "I think so? He's tall and blonde, right?"

"He is more than tall and blonde; he is a Grecian god." Sabina thrust her phone under Lilly's nose. The display showed a man with piercing blue eyes and a smile that could melt an iceberg.

Lilly tried to appear disinterested in the photograph, but the actor was mouthwatering. Something about his potent gaze made her weak in the knees, and this was only a picture. "I'm not into blonde men," she lied.

"Is that a fact? Then why are you blushing? What kind of naughty thoughts are you having about Mr. Edmonton right now?"

Lilly felt her face go bright red. "Shush! I'm not having any dirty thoughts."

"Right, not picturing him butt ass naked, six-pack on display, pushing you against a wall and having his way with you?"

I'm picturing much more than that, but hell, it's a start, Lilly thought, focusing her gaze on the patient chart.

"You've read that same page for the last five minutes."

Lilly snapped the binder shut, yanking out another patient chart and flipping through it with aimless abandon. "Quiet, or I'll make you work overtime."

"Admit it, he's hot as hell."

"I told you, I don't like blonde men."

"Girl, how are we friends? You'll overlook all his perfection because of his hair color? I'll buy him some black hair dye; does that help?"

Lilly giggled, hugging her friend around the shoulders. "We're friends because I'm the only one who actually supports your dreams of karaoke stardom...and I'll take your word on Edmonton's sex appeal."

"When I'm a karaoke star, I'll be sure to remember you and all the little people."

"At the rate you're going, you might wind up in the looney bin first." Lilly closed the chart. "Back to our dull, dreary and Jacob-less lives; any emergent cases in the operating theater?"

"My friend in Accident and Emergency said a cardiac patient tanked down there about thirty minutes ago."

"Odd we haven't heard anything." Lilly glanced at her pager as it went off. "Ask, and ye shall receive. Emergent open-heart patient being prepped in OR 5 as we speak."

"Who's doing the surgery? Is it that beautiful new surgeon, or haven't you noticed Cary Grant's doppelgänger either?"

Lilly's brown eyes narrowed. "I assume you mean Dr. Torres? Sabina, I'm selective, I'm not dead. He's gorgeous. But he's also a surgeon, and you know what they say about surgeons."

"And what is that exactly?" A baritone voice reverberated behind her, causing Lilly to flush bright red.

Pointing in the voice's general direction, Lilly mouthed to Sabina, 'Dr. Torres, right?', getting her answer when Sabina collapsed into giggles.

Turning, Lilly smiled at the young surgeon, hoping he missed the first part of her statement. "Dr. Torres, I was headed down to the OR Theater. Are you assisting with the emergent case?"

"I'm the lead surgeon actually. I wanted to speak with you, Ms. Staver, before I scrubbed in for surgery."

6

Walking from the nurses station, Dr. Torres and Lilly were met by Ben, the hospital's administrator. Ben and Lilly maintained a long-distance friendship for twenty years, and it was at his behest that Lilly was working in the UK. St. Luke was expanding from a community hospital to a trauma facility, and their fledgling critical care team needed an experienced manager to get the unit up to speed. It didn't hurt that Lilly needed an escape from New York at the exact same time. The situation was kismet for both parties.

"Ben, is there a problem?" Lilly looked up at her friend, his face unreadable.

"This case is complicated," Dr. Torres began. "The patient is young, but I'm not sure what the outcome will be after surgery. She may require a balloon pump, perhaps even a VAD."

Lilly's face paled; doctors only used these devices for the sickest heart patients. "A congenital defect, I'm assuming. How old is the patient?"

Ben squeezed Lilly's shoulder. "She's 34 and in otherwise perfect health, which is to her advantage. But our nurses are not equipped to handle this case without supervision. That's where you come in; we need you to recover the patient until she's stabilized."

Dr. Torres smiled at Lilly. "Ben tells me you're the best nurse at this hospital. Besides, I've watched you work, you know this specialty inside and out."

Lilly pushed a lock of straight brown hair from her face and chuckled. "Ben is biased, but I'll gladly supervise this case."

"Thank you, I feel better knowing that." There was a solemnity in the surgeon's dark eyes. This case was weighing on his mind.

"Never a problem. I'll go get changed, skirt and heels are a bit of an overstatement at the bedside. Ben, I'll catch up with you in a few minutes?" Lilly walked into the locker room, grabbing surgical scrubs off the cart. She thought she was alone, save for a few knapsacks and random pairs of shoes.

"Lilly."

Lilly turned to see the young surgeon only inches behind her; his dark gaze focused on her face. "Yes, Dr. Torres?"

He held up a necklace. "You dropped this."

Lilly's hand flew to her neck. "I didn't feel it fall off, thank you so much! That's my talisman, it's so important to me." She reached her hand out to grasp the chain, but he held it out of her reach.

"Turn around, I'll put it on you."

Lilly's heart beat faster, but she obliged, pulling her long dark hair over one shoulder. She trembled when his fingers slid along her neck, pushing a few errant strands out of the way. "Thank you."

"You smell amazing, I always meant to tell you. Absolutely intoxicating." He leaned in closer, his lips hovering at her ear.

Now Lilly's heart raced like a freight train. "I'm not wearing anything."

She felt his breath against her skin, his lips barely brushing her neck. "It's you that's intoxicating."

Lilly's mind went blank as she struggled to think of some response, any response. His fingers were warm against her skin, and Lilly's body reminded her how many months it had been since she last engaged in any type of sexual activity. She turned to face him, their bodies mere inches apart. "I'm just ordinary, Dr. Torres."

He ran a finger along her jaw, a smile drawing up the corners of his mouth. "Lilly, there isn't anything ordinary about you."

Damn, but he was beautiful. His dark, almond eyes, perfectly chiseled face, thick, dark hair—a perfect specimen. "I'm afraid you're mistaken, sir," Lilly murmured.

Dr. Torres chuckled. "I'm never wrong about these matters, and I think you're gorgeous too, Lilly."

Lilly's flush increased. He *had* heard her statement to Sabina about his classic good looks. "Oh God, you heard that."

"It made my day. I've been dying to get to know more about you since my first day at St. Luke."

"Me?"

"Yes, Lilly, you." He drew closer, and Lilly realized he was going to kiss her—in the middle of the damn locker room. *Do I want to kiss him?* Her body screamed in the affirmative, but her heart balked at the action.

"Lilly, are you in here?" The door flew open, and the couple jumped apart. Ben stood in the doorway, a knowing smirk on his face. "I hope I'm not interrupting anything."

Lilly sent her friend a look of death, her face turning fifty shades of red. "Of course not—"

"Lilly dropped her necklace. I returned it to her," Dr. Torres interjected, a rueful grin on his lips. "I need to get scrubbed in for surgery. I'll see you both later."

Lilly averted her eyes from Ben's stare. "Can I help you with something?"

"I didn't realize you and Enrique were so friendly," Ben chortled.

"I don't know what you're talking about." God, she was an atrocious liar.

"Sure, you don't. I figured the good doctor had a thing for you."

Lilly huffed. "He doesn't have a thing for me."

"You were kissing just now."

Lilly spun on her heel, mouth wide open and gaping, as she searched for a retort. "We weren't kissing!"

"You would have been kissing in another five seconds. I've got impeccable timing," Ben quipped.

"We weren't—"

Ben pulled his friend into a hug. "I'm all for it. The man is gorgeous, brilliant, talented and single. What's not to love?"

"It's *not* a match-up. Anyway, why don't you pursue Dr. Torres if he's such a catch?"

Ben leaned close, whispering, "I'm not his type, he prefers petite brunettes."

"His loss, then. You're an even better catch," Lilly grinned. Ben had only recently opened-up about his sexuality after 38 years of hiding in plain sight. Lilly was as determined to find him a perfect match as he was to find her a husband. "I've got to change, now scoot."

Ben placed a hand on her arm. "Thank you, I know this will be a long day for you. I hope it isn't cutting into any plans."

Lilly laughed, shaking her head. "My cats will be sorely disappointed, but they'll forgive me after a can of tuna."

"One last thing—and I know how you feel about this—the patient is a VIP. She's getting the largest room."

Lilly scoffed in disgust. "All patients are VIPs, I don't see why one deserves preferential treatment. But, if they want to pay the fees for added amenities, that's their prerogative."

"Her brother is a famous actor, and the family wants to avoid the fanfare that will accompany his arrival."

Lilly nodded in agreement. "The last thing the staff needs is a bunch of fans blocking corridors." She glared pointedly at Ben. "Are you going to give me some privacy?"

Ben smirked. "The same kind Dr. Torres gave you?" He ducked out the door, narrowly missing the t-shirt Lilly volleyed in his direction.

Lilly changed and walked back to the nurses station. She cast a glance at Sabina who looked ready to faint. "Are you okay? What's wrong?"

"Do you know who this emergent case is? It's Janie Edmonton, Jacob Edmonton's sister. Jacob Edmonton will be in our unit!" She fanned herself as

9

if every mention of his name raised her blood pressure.

"Oh, wonderful," Lilly muttered, ignoring the squeeze in her stomach at the realization. "Don't get too excited, he might not even show up."

"It's his sister. Holy shit, I wish I'd put on makeup this morning."

Lilly shot her a stern but loving look. "Sabina, this woman is sick. Our focus has to be on her recovery, not some Hollywood actor."

Sabina straightened, her smile fading. "Is that why you're recovering her? Is her case that complicated?"

Lilly's expression was somber, but her voice maintained a positive tone. "Dr. Torres is an excellent surgeon. Let's hope it isn't too difficult when he gets in there."

She had recovered countless surgical patients, but something about this case felt different. She couldn't put it into words. The severity coupled with a Hollywood actor creating chaos at the community hospital was more than Lilly bargained for on a Monday afternoon. She only hoped her frayed nerves resulted from an overload of caffeine and not a premonition of the future.

CHAPTER TWO

Jacob

A string of cars snarled along the London highway, bringing traffic to a standstill; Jacob wanted to forgo the limousine and run the rest of the way. The driver noted Jacob's agitated movements in the rearview and stated, "Traffic should be moving fine now, sir. No problem."

Jacob's eyes smoldered, his tone sharp. "No problem? You're taking me to a hospital. That's a problem."

"I'm sorry sir, I meant no disrespect. I thought the traffic was agitating you."

Jacob sighed, his heated demeanor turning to defeat. "No, I'm sorry. I wasn't prepared for this and...I'm not sure what to think."

The driver nodded. "I'll send prayers for your family, Mr. Edmonton. We've arrived."

Jacob leapt from the vehicle as it neared the hospital entrance and darted into St. Luke's lobby. His head was spinning. He leaned against the wall to steady himself and catch his breath.

His voicemail was full when he landed at Heathrow. There were numerous calls from Audrey and his Mum, barely intelligible over their sobbing. All he gleaned was Janie was rushed to the hospital and needed emergency surgery. He didn't know the gravity of the situation or what to expect, and the drive from the airport took forever and a day.

He'd been calling everyone since he heard the messages, but their phones went straight to voicemail. It was all Jacob could do to keep from pitching his mobile across the room.

He hurried to the information desk, drumming his fingers on the countertop while a robust clerk assisted another patron. She turned to him and her jaw dropped in recognition. "Mr. Edmonton, my goodness, how may I help you? What an honor, sir."

He was usually charming with his fans, but today was not a typical day. "My sister, Janie Edmonton, was admitted through Accident and Emergency a few hours ago."

The clerk typed the name into the database, her eyes shifting between his face and the screen. "Yes, she was admitted at two-thirty this afternoon. Go to the third floor and ask for the surgical waiting room within the critical care unit."

His eyes widened. "Critical care unit? How sick is she?"

"I'm sorry sir, I can't provide any additional information but if you go to the third floor and ask for the—"

"The surgical waiting area for the critical care unit—got it." He smacked the counter and started to walk off when the female patron grabbed his arm.

"Sir, I know this may not be the best time, but my daughter would never forgive me if I didn't ask for an autograph."

Jacob shook his head in disbelief as he snatched his arm from her grasp, bolting for the lift. He followed the signs to the surgical waiting area, and found his family huddled in a corner. His mother dabbed her eyes with a tissue, his father paced in circles, and Audrey sat with her head buried in her hands.

His mother, Caroline, noted his arrival and attempted a smile, failing miserably. "Jacob, you're here. Thank God." She lifted her cheek for a kiss and Jacob obliged, but her embrace was like a limp dishrag.

"What's happening? I tried calling, but no one answered their phones. Where's Janie?"

Audrey lifted her head, her eyes red-rimmed. "She's in surgery. Her heart failed, they don't know..." She broke off, sobs overwhelming her body.

Jacob placed his arm around Audrey; she stiffened but eventually relaxed into his embrace. "She has to be okay, Jacob. She has to get through this—it's Janie."

Her words sprung a leak in his damned-up emotions, and tears rolled down his cheeks.

When Audrey realized he was crying, she jerked away, anger clouding her distraught face. "No, don't you do that Jacob! You don't get to stay away for months on end and never call and then when she might...you don't get to be the big brother now, you gave up that role for your acting career."

Jacob jolted back, shocked by the venom pouring from his sister-in-law. They might not see eye-to-eye, but how could Audrey question his love for Janie?

"Audrey, please stop. Jacob has every right to be upset," implored Caroline, always the peacemaker.

Audrey jumped to her feet, shaking her head. "No, he doesn't. Love isn't conditional, and it isn't just on his timeline. Screw this, I'm going to smoke a fag." She grabbed her purse, storming towards the exit.

"Where's Elizabeth?" Jacob asked, searching the room for his niece.

"With my Mum," Audrey muttered as she stormed out.

Jacob glared at her retreating form before shifting his focus to his mother. "How are you holding up, Mum?"

She shrugged, her eyes glassy. "I have to believe Janie will get through this."

Jacob nodded his agreement, and they fell silent. He watched two young women approaching his family and he fixed his piercing blue glare on them, but they were determined in their mission.

You have got to be joking. Have people no heart? I'm in a hospital waiting room!

The smaller of the two approached first, whispering, "You're Jacob Edmonton, aren't you? The actor? It's amazing to meet you!"

"Thank you. My family has a personal emergency, so it's not a good time." Although his words were calm, his tone held an implicit warning.

Unfortunately, that warning sailed right over the woman as she pulled out her phone. "Can I take a picture, please? My friends will be so excited!"

Sighing in resignation, Jacob posed for the picture, his expression stern. As the young women departed, he saw Audrey standing in the doorway, shaking her head in disgust. "You're incorrigible. You can't think of anyone else for one minute, can you?" Her words fell like ice shards, shattering as they hit Jacob's armor.

Jacob grabbed her arm and pulled her close, his voice low but firm. "Let's not do this here, shall we?"

"Me? I'm not the one turning it into a personal autograph signing, comforting my precious ego while Janie lays on an operating slab. You'll never change."

"You know nothing about me, Audrey. You only know what you choose to believe but I love my sister, and I have as much of a right to be here as you do, so back off." He growled the warning, and Audrey scoffed with derision as she sank into the chair farthest from Jacob.

"Will you two stop? Can't you see how you're upsetting your Mother?" Jacob's father thundered in their direction. "This is not the time nor the place, so leave it."

Jacob's exhalation was slow and deliberate as he willed himself to calm down. "You're right, I'm sorry Mum, and I'm sorry Audrey." Audrey's steely countenance didn't shift. Jacob was about to offer a sarcastic retort when a woman in gray scrubs strode toward them.

He stood, hopeful she came with news of Janie's condition, but she giggled and requested an autograph. Audrey shook her head in disbelief and the intrusion brought on another rush of tears for Jacob's mother.

He almost let his frustration pour into the waiting room when he heard a laugh; the low, seductive chuckle reverberated through his body. His head

13

swung up, searching for the owner of that sexy sound.

She was tiny, encased in green scrubs with dark-rimmed glasses and a low ponytail; the complete opposite of his usual type. The woman was conversing with other employees, and he smiled in spite of himself when her laughter carried. God, he loved her laugh. It was so genuine.

Then she smiled, and Jacob's breath caught. The woman was stunning and headed in his direction. He tore his gaze away, hoping she wasn't another fan looking for a photo opportunity.

"Mr. Edmonton?" The girl in gray scrubs asked, holding out a piece of paper. "Your autograph, please?"

Jacob fought to maintain control, looking up to see a look of horror crossing the petite brunette's face as she quickened her pace across the waiting room.

"Mr. Edmonton?" The autograph seeker repeated, and Jacob only prayed he could hold his temper and survive this madness until Janie made it out of the operating suite.

Lilly

L illy's eyes widened in disbelief when she spotted a fellow nurse requesting Jacob Edmonton's autograph.

She rushed over, placing her hand on the nurse's arm. "Not the time, not the place, do we understand?"

Her words were low enough that only the nurse heard her, but her body language made it clear she was not joking about the matter. Mumbling an apology, the nurse hurried off, and Lilly took a deep breath before facing the family.

"My name is Lilly, I'm the nurse who will be taking care of Janie." Her eyes moved to each family member, holding Jacob's gaze the longest. His blue eyes were more piercing in real life than the photo Sabina showed her earlier. The picture that showcased his fantastic abs and chest...shit. *Focus, Lilly. Pull it together.*

Lilly walked past Jacob and squatted in front of Audrey. "Are you Audrey?"

When the young woman nodded, Lilly took her hands and held them for a moment, giving them a gentle squeeze. She did the same to the parents before turning and facing Jacob.

Gazing up at his muscular frame, Lilly extended her hand. "Mr. Edmonton, I'd like to take your family somewhere more private, if that's all right with you. I apologize for the behavior of some of our staff. There's no excuse for it given the situation, and I want to ensure it doesn't happen again. There's a private room down the hall where you won't be bothered." Lilly's eyes moved to her hand, still enveloped in his. She pulled back in haste.

Jacob nodded, offering her a gracious smile. "That would be wonderful, thank you."

Lilly escorted the family down the hall. "It's nothing fancy, but it's away from prying eyes."

Caroline grasped Lilly's hand. "Do you have any news on Janie?"

"She's still in the operating theater; I'm headed there to get an update on the surgery. Before I do, would anyone like coffee?" Lilly scoffed at her faux pas. "I mean tea. It's England; everyone drinks tea, don't they?"

Jacob's father chuckled. "Tea would be wonderful. Thank you, Lilly."

"Tea it is; I'll be back in a moment."

Audrey smiled at Lilly. "You're a Yank." It was a declaration, not a question, one Lilly was quite used to after three months in England.

Lilly nodded and smiled. "A New York Yank at that, but I hope you won't hold it against me." She felt Jacob's intense gaze on her, and her cheeks reddened. Damn her fair complexion. "But despite being born on the wrong side of the pond, I've been a nurse for a long time, and I assure you Janie will receive the best care possible. Please sit, try to make yourselves comfortable."

Lilly requested the teas from the concierge station, then continued to the operating theater. She donned a face mask and pushed open the door of OR 5; inside Jimi Hendrix's guitar strummed through the stereo as Dr. Torres traded lighthearted banter with the anesthesiologist.

They're joking, always a good sign.

Lilly turned to the circulating nurse. "Any update on Ms. Edmonton?"

The nurse glanced up at her. "Surgery is moving along well; some arrhythmia noted, hypotensive issues. She should be moving to recovery in an hour." The nurse confirmed the information with Dr. Torres, who glanced in Lilly's direction.

"Come to see how the other half lives, Lilly?" Dr. Torres inquired, his dark eyes crinkling. It was a long-standing joke that no one truly understood medicine until you worked within the confines of the operating room.

"Sadly, no, but I'll be waiting for you at the finish line, where the real work begins," Lilly retorted, her cheeks flushing under his gaze as she left the theater.

Lilly walked toward the waiting area, hearing a heated one-sided conversation. As she rounded the corner, she saw Jacob Edmonton leaning against the wall, his phone in a death grip by his ear.

She paused by him; she hated breaking into a conversation, particularly an argument, but this news was important. "I have information on Janie," Lilly whispered, placing a hand on his arm.

"Just hold on a second," Jacob barked into the phone. His expression softened as he looked at her, an embarrassed smile on his gorgeous mouth. "I'm sorry, Lilly. You have news about Janie?"

Lilly opened her mouth to respond when unintelligible squawking sounded from the phone. "I'll be in the room with your family."

"I'll be there in a moment. Thank you, for all your help."

"It's my job."

His blue eyes warmed as he looked at Lilly. "You're good at it."

All eyes swung to Lilly as she opened the door. "I have news. The surgery is going well, and the doctors expect that Janie will be in recovery within the hour. From there—" Lilly was cut off as Jacob entered the room.

"Sorry, what were you saying?" Jacob adjusted his glasses, his eyes glued to his phone.

"I was telling your family that the surgery is going well, and she should be in—" The ringing of Jacob's phone cut her off a second time, and Jacob mumbled an apology before exiting the room.

Audrey sighed, shaking her head. "He has to ensure his one million Instagram fans are present and accounted for."

"He does seem very popular. I guess that's part of the job," Lilly murmured, wondering who had gotten him so heated during such a stressful family time.

"He's a selfish asshole; thinks he's God's gift to women. A different one every night; they line up to sleep with him," Audrey huffed.

"Right...okay." Lilly wished she could evaporate into thin air and reappear in a war zone, where the tension wasn't running as high.

"Really Audrey? Why don't you tell Lilly exactly what you think of me?" Jacob ran a hand through his curls, his jaw tightening.

"Let me guess, little Ms. Victoria on the line?" Audrey seethed at Jacob, narrowing her eyes at him. "Bingo, I fucking knew it."

Lilly backed herself into a corner, praying this melee would soon end.

"It's none of your damn business who was on the phone, and it wasn't Victoria."

"One of your other sluts? I suppose we should be honored that you deign us worthy at all, when else do we see you? Hell, Janie has to undergo emergency heart surgery to be a candidate for your time."

"Everyone, please stop. This is not healthy for anyone right now," Lilly pleaded.

"You know nothing, Audrey!" Jacob hissed as he exited, slamming the door behind him.

Lilly stared at the waiting room door, uncertain how to proceed after the family squabble. When it became obvious no one else was going to open the conversation, she sighed, settling into a chair.

"Let me tell you what to expect when Janie comes out of surgery. I find it helpful to let families know about the machinery used during recovery, so it's less of a shock. Does that sound good to everyone?"

Lilly left the waiting room ten minutes later and found Jacob slouched in a corner, his face in his hands. Despite Audrey's accusations, he didn't appear like a spoiled playboy, but rather a brokenhearted man struggling to comprehend the events of the day. Her heart softened and she was tempted to hug him.

She knelt in front of him. "Mr. Edmonton?"

Jacob looked up, his eyes red-rimmed. "Sorry about that display, you didn't need to see that."

"Trust me, I've seen far worse. Chairs being thrown, tables overturned, a planter halfway through a window—"

Jacob smiled at her, shaking his head. "You're joking."

"Unfortunately not, your family is tame comparatively. Although, I'm sorry to see such animosity during an already difficult time." She shifted under his gaze, his sapphire eyes were unnerving. "I thought since you didn't hear my spiel, you might like to grab a cup of coffee, so I can fill you in on the details. You look like you could use it."

"That's a great idea, thank you. And please, call me Jacob."

"Jacob it is." Lilly held out her hand to him, and he grasped it, pulling himself to a standing position. She tried to ignore the warmth that shot up her arm when his fingers enveloped hers.

Jacob gazed down at her, a wry smile on his lips. "God, you're tiny. How tall are you?"

"Not very," Lilly chuckled. "Just under five feet, or one and a half meters as they say in England."

Jacob returned her laugh. "So, not very tall."

Her laughter died in her throat as she looked at the ground, suddenly self-conscious of her diminutive stature.

"I love your laugh."

Lilly smiled up at him. "I don't sound like a member of the Lollipop Guild, do I?"

"Not at all, your laugh is beautiful and genuine and sexy as hell—" He stopped speaking abruptly, letting out an embarrassed huff. "I'm saying all the wrong things today."

"Thanks for the compliment." Lilly knew her face was bright red, but it was a minor issue compared to the sparks going off inside her body.

"I meant it," Jacob murmured as he placed a hand on her shoulder, and Lilly fought to ignore the butterflies in her stomach.

"Here we are." Lilly pushed open the door to a small doctor's lounge and poured them both some coffee before joining Jacob at a table.

"This," Jacob began, sipping the brew, "is truly terrible coffee."

Lilly laughed, almost spitting her coffee in his direction. "It's like old shoe leather, but the sludgier it is, the longer it keeps you awake, at least that's the rumor."

"I'll be awake for weeks, if that's the case." Jacob smiled broadly, and Lilly understood what Sabina meant about his effortless sex appeal.

"Let me tell what to expect after Janie comes out of surgery." Lilly segued into her well-practiced dialogue about post-operative expectations; pausing half a dozen times to allow Jacob to take one of his endless phone calls. His public needed him incessantly, it seemed.

The interruptions helped her regain her bearings and not fall into the sensual gravitational pull surrounding this man. She didn't understand it. He was not her type. He was tall and lean and blonde and fucking gorgeous. *What is wrong with me? Get it together, Lilly. This man is a damn movie star, he isn't going to think twice about someone like you.* Her pager sounded, and she gazed at the number, Janie would be moving to recovery within twenty minutes.

"I'm so sorry Lilly, my phone is never this crazy." Jacob's hand touched her arm and Lilly jumped. "Are you okay?"

"You startled me." Lilly looked up, offering a small smile. "Shall I continue?"

"Please."

She tried to ignore his sudden laser focus on her, or the fact that his hand still rested on her arm, moving in almost imperceptible circles. "I know I bombarded you with a ton of information, but do you have any questions for me at this point?"

Jacob blinked, digesting the information. "It sounds so complicated, but it also sounds like you've done this a few times before."

"More than a few. Here's my best advice, it's terrifying because it's unfamiliar. But if I don't look worried, you don't need to worry."

Jacob smiled and thanked her as his phone rang for what seemed to be the umpteenth time. He silenced it, sliding it into his pocket.

Lilly straightened, her expression turning somber. "You know—never mind."

"No, please; what were you going to say?"

Lilly bit her lip. "Janie will need help when she gets out of the hospital. She'll need people she can depend on to assist with her recovery."

"I'll hire the best help in London—maids, nurses—whatever she needs."

"That's all well and good, but she really needs her family during her recuperation. She'll need you to be present and I noticed you couldn't stay in a

19

conversation two minutes without your phone going off—"

Jacob leaned forward, his hand tightening on her arm. "Those were important phone calls—"

"I'm sure they were, but isn't your sister far more important than anyone on the end of that line? This is her health we're discussing; she's undergone a very serious surgery, and I want you to understand the gravity of her recovery period." Lilly's voice was gentle but firm as she held his gaze, unrelenting. She couldn't believe she spoke to him in such a forward manner, but he needed to stay in the present moment.

Jacob scoffed, shaking his head. "Another one, trying to demean me because my priorities aren't what you think they should be. I guess Audrey got to you, after all. I suppose you think I'm nothing more than a washed-up playboy, right?"

Lilly sat back, flabbergasted by Jacob's sudden anger. "I don't think that at all, I don't know you. I didn't mean to hurt your feelings, I just—"

"Of course you didn't. No one ever does when they're cutting you down."

"I know you love your sister and I want to ensure she gets the best care possible—"

His eyes flashed daggers in her direction. "Isn't that your job, Lilly? Why don't you focus on what *you're* supposed to be doing instead of *my* life?"

Lilly clenched her fists under the table. He was a genuine asshole. "My job is to protect and care for Janie during the duration of her hospital stay. Once she's discharged, she'll need help from her family. I don't understand—"

"No, you don't understand! You don't have a clue how it feels to have the world watching your every move, writing about everything you do. Going to the market shouldn't be an event, but when you're me, it becomes one. So, until you have any concept of what my life looks like, you should stick to things you understand."

That was enough verbal abuse for one day. Lilly stood, throwing her coffee cup into the garbage. "Well, you've got me there; I don't have any idea what it's like to be you. I do know when you're lucky enough to have a family that loves you, you ought to love them back. If you'll excuse me, I need to get Janie's room ready for her arrival."

Lilly exited the doctor's lounge, her heart racing and fists clenched. *What a pompous ass!*

"Have you met our VIP's brother yet?" Sabina inquired as she passed the nurses station, the smile fading when she noticed Lilly's expression.

"You mean the most pretentious prick I've ever had the displeasure of dealing with? Yes, I've met Jacob Edmonton, and he's a full-fledged asshole."

20

With a final huff, Lilly stomped into the clean utility room.

CHAPTER THREE

Jacob

Jacob regretted the words the moment they exited his mouth, but it was too late. Lilly was gone. He stayed in the break room a few moments longer, questioning why he jumped all over her in that way. It was entirely out of character. He was renowned for exceptional politeness, yet he had shown every lousy trait he possessed in less than ten minutes with this petite nurse.

He couldn't stand the way she held his gaze when she questioned his lifestyle choices. It was as if Lilly could see right through his facade and she wasn't about to let him slide with any excuses.

This is ridiculous; I have more important things to worry about, Jacob reflected as he walked back to the private waiting area. No words were exchanged as he returned to his family, so he slumped into a chair, shoved his sunglasses onto his face and pulled his hood over his head.

He had no idea how much time had passed when his mother woke him, shaking his arm. "Jacob, it's time. Lilly says we can see Janie now."

Momentarily dazed, Jacob nodded, following his family into the unit. His knees buckled as he neared his sister's bed, unprepared for the cacophony of beeping machines.

As he faltered, he felt a hand on his arm, directing him to a waiting chair. "There you go, do you need some water?" He looked up into Lilly's face, her thoughtful eyes scanning him. She had the most beautiful brown eyes, and they were warm and reassuring where Victoria's were cold and hard as emeralds.

"No, thank you, I wasn't ready—"

"What you're feeling is normal." Lilly shot him a forced smile before turning her attention to the rest of the family. "I know it's terrifying with all the tubes and wires, but if recovery goes according to plan, she will look totally different within the next twelve hours. Our goal is to wake her up and get her breathing without the ventilator, then see how she tolerates liquids. By tomorrow, she'll be out of bed and walking."

"You're joking!" Audrey exclaimed. "She'll be walking by tomorrow?"

Lilly smiled. "I didn't say she's going to *want* to get up and walk, but that's the plan."

A young doctor entered the ICU bay, interrupting the conversation. Jacob watched as he placed his hand on the small of Lilly's back and tightened at the intimacy of the gesture. For all he knew, the two were married a decade and had a gaggle of children; that thought made his nausea return. He stared at the floor to avoid glaring in Lilly's direction.

Lilly returned to Janie's side with the doctor in tow. "This is Dr. Torres. He was the lead surgeon on Janie's case, and wanted to speak with all of you for a few moments."

Jacob turned his attention to Dr. Torres, a surgeon of about thirty-five who looked remarkably like Cary Grant. Jacob brushed aside his preoccupation and focused on the doctor's words. He seemed competent, and the operation had gone smoothly. Janie wasn't out of the woods yet, but things looked hopeful for a full recovery.

"Ah, and this lady—you have the best nurse at St. Luke. Lilly will take excellent care of Janie through her initial recovery." Dr. Torres placed his arm around Lilly's shoulder, and Jacob felt that intractable jaw twitch again, particularly when Lilly beamed at the surgeon.

"I appreciate your vote of confidence, Dr. Torres." She nodded as he left the bay before returning her attention to the family. "I know you want to stay close to Janie, but our medical team needs to focus on waking her up and getting her off the ventilator over the next few hours. So, after taking a moment to speak to her, I'll ask that you either return to the waiting room or better yet, head on home. She'll need your strength once she's awake and you can't pour from an empty cup." Her fawn eyes focused on Jacob, her gaze speaking volumes only he could hear.

"We just got here. I can't stay with my daughter?" Caroline dabbed her eyes again, fresh tears welling. "Lilly?"

But Lilly was focused on Janie's bedside monitor, the only sign of trouble a slight widening of her pupils. Before she could reply, the machines squawked a frenzied tempo, and red lights pulsated. "I've got a code! Get the cart!" Lilly slammed the bed into a flat position and began administering compressions.

Jacob's head spun as medical personnel poured into the room from every angle. Hands tugged him outside the bay, leading him to the waiting area. "Wait! That's my sister in there! What in bloody hell is going on?"

The nurse, Sabina according to her nametag, held up her hands to calm him. "Something's happened with your sister's heart, and it stopped pumping. Lilly caught it immediately, and they are working on her now."

"What do you mean, her heart stopped pumping? She's not dead, damn it, she's not dead!" He heard his family's anguished cries in the background, but his mind couldn't comprehend Sabina's statement.

"Let me get back in there and see what's happening. We've called the chaplain, and he's coming to speak with you." Sabina patted Jacob's shoulder before returning to the unit.

Jacob's breaths came in short, ragged gasps. This had to be a nightmare. His sister was not laying in a hospital bed without a heartbeat or a future. He didn't know how long he stayed crouched against the wall like a beaten child, it could have been two minutes or two hours, the clock hands ceased their movement and time held no meaning.

"Janie's stabilized. You can go in for a moment." Jacob looked up and saw Sabina standing over him, offering her hand, which he feebly accepted.

The steps back to the unit took an eternity, the uncertainty only solidified by earlier events. Jacob hesitated outside the bay. His sister looked so peaceful while Lilly and Dr. Torres seemed exhausted. Lilly was sweating, out of breath and her ponytail had fallen loose, brown hair tumbling over one shoulder.

Dr. Torres guided Jacob and his family to Janie's bedside and explained the situation. Janie's heart, irritable from surgery, suffered an arrhythmia, or abnormal heart rhythm, but Lilly kept her blood pumping until they could shock her heart into a normal rhythm.

Jacob leaned against the bay wall, tears forming as he looked between Janie and Lilly. "You saved her life."

Lilly's chin raised as she looked him square in the face. "I did my job, Mr. Edmonton." She turned to his family. "I know it was an awful scare, but she's on medication that will hopefully prevent anything else from occurring. All things considered, I understand if you don't want to go home. There are rooms in the building next door where you can sleep and shower. It's not the Four Seasons, you must realize," Lilly's eyes darted back to Jacob, "but a meal and a couple hours' shuteye can do wonders. We'll call you if anything changes but no news is good news in the medical world."

The family spent the next few minutes fluttering around Janie, sending love and shedding a few tears. Jacob waited until they departed to approach the bedside, gazing down at his sister, so frail and small. Grabbing her hand, he noticed a three stone pendant pressed into her palm.

"What—"

"It's mine; it's my talisman. It always brought me luck. She needs it more than I do now." Lilly's voice was soft across the bed as she smoothed Janie's matted hair, avoiding Jacob's gaze.

"You gave it to her?"

Lilly nodded. "As I said, it always brought me luck. You should rest, Mr. Edmonton—"

"It's Jacob."

Lilly's jaw twitched. "I prefer Mr. Edmonton, if it's all the same to you."

Her words hit like fists. He hated that she erected a wall to protect herself from another verbal onslaught. His brain blanked as he looked at her, noting how she refused to meet his gaze. *How do I apologize for being a total cad to the first person who has ever seen through my bullshit excuses?*

Jacob didn't have an answer, or an apology, for Lilly, but he would make certain to come up with one. She deserved one. "If that's your preference... thank you for saving my sister." Giving Janie's hand one last squeeze, he trudged out of the critical care unit.

Lilly

"Lilly, hold up a moment."

Lilly turned, smiling at Dr. Torres as he leaned against the counter in the critical care unit. He finished his notations and closed the patient binder, handing it off to a staff nurse. Lilly smirked behind her hand as the young redhead blushed and cooed at the surgeon, her amusement increased only by Dr. Torre's blithe ignorance of the nurse's flirtation.

"What can I do for you, Dr. Torres?"

"Do you think you can call me Enrique?"

"Perhaps I can manage it."

His hand pressed against her lower back as he smiled down at her. "Have a drink with me. It's been a shit day."

Lilly glanced at her watch. Not only had it been a shit day, but it had also been a fourteen-hour day. "It's almost ten."

The surgeon chuckled. "You think I don't know that? I arrived just after you this morning."

Lilly realized he had the most endearing smile and lips; lips that damn near kissed her earlier that day. She returned his laugh. "One drink, but if I fall asleep, you'd better not leave me in the pub!"

"I wouldn't dream of it," Dr. Torres murmured.

The pub was relatively quiet, with only a smattering of locals playing billiards. Lilly and Dr. Torres fell into a booth across from the bar, ordering up whiskey and burger platters.

He handed her a glass and she smiled, taking a sip. "Dinner of champions; thank you, Enrique."

"I like how you say my name."

Lilly blushed, but she didn't know why, it was hardly an intimate conversation. "My New York accent is hardly known for its fluidity. Yours, on the other hand, is lovely."

Enrique slid his hand across the table and clasped Lilly's fingers. "I hope you aren't angry at my behavior earlier. I seldom act so rashly, I got lost in the moment."

Lilly chewed her lip, staring at the table. "Nothing happened, so don't worry about it; no harm, no foul."

His fingers tightened around hers. "Something would have happened. My regret is that it didn't…or that you would be angry because it did."

Lilly met his dark brown eyes and smiled, wondering when the fireworks and sparks would show up. This man was magical, everyone thought so, and he was interested in her. She should be melting on the spot. Perhaps she truly was frigid after her last relationship. "I'm not angry." She swirled her whiskey and took a sip. "You did an amazing job with Janie."

"Thank you, God was smiling on us today. Enough about work, tell me about you. What's your story?"

Lilly nearly choked on her drink. He was direct. "Not much to tell, I grew up in New York. I've been a nurse for 15 years and only arrived in England a few months ago to help establish the critical care units at St. Luke."

Enrique's mouth twitched as he nodded.

"What's so funny?"

"I asked you about yourself, and you responded with a detailed explanation of your work history."

Now she was red to the tops of her ears. Thank god for darkened pubs. She leaned back against the booth, finally meeting his dark gaze. "What would you like to know?"

"I asked some colleagues about your marital status, before today, I might add. They said you're single."

"Yes."

"How is that possible?"

Lilly's heart flipped, but she wasn't certain if it was because of the question or the sight of Jacob walking through the pub door. She slid down in the seat, averting her gaze and praying the actor didn't see them.

No such luck.

Just as Enrique looked over his shoulder to signal the server, Jacob looked directly into the booth.

Maybe he'll pretend he doesn't see us and go about his business.

Luck was not her friend tonight.

"Dr. Torres, Lilly, good evening."

Lilly peered up at Jacob through her glasses, his blue gaze affixed to her face. "Hello, Mr. Edmonton. Janie was stable when we left and we were starving…I know this looks odd after today…"

Enrique quirked a brow at her verbal rambling and Lilly sighed. She sounded like an idiot. The surgeon extended his hand to Jacob. "Your sister is progressing wonderfully. We'll have her out of bed tomorrow morning."

27

"I'm so grateful to you both. It's been one hell of a day." Jacob drummed his fingers on the edge of the table, shadows playing under his eyes.

"Would you like to join us for a drink? Looks like you could use one," Enrique offered.

Please say no, please say no, Lilly repeated internally, trying to ignore the butterflies flapping like blooming fools in her stomach.

"I would love to, some might think it's bad form, but I know what Janie would say—bottoms up, big brother."

"Lilly, why don't you move over here and let Jacob—"

"She's fine right there, I'll sit next to her...if she doesn't mind." Jacob's eyes focused on Lilly again.

"Of course," Lilly mumbled, scooting over in the booth. She glanced to Enrique, who pursed his lips but said nothing. He looked aggravated by Jacob's seating choice, not that it was Lilly's decision. Maybe she was reading too much into it. Her eyes focused on her whiskey while she tried desperately to ignore the flush racing through every pore in her body. Christ, just being near the man affected her. She must be a bloody masochist.

The server brought Jacob a glass of whiskey. "I hope it isn't premature, but I'd like to propose a toast to the man and woman who saved my sister's life. Dr. Torres, you're an amazing surgeon. Thank you for working your magic. And Lilly," Jacob turned to her, grasping her hand, "you're exquisite, in every way."

Lilly couldn't breathe, time stopped as she stared into Jacob's eyes. She must have fallen into an alternate universe because this man detested everything about her. Had she finally gone mad? He was probably being sarcastic, knowing she wouldn't say anything in front of Enrique.

She pulled her hand back and grabbed her whiskey, clinking glasses with the men.

Enrique watched their interaction with a great deal of interest. "Do you two know each other?"

"No, not at all," Lilly blurted, taking another swig of whiskey.

"She's the most insightful person I've ever met; gave me much to think about today," Jacob retorted.

Lilly closed her eyes, praying that reality would snap back into play. This alternate world was far too off kilter for her liking.

"Certainly sounds like you know each other," Enrique muttered, leaning back against the booth.

"We met today, just a few hours ago," Lilly retorted. How much longer until she could make her escape?

"Enrique, darling, what are you doing here?" A tall blonde stood at the edge of the booth, a broad smile splitting her face.

Enrique's eyes widened. He was definitely not expecting this woman. "Emma, what a surprise. When did you get back to London?"

"I came back early, tried calling your flat, but there was no answer. I hoped we might grab a late dinner, but I see you've already eaten." She suddenly realized there were other people at the table and her jaw slackened when she saw Jacob. "My goodness, you look exactly like—"

"Jacob Edmonton?"

"Yes, a dead ringer," Emma laughed, shaking her head.

"I suppose I would resemble him." Jacob slid further into the booth, his body now pressed against Lilly.

Lilly watched the interaction, her breath halting when Jacob's fingers brushed her thigh. *Figures, now the damn fireworks show up.*

"Oh my word, you *are* Jacob Edmonton, my apologies. I'm a huge fan." Emma held out her lithe, manicured hand. The woman had never done a day's hard labor in her life.

"Pleased to meet you."

The blonde's eyes moved to Lilly, an uncertain smile on her lips. "I assume you're Jacob's wife? My name is Emma."

Lilly wanted to die, right at that very moment. "I most certainly am not!"

Jacob turned and shot her a startled look; apparently, he wasn't used to women *not* wanting to be his significant other. Then an impish smile crossed his face and Lilly knew she was in trouble. "Now darling, don't forget our earlier discussion, you shouldn't be ashamed of our relationship."

Lilly's eyes were as big as saucers, slack-jawed after his statement. "What the hell are you talking about?"

Jacob turned to Emma, smiling at the blonde as he slipped an arm around Lilly's shoulders. "She's shy around strangers."

Enrique scoffed, his face marred with a frown. Lilly wasn't sure if he was angry about Emma's sudden appearance, Jacob's charade, or both. "Will you excuse me for a moment? I need to speak with Emma."

"Certainly." Lilly forced a smile, wishing she was anywhere but next to Jacob Edmonton.

"I'll take good care of Lilly," Jacob whispered, squeezing Lilly's shoulder.

It was time to go. Enough of this arrogant prick and his mind games. "You are such an asshole."

Jacob smirked, sipping his whiskey. "Is that your pet name for me, luv?

I just want you to be true to your feelings."

Lilly considered dousing him with her remaining whiskey, glass and all. Anything to remove that smirk from his mouth. His luscious, gorgeous mouth. Or…she could play his game and up the ante.

Turning in her seat, she curled her lips in a smile, running her hand along his jaw. His beard was surprisingly soft under her fingers, but it was the light in his eyes that pushed her forward with the farce. "You're right darling, we've kept our feelings secret long enough."

"I'm so glad you agree," Jacob murmured, his hand clasping her thigh.

"I more than agree. I think it's time to take it to the next level." Lilly moved closer to that spectacular mouth as her eyes drifted close, starting when their mouths connected.

Lilly's mind reeled. She hadn't planned on actually kissing him, her lips weren't that close to his mouth…unless…Jacob leaned into the kiss. And *that* was not the reaction she expected.

His lips were soft and warm, and for an instant, she forgot everything beyond that kiss, beyond their physical connection.

Jacob's mouth opened as his hand tightened on her thigh. He took her bottom lip between his teeth and Lilly gasped.

This was moving into unfamiliar territory, and quick. Lilly snapped back to reality, and pulled away, a triumphant smirk on her face. "Sorry darling, I'm not quite there yet."

Jacob's eyes flew open, shooting darts at her as she finished her whiskey, but he quickly regained his composure. "Something we'll have to work on… sweetheart." His hand squeezed her thigh, his fingers trailing upwards against her leg.

Lilly gasped as she tossed his hand away, noting his smile and the glint in his eye. This man was enjoying the hell out of this game, and he wanted the last word. Fine, let him have it. She had proven her point, whatever it was.

Jacob leaned back against the booth, a genuine smile crossing his lips. "Touché, Lilly."

Lilly smiled and shrugged. "Two can play your game. You didn't invent it, you know."

Jacob leaned over and pressed his lips to her ear, his breath stirring up those butterflies again. "Too bad you pulled away before I got to find out what an amazing kisser you are."

This man was incorrigible. "Your loss."

He pulled back, staring at his whiskey, a frown creasing his Grecian profile. "Yes, it is."

Lilly paused. What the hell caused his sudden about-face? The reality of her actions sank in. She had two options—bury her face in her hands and never look up or change the subject and pretend the kiss never happened. That soft but magical kiss.

Lilly went with option two. She stirred her drink, searching for answers in her ice cubes. "How's your family?"

"Mum and Audrey finally fell asleep. My Dad is watching the news on a loop, and my niece is wondering when her Mum is coming home."

"How old is she?"

"Elizabeth is five." Jacob pulled out his phone, flipping through photos. He opened one, but it wasn't his niece, rather him shirtless on a beach; a tall blonde draped over his body like a boa constrictor. The two combined were the epitome of all things considered beautiful. Lilly wanted to vomit. "Sorry, wrong photo."

Lilly sipped her whiskey through the stirrer straw. "Your wife is beautiful."

Jacob scoffed. "She is definitely not my wife."

Lilly shrugged, the whiskey was making an appearance. "She's still beautiful. You two look good together, but I'm sure you knew that already."

"Her beauty is only skin deep. She made me realize how stupid it is to commit your heart to another person. It's far safer to focus on my career, interspersed with numerous romps and meaningless sex. Screw romance and happily ever after."

"Words to live by," Lilly breathed, her sarcasm evident.

"It's better than being a fool in love."

"Love is never stupid," Lilly blurted, immediately wishing she could pull the words back.

Jacob's gaze held hers, damn, that fire was back in his eyes again. "It was in this case."

"Did you learn something from your time with her?" She shouldn't keep pushing, but she knew his answer was a facade, hiding the truth.

Jacob drummed his fingers on the table. He was aggravated. "Yes, I learned that it's stupid to commit your heart to another person. I pity anyone dumb enough to fall in love."

Lilly opened her mouth to retort but scoffed at that foolish idea. Time for her to leave, this night was more fun than a root canal. "On that happy note, can you let me up? I'm calling it a night."

"I can walk you to your car."

Lilly shook her head. "I don't have a car, I take the Tube."

"I can drive you—shit, no I can't—I don't have my car. Let me call you a cab."

"It's not necessary."

"I insist." Jacob called in a taxi before motioning towards the front of the bar. "Won't Dr. Torres be angry that you're leaving?"

Lilly shrugged. "I doubt it. He's busy with Emma."

Jacob kept his focus on his phone. "I thought you and Dr. Torres were an item."

"Why would you think that? We're work colleagues."

Jacob captured her gaze, his azure eyes deep and probing. "The way he looks at you. But you deserve better than being a side piece."

Lilly squinted in confusion. "A side piece?"

"Yes, someone he's with on the side when he isn't with Emma."

"This from a man who advocates for meaningless romps?" Lilly's eyebrows raised in disbelief.

"I believe my exact words were numerous romps and meaningless sex."

"Because that makes *all* the difference."

Jacob chuckled, and Lilly wasn't certain if he was endearing or exasperating. "I take it you don't approve."

Lilly shrugged, although his crass statement bothered the hell out of her. "It's not my business who you're sleeping with; I'm just glad I'm not programmed that way. I would hate to think my existence was centered around such shallow banalities."

The energy in the room changed as Jacob's fingers drummed the table again, his blue eyes darkening.

Lilly opted to back off. This man was not happy. "I appreciate your concern regarding Enrique, but we're not an item, in any way." The memory of Enrique's behavior earlier in the day flashed in her mind, apparently he liked to keep multiple women hanging by a thread, too. "You didn't need to call a cab."

Jacob stood, allowing Lilly to slide out. "Yes, I did. It will be here in five minutes."

Enrique reappeared, his gaze moving between Lilly and Jacob. "Lilly, I'm so sorry; I didn't think I would see Emma tonight."

Another shrug, Lilly was getting this gesture down pat. "No problem. I'm heading home. Jacob was kind enough to call me a taxi."

"I can take you home," Enrique implored.

"I'm fine. Have a nice night with Emma." Lilly kissed the surgeon's cheek. "I'll see you tomorrow."

"I'll walk you out, let me pick up my food." Jacob excused himself and headed for the bar.

Enrique's eyes narrowed, and he huffed. "You're leaving with him?"

Lilly scoffed—was he serious? "What? No."

"You came here with me."

"And you walked off with your girlfriend, whom you *weren't* expecting."

"She's not my girlfriend, she's—"

Lilly held up a hand, she was beyond done with this conversation. "I don't care. It's late, and I'm exhausted."

"Lilly…" Enrique beseeched.

She kissed his cheek again. "Hey, I'm not angry. Have a good evening."

"Are you ready?" Jacob's voice interjected into the moment.

Lilly nodded, and the two walked outside, pulling their coats tight against the chill. "Thanks again for the cab." Christ, could she come up with anything else to say?

Jacob set down the bag of food on an outdoor table, putting his hands on Lilly's arms and turning her towards him. "What were you thinking before?"

Fuck, he's touching me again, my brain doesn't function when this man touches me. "Before when?"

"Right after I said how I pity the fool dumb enough to fall in love. You had this look on your face, but at the last second you held back and asked me to let you up." His grip tightened slightly. "What were you going to say?"

"I don't remember," Lilly lied.

"Yes, you do, Lilly. What were you going to say?"

"The cab's here."

Jacob dropped his hands, letting out a resigned huff. "Right." Then he rolled his eyes. The bastard rolled his eyes.

Lilly paused against the taxi door, knowing her mother would roll over in her grave as her daughter threw every bit of manners out the window in lieu of brutal honesty. "I was going to call bullshit on your statement."

Jacob's eyes widened as he walked over. "Excuse me?"

"There is nothing like love. Sure, sometimes it hurts like hell, but it's worth every second. Maybe you just fell in love with the wrong woman. Next time, you'll fall in love with the right one."

"You're such an expert?"

"Not by a long shot, but I know if you gave it a chance, you'd be a happier person."

"I'm happy," Jacob growled, an inner fire emanating from him.

Lilly laughed at the blatant lie. She saw right through this man. "Successful, yes. Talented, sure. Gorgeous, you're adored by millions. But

33

happy? Not a whit."

Jacob leaned in, their faces only inches apart. "You don't know anything about it—"

Lilly's eyes blazed as she leaned forward. "Don't I? I think I hit the nail right on the head, you're just too scared to admit it."

She saw his jaw tick, his fists clench and his nostrils flare. She waited for his retort, round two of his verbal assault.

"God damn it, Lilly." Without warning, Jacob set down the bag of food, grabbed her arms and pulled her against him, claiming her mouth with a savage kiss.

This kiss was unlike the earlier theatrics in the bar; this kiss bled emotion. It was raw, angry and needy. Lilly's hands moved up to push him away, but Jacob grabbed her wrists as he delivered a bite to her lower lip. Lilly gasped, and Jacob took that opportunity to slide his tongue into her mouth, possessing her completely.

She released a soft moan and Jacob deepened the kiss, one hand coming up to hold her head, tangling in her hair. As the shock wore off, the sparks set in, flooding her every cell.

Just as suddenly as it began, Jacob pulled away; his breath coming in ragged gasps. He looked over her shoulder, his face a sea of conflicting emotions.

Lilly stood there, frozen, her fingers on her lips. Her insides churned like the sea during a hurricane, she had to escape. "I have to go."

"Lilly—"

Lilly jumped into the taxi and gave her address, refusing to look back at Jacob.

CHAPTER FOUR

Jacob

Jacob watched the taxi leave, uncertain what transpired moments earlier. He hadn't intended to kiss her—again—but his emotions and need for Lilly took over, fuck, but she could kiss.

His thumb traced his mouth, her lips were so soft, and she tasted so damn good. He chuckled to himself—in an effort to prove love was meant only for fools, he had behaved like one instead. And he enjoyed every second of it.

"What the hell was that?" An agitated voice bellowed over his shoulder.

Jacob jumped at the sudden question, he hadn't heard anyone come outside. "You startled me, mate."

"I am not your mate. I'll ask again, what the hell was that with Lilly?"

Jacob closed his eyes and sighed, time to do battle with the good doctor. He turned to face Enrique, noting the scowl and glare emanating from his dark eyes. "What did it look like?"

Enrique inched forward. "She's too good for the likes of you. I know your reputation, how you treat women."

Jacob scoffed, this was brilliant. "You don't know a damn thing about me. You know what you read in magazines, which is bullshit, by the way. And you're one to talk. At least my girlfriend didn't show up while I was making a move on someone else."

"She's not my girlfriend. You don't know anything about me either."

Jacob held up his hands, he wasn't in the mood to do battle. "Fair enough. I don't care if Emma is your girlfriend or not, but Lilly might have an opinion."

"Stay away from Lilly."

Usually, Jacob would have agreed, considering he barely knew Lilly and had his pick of eligible women, but something wrenched in his gut at the idea of passing up an opportunity with the petite brunette. He shook his head and chuckled. "I don't think so, Dr. Torres."

Enrique got in his face. "Do I have to make you stay away from her?"

"Are you insane? Shall we duel at dawn? Fight for her hand?" Jacob met the surgeon's glare, aware that people were gathering on the sidewalk.

"Enrique? What's going on? What are you two fighting about?" Enrique's friend, Emma, placed a hand on the doctor's shoulder.

Enrique jerked his arm from her grasp, raking a hand through his dark hair. "Nothing."

Emma's gaze moved to Jacob, looking for answers. "What am I missing here? Did your wife leave, Mr. Edmonton?"

Jacob nodded, volleying back Enrique's unwavering stare. "Lilly went home, and I am headed back to my family. Lovely meeting you, Emma. Enrique." With a final scowl, he turned in the direction of the hospital.

The hotel suite was a bevy of activity when he arrived, far different from when he left.

"Uncle Jacob!" A small blonde girl raced out of one of the bedrooms.

Jacob grinned, scooping up his niece. "Hello, beautiful. I missed you."

"I missed you too." The little girl buried her face in the crook of his neck and Jacob carried her and the bag of food to the kitchen area.

Audrey walked out of the bedroom, hairbrush in hand. "Elizabeth, we weren't finished." She straightened when she saw her brother-in-law. "You're back."

Jacob set Elizabeth down and began unloading the contents of the bag. "I stopped to get us food at the pub."

"You smell like whiskey. Did you drink your dinner?"

Jacob sent Audrey a scathing look. "I saw Dr. Torres and Lilly; they bought me a drink."

Audrey softened. "Did they have any news on Janie?"

"They said she's progressing beautifully. She'll be out of bed tomorrow."

Tears filled Audrey's eyes, and she wrapped her arms around Jacob. "Thank God."

"She's going to get through this, Audrey. I promise you. She has too much to live for with you and Elizabeth."

Audrey pulled back, her cheeks wet with tears, a smile playing on her mouth. "And a pain in the ass big brother."

"That too. Come on, I got you bangers and mash."

"Whiskey too?"

"I knew I forgot something."

Audrey laughed, calling Elizabeth to the table. "I should send you back for it."

"Good thing I remembered *before* I left the pub."

"Oh, good man. I knew we kept you around for a reason."

Elizabeth hopped onto Jacob's lap, her excitement boundless. "Do you know there's a whirlpool tub here just like your house?"

Jacob stroked his niece's hair. "Is that a fact?"

36

Elizabeth nodded, chewing her chip thoughtfully.

Audrey offered Jacob a strange smile. "You're a natural with children; perhaps you should consider finding a good woman and settling down. Or is that too bourgeoisie for you?"

Jacob chuckled, he was surprised how much Audrey's attitude changed when he brought good news about Janie. But he opted not to look a gift horse in the mouth, choosing to enjoy a civil dinner with his sister-in-law.

Jacob dropped a kiss on Elizabeth's head as she scrambled into her own seat. "Finding a good woman is the trick. I'm fabulous at finding one-night stands and serpents disguised as women. You and Janie are lucky."

"We are lucky. But we were willing to take a chance on each other. That's where you and I differ."

"We both like beautiful women," Jacob joked, earning a guffaw from Audrey.

"Truer words have never been spoken."

"How did you know Janie was the one?" Jacob had never inquired about their relationship. Hell, he was usually too busy worrying about himself.

"It wasn't just one moment, it was a collection of moments that equaled her being the one woman I couldn't live without. And your sister threw a lot of obstacles at me, for kicks, I think. But I bashed through them with a battering ram. Nothing she could throw at me would deter my quest to make her mine."

Jacob poured them both a glass of whiskey and sat back, listening to Audrey regale him with the tale of her courtship with Janie. "You knew right away, then."

Audrey nodded. "I did. Another woman was interested in her and asked me to back off. Any other time, I would have done just that. But with Janie, I told that woman to kiss off. She was mine."

Jacob choked on his whiskey, realizing his sister-in-law's tale echoed his own spat over Lilly.

"You okay?"

Jacob nodded. "Went down the wrong pipe."

"Why the sudden interest in mine and Janie's romance?"

Jacob stroked his beard, recalling his earlier kiss with Lilly. "They say the best way to achieve anything in life is to find someone successful in that arena and mimic their behavior. You and Janie are a prime example."

"Since when are you looking for a successful relationship? I thought you had a four-week timeline with any of your ladies."

"They're lucky to make it that far. Damn, I sound like a cad."

Audrey shrugged. "To be sure, but at least you're an honest cad."

37

Jacob swigged his whiskey, feeling the warm burn move through his body. That same burn swept through him when his lips pressed against Lilly's sensual mouth. "I'm getting tired of being a cad, honest or otherwise."

They finished their dinner and Audrey put Elizabeth to bed while Jacob checked on his Mum. Then he settled in the living room, his fingers wrapped around his third glass of whiskey. "Is she asleep?"

Audrey nodded. "Out like a light. The excitement of today wore her out. It wore all of us out." She sat next to Jacob, a refill in her hand. "So, you hung out with Dr. Torres and Lilly? I figured those two were dating."

Jacob snorted. "They're not dating."

"That was a speedy retort."

"He wants to date her, he made that point clear to me tonight."

Audrey sat up, staring at Jacob. "What aren't you telling me?"

"Bugger." Jacob buried his head in his hands. "I went off on Lilly earlier today."

"Why?"

"She claimed I had screwed up priorities." He looked to Audrey, a smirk on her face. "I got pissed because she was right. The woman knew me five minutes and saw right through me. I let her have it, and she let me have it right back."

Audrey chuckled. "I like this girl, standing up to you."

"All one and a half meters of her," Jacob grumbled.

"You like her."

"I do not—"

"Bullshit. Yes, you do; you like her." She swirled the whiskey in the glass. "Did you play nice at the bar or did you throw some more zingers her way?"

"I was a total asshole, but she outmaneuvered me. She's a hell of a kisser though." He finished off his whiskey.

You could have heard a pin drop. "You kissed Lilly? How in the world did that happen?"

"I've got skills." The cad exterior was firmly in place again.

"Oh for God's sake." Audrey stood up, heading towards one of the bedrooms. "Be careful, or you might fall in love for real this time."

"I think I'm safe." Jacob stared at the bottom of his glass, feeling the weight of his lie. He wasn't safe at all. "Audrey?"

"Yeah?"

"How would I know?"

"You'll know. All other women will fail to shine as brightly as she does."

With a final wave, Audrey slipped into the bedroom, leaving Jacob alone with his thoughts.

His phone flashed, and for a brief instant he wondered if it might be Lilly; a ridiculous thought, they hadn't exchanged numbers. His breath caught when he saw who sent the message. It was Victoria.

'Hey Jacob, miss me? I miss you. We need to have a chat, discuss our situation. Love and stuff, V.'

This was the first time she reached out since he found her in his bed with another man. The same day his unfortunate 'groveling incident' achieved worldwide publication. He cringed when he recalled how brokenhearted he was at her infidelity. Christ he'd been a fool.

He hit the button to reply to her message but paused. What was there to say to each other at this point? A month ago, he would have given his right arm for such a text, but tonight he tossed the phone aside without answering. Maybe it was Janie's surgery bringing about his change of heart. Who was he kidding, he hadn't been able to push Lilly from his mind since they met.

Lilly

Lilly didn't care what time it was; she deserved a bubble bath. She sank into the bathtub, the warm water soothing her aching muscles. Unfortunately, it did nothing for the irritation she felt towards Jacob Edmonton, or the way her body reacted whenever she thought of the man. And that kiss, that damn kiss. It was amazing she didn't orgasm from his kiss alone.

She closed her eyes, reliving the moment, the pressure of his mouth against hers, his tongue working its magic. Damn him for being so talented in that department. Why did the best kiss she'd ever experienced have to be with a man who only valued women for their erotic abilities?

Before she could ponder the issue further, the phone rang, and Lilly mentally prepared herself before answering. It was after midnight. It wasn't likely to be good news on the other end of the phone. "Hello?"

Sabina's voice was a welcome sound to her ears. "Hey girl, I wanted to check on you. I left a couple of messages, but I hadn't heard back, and I was worried. How's our VIP?"

Lilly sipped her Chardonnay. "She was doing great when I left."

"And when was that exactly?"

"Enrique and I left about ten."

Sabina mewed appreciatively. "Really? How interesting."

Lilly chortled. "No, it's not. Ben already told you about catching us in the locker room?"

"Whatever do you mean?" Sabina feigned innocence.

"Save it. Sorry to break it to you, but nothing happened."

"Ben said you two looked mighty cozy together before he accidentally busted up the moment. Did you two pick up where you left off?"

Lilly snorted in laughter. "Yeah right. His girlfriend showed up, which left me alone with Jacob Edmonton, and it was all downhill from there."

"Hold up, you were with Jacob Edmonton? And you didn't call me?"

"It wasn't planned. Enrique and I went to the pub for a drink—"

"With his girlfriend? Wasn't that a bit awkward?"

"No, she showed up later. Jacob came in to pick up food and Enrique invited him for a drink. Then his girlfriend showed up, Enrique left me with Jacob and..." Lilly trailed off, her face flushing.

"And what? You better not withhold juicy information, girl." Lilly could almost see Sabina sitting on the edge of her seat. She lived for this dramatic crap.

"We kissed twice, and then I left," Lilly blurted out, speaking so quickly that the words ran together.

"You kissed Jacob Edmonton? Holy shit."

"Not exactly. Jacob kissed me, but he didn't mean it."

"I can't even pretend to know what that means. Was he out of his tree?"

Lilly giggled, this conversation had gone down the rabbit hole. "No, he wasn't drunk."

"Let me see if I've got this right, a sober Jacob Edmonton kissed you, not once but twice, but he didn't mean it. Did he just keep falling against your mouth?"

"The first time he was pretending we were a couple in front of Emma."

"Who the hell is Emma?"

"Enrique's girlfriend. You wanted the story, keep up." Lilly giggled again. "Jacob figured he could embarrass me by putting on a show and putting me on the spot, but I upped the ante and pretended to be his wife. I even leaned in to kiss him, and before I knew it, we *were* kissing."

"So you kissed him?" Sabina qualified.

"I moved forward, but I planned on pulling back at the last second. Apparently, he moved forward as well."

"Crikey. Was he any good? He must be an amazing kisser."

"The kiss was pleasant."

"Pleasant? Do you know how many women would kill to be in your shoes right now?"

"He's an asshole and a self-proclaimed womanizer. He said that he pities anyone foolish enough to fall in love."

"And that made you want to kiss him again?" Sabina's question echoed her disbelief.

"I told you, he kissed me. Both times. The second time was to shut me up. He didn't like me telling him that I thought his bad boy image was a load of crap."

"I can't believe I wasn't there. Was this another one of those pleasant kisses?"

Lilly's body tingled as she relived the kiss. "It was a soul-wrenching kiss, hot as Hades."

"Damn girl, how did you leave it? And what does Enrique think of all this?"

"I got into a taxi and left immediately after the kiss and Enrique has no

41

idea it happened. There you go, my night in a nutshell."

"Enrique up and left with his girlfriend, no goodbye? That's rude."

"He claimed Emma wasn't his girlfriend, but her body language said otherwise. He offered to drive me home, but I declined."

Sabina guffawed. "You passed on an opportunity to soak in a tub with a gorgeous surgeon? Girl, were you dropped on your head as a child?"

Lilly giggled. "Definitely not. And I have a date. A glass of Chardonnay and two tabby cats who want nothing to do with me."

This answer did not satisfy Sabina. "What woman doesn't want a strong, sexy, Spaniard as her personal masseuse? Oh wait, this is you I'm talking to—"

"Hilarious, Sabina. I'm not getting involved in whatever his situation is with Emma. It's far too complex for my liking. Besides, he doesn't need another wide-eyed fan for his club."

Sabina paused. "Are we still talking about Dr. Torres or have we segued to a certain blue-eyed actor who couldn't stop kissing you?"

Lilly scoffed into the receiver. "Both, honestly. I don't get the impression that Enrique sets out to break hearts, but Jacob seems to enjoy the sport. He's a total player. Ugh."

"He isn't that bad, Lilly. Don't forget he's had an awful day."

"Of course you don't think he's that bad. You were drooling over him earlier."

"That's beside the point, and you better not tell him that factoid." Sabina cleared her throat. "He returned to the unit about seven, he was looking for you. He brought you a delicious pasta dinner, which I told him you couldn't eat."

Lilly's voice rose in curiosity. "He brought me dinner?"

"Which I kindly ate for you."

"What a pal." Lilly paused before mumbling, "Why would Jacob bring me dinner?"

"He figured you were exhausted, and he doubted you had eaten since breakfast. He then went on for five minutes bumbling all over the place about what a jerk he was to you and how awful he felt."

Now Lilly's interest was really piqued. "Jacob Edmonton said that? I find that hard to believe."

"Well he did, and he seemed genuinely upset you weren't around for him to apologize. He even inquired about you and Dr. Torres. He seemed to think you two were married but looked infinitely relieved to learn that wasn't the case. Then he got a call and left; you missed him by not more than five minutes."

"It makes no sense! Why did he act like a jerk at the pub? Why didn't he try being nice if he felt so damn bad about his behavior earlier?"

Sabina laughed. "It reminds me of a boy on the playground pulling a little girl's braids because he likes her, but he doesn't know how to show it."

"There is no way in hell that man likes me. He made it abundantly clear what his views on love and romance are, and they're the complete opposite of mine."

"Meaning he sleeps with everyone and you sleep with no one?" Sabina asked pointedly.

Lilly's stomach turned at the thought of Jacob having sex with countless, faceless women. "Something like that," she muttered.

"You're an amazing catch. It's about time you put yourself back in the game. There's no shortage of men who want to date you. Why do you refuse to go out with any of them?"

"Are we really going to discuss this now?"

"Yes, because you are letting two gorgeous men slide by the wayside. Don't you know that's Adonis abuse?"

Lilly choked on her wine. "Why don't you date them?"

"Spill it. Why are you so unwilling to date?"

Lilly sighed as she popped bubbles with her fingers. "I dated a musician for five years, thought we were going to get married, have babies, the whole white picket fence scenario. His band was gaining notoriety, so I supported us. I worked two jobs and put my dreams on hold…I thought it would be a temporary hold. He was brilliant, and he knew it, and so did his adoring fans." She took another swig of wine, steeling herself to continue. "I came home to his empty closets and a note. He claimed he needed to focus on his work and I was a distraction."

"Bastard," Sabina breathed.

"But that wasn't the truth. He had taken up with a PR rep at Sony Music. She could advance his career, so I guess she was the right kind of distraction." Lilly finished her wine. "Apparently, everyone associated with the band knew they were having an affair. Everyone but me. I was blindsided. It was utter humiliation."

"When did this happen? You never talk about it."

"It was a year ago. I walked around in a kind of daze for the first nine months, so angry at myself for believing in him, letting someone get that close. The worst part? I loved him but not in some earth-shattering manner; I figured it was a good, solid relationship and fireworks were meant for romance novels. I gave up five years and my chance to have a family…did I mention they had

43

a baby girl last year?" Lilly chewed her lip, willing the memory back to the recesses of her mind.

"And there's been no one since then?"

"No, although I have to admit I still look for fireworks." Lilly rubbed her throbbing head. "I'm terrified to let anyone that close again, especially someone whose work is their life. I would always wind up second best or dumped when someone better came along."

Sabina sighed into the phone. "Luv, not everyone is like that wanker. There are good men out there. Hell, at least go out and get laid."

Lilly giggled. "And just like that, it comes back round to sex."

"Doesn't everything?"

"I'm not looking for sex, that's why God made vibrators. I'm looking for a love that sinks its claws into your soul and won't let go. A feeling so strong you couldn't fight it if you tried."

Sabina scoffed. "Is that all?"

"Go big or go home."

"So, if you find fireworks, all celibate bets are off?"

Lilly hesitated, recalling the fireworks display when she and Jacob kissed. "I'll let you know when I feel them. But until then, are we done dredging up my past?"

"Sure, for now at least. It's late, get some rest. You'll be at work tomorrow?"

Lilly sighed as she heaved herself out of the tub and grabbed a nearby towel. "I'm teaching a class in the morning, so I'll be there, besides, I want to check on Janie and make certain she's doing okay. I promised her family. I'll see you tomorrow?"

"Absolutely. Here's to some spicy hot dreams involving one of two gorgeous men; both of whom are besotted with you." Sabina hung up the phone before Lilly could reply.

What nonsense, Lilly surmised, padding into her kitchen. Her tabby cats still weren't speaking to her after their delayed dinner, so she opened another can of cat food in an effort to bribe their good will.

As she slid under her covers, Lilly willed her mind to think of anything but Jacob Edmonton, but her final thought before sleep took hold was how it felt to be held in his arms.

CHAPTER FIVE

Jacob

Jacob strolled into the critical care unit, balancing boxes of pastries and bouquets of flowers with the grace of a ballroom dancer. He stopped at the nurses station and presented a tray of baked goodies, posing for a picture with a few of the staff nurses.

And then he heard it—the most beautiful sound—Janie's laughter. He hurried into his sister's room where he stopped in his tracks. Lilly was perched on the side of Janie's bed, the two women giggling about something on Lilly's phone.

His body clenched at the sight of Lilly, the memory of their kiss fresh in his mind. His eyes roved over her body, she looked so different from the other day. Instead of scrubs, she wore a light gray skirt that showcased her ridiculously long legs and a fitted sweater that played up her ample breasts. His fingers twitched at his side with an uncontrollable urge to tangle his hands in her dark hair and press that luscious body against him.

Janie giggled when she glanced up and caught her brother openly ogling Lilly. "Jakey! You're here!" Jacob swooped in for a hug, careful not to dislodge any of the remaining wires and stood back to admire his sister. In his haste, his hand brushed against Lilly, and he faltered, grabbing her leg to maintain his balance.

"Sorry Lilly, I—" He halted when his gaze met hers; and she blushed. At least she was equally flustered.

"Are you quite alright, Mr. Edmonton?" Lilly inquired, moving to the opposite side of the bed. "Doesn't Janie look wonderful? She's already walked the length of the hallway today. Soon I'll be running to keep pace with her."

Jacob realized he was staring at Lilly and switched his gaze to his sister, who winked knowingly in his direction. "You're gorgeous Janie, ready to hit the catwalk."

Janie giggled, squeezing Jacob's hand. "You're a terrible liar, but I do look tons better than two days ago. What craziness. I thought I had the flu." She fingered the necklace around her neck. "Isn't this beautiful? Lilly gave it to me. She said it would bring me love and luck."

Jacob dropped a kiss on Janie's forehead before meeting Lilly's gaze again. "I've seen it, and I believe it will bring you both those things." He presented a bouquet with a flourish. "These are for you."

45

Janie buried her nose in the flowers. "Tulips, my favorite. Thank you." Spotting the other bouquet, she inquired, "And who are those for? My invisible roommate?"

For the second time in a matter of minutes, Jacob felt a flush rise in his face. "Actually, they're for Lilly."

Lilly choked on her sip of coffee. "Me? What in the world for?"

Jacob handed Lilly the bouquet with a smile. "For being you."

Lilly accepted the flowers, surprise evident on her face. "That's really kind, thank you. I'll leave you two to visit while I find a …a vase." Lilly squeezed Janie's hand and nodded at Jacob before skittering out of the bay.

Janie collapsed in a fit of giggles when Lilly left the room, and Jacob glared at his sister in mock anger. "And what exactly do you find so funny?"

"You, my always put together and polished brother, bumbling around like a fresher in university. Make it a bit more obvious, why don't you?"

"I tripped Janie, it could happen to anyone. These rooms are full of hazards with all the wires and tubes and—" He broke off as her laugh turned into a cough. She grabbed a heart-shaped pillow and held it to her chest incision, slowing her breathing. "Should I get some help?"

"No, Lilly said its normal during the recovery period. It hurts when I laugh or cough, but the pillow helps."

"I'll let you rest." Jacob rose from the bed, but Janie grabbed his wrist.

"Please stay, I've missed you. You must fill me in on everything in your life. I live vicariously through you."

Jacob guffawed at her statement, but Janie continued, undeterred. "It's true, you're adored everywhere you go. They roll out the red carpet for you and upgrade you the moment they see you."

"I'm adored by people that don't matter. The ones who do, can't seem to stand me." Jacob's words hung as heavy as a wet blanket on a summer day.

"I adore you, and I hope I matter."

Jacob kissed his sister's cheek. "You matter most of all, Little Bit."

"Have you heard from her?" Janie's gaze was pointed as she addressed the elephant in the room.

"I'm assuming you mean Victoria?" Jacob shifted on the bed, uncertain he wanted to broach this topic.

"No, Oprah Winfrey. Of course I mean Victoria. Did she send regrets after the awards show? Perhaps a photo of her latest lover?" Janie didn't bother to hide the disgust in her voice.

"She texted the other night and wanted to talk. I returned the call the following day, explained your health situation. She sends her love and wishes for a speedy recovery."

Janie snorted. "I'll bet she does. Why are you still speaking to her, Jakey? She's not good enough for you. You deserve someone who really loves you—the person you are inside—not just the exterior facade."

To be honest, Victoria was the furthest thing from Jacob's mind. Beyond his shock over her random text and their brief phone call, his thoughts circulated between worry over his sister, strained family relations, his ruined reputation...and Lilly. Despite his best efforts that little nurse filled his thoughts since she first walked into his world, and it went deeper than the glaring physical chemistry. She looked right through his armor and saw the pain hiding underneath. In thirty minutes Lilly understood his inner workings better than Victoria had in six months, and that idea made Jacob uneasy. Lilly could strip him bare—body and soul.

"I don't hope for reconciliation anymore. I simply thought Victoria should know about your situation. Her reaction was practiced, her delivery perfect, but there wasn't a speck of emotion behind it. You were always right about her. However, she claims to have a lead on that new action movie, and if I were to land that role, it would secure my career."

"By crawling back into bed with a black widow?" Janie sat up and looked into her brother's eyes, her blue depths mirroring his own. "You don't need her help. You are unbelievably talented. You just need to stand the hell back up and remember who you are, remember Jacob before Victoria came along. I miss that guy."

Jacob smiled, ruffling Janie's hair. "You always were my greatest cheerleader."

"And president of your fan club."

"Probably the only member at this point."

Janie giggled. "You need someone outside the business, someone...like Lilly. She's fabulous, isn't she? She's been so helpful throughout this entire ordeal, a real lifesaver." She plucked at her blanket, a smirk crossing her delicate features. "And damn easy on the eyes."

That's the understatement of the century, Jacob thought, keeping that fact to himself. "I assume you're referring to the nurse?"

Janie glared at her brother's futile attempt at disinterest. "Don't be daft, you're not that good an actor. You brought her flowers, and I presume whatever is in that box is for her. I saw the way you looked at Lilly. I've never seen you look at someone like that."

"I'm thrilled she's taking good care of you, Janie. Can't I show my appreciation?"

"By gawking at her legs? Sure, if that's how you show gratitude."

Jacob huffed. "Besides, she has something brewing with your surgeon, Dr. Torres."

"And how would such a disinterested party know this?" Janie smirked, her lips curling at her brother. "There's nothing brewing between them."

Jacob straightened, his curiosity piqued. "How do you know?"

"I asked her. I saw how Dr. Torres was around her, and I surmised the same thing, but Lilly said they barely know each other. Apparently, he acted like a bit of a cad the other night. You aren't the only man falling all over her today."

"He behaved like a total ass." He surprised himself with his quick retort. "Did she mention me?"

Janie's eyebrows shot up. "Now why would she mention you?" Another giggle, ending in a cough. "You could try being charming, it might serve you better than being prickly as a cactus."

Before Jacob could respond, a nurse entered the room, needing to draw blood for labs. Jacob stole another kiss and excused himself, walking to the nurses station.

Sabina grinned broadly upon seeing Jacob. "Well hello, Mr. Edmonton; don't you look fine this morning?"

Jacob laughed, running a hand over his beard. "I suppose better than I did a couple days ago; showered, at least. I wanted to speak with Lilly, but I don't see her on the floor. Is she working in another unit today?"

Sabina tilted her head and smiled again, this time with a mischievous glint. "Lilly isn't a staff nurse."

Jacob's heart dropped. "She isn't a nurse?"

"Of course, she's a nurse, she's the coordinator and educator of the units. Her office is at the end of the hall."

Jacob nodded, strolling in that direction when Sabina added, "I'm assuming it's gluten-free this time?"

Jacob chuckled over his shoulder. "Completely and utterly free of gluten."

"Good man. I knew there was hope for you yet." With a final smile and wave, Jacob made his way towards Lilly's office.

Lilly

L illy settled into her chair for the first time in two days, turning her radio to Stevie Nicks and opening her salad. The first bite was halfway to her mouth when someone knocked.

"Just perfect," Lilly muttered under her breath, swinging open the door. Jacob stood on the other side, and Lilly felt her pulse quicken. Damn her body's reaction to this insufferable man! "Mr. Edmonton, what can I do for you?"

Jacob shifted his weight, and if Lilly didn't know better, she would swear he was nervous. "If I apologize for being a total ass the other day, will you stop calling me Mr. Edmonton?"

Lilly laughed in spite of herself. "I might be able to accommodate that request, depending on the strength of the apology."

Jacob smiled, and Lilly's stomach flipped with how it lit up his face. "I'm fully committed to groveling."

"Always up for a good grovel, come in." Lilly stepped aside, allowing him access to her office. "Have a seat." She was aware of his lingering gaze on her legs and tugged at her skirt in a futile attempt to provide more coverage.

Jacob handed her a tea, which she gratefully accepted.

"One caveat."

Lilly raised her eyebrows. This should be interesting. "Caveat to what?"

Jacob's eyes darkened as he leaned forward, his arms resting on his knees. "The apology."

Great, here it comes. Lilly shook her head and closed her eyes, mentally preparing for another round with the A-list actor.

"I won't apologize for kissing you."

Lilly's breath caught, her palms sweaty. "Really?"

Jacob shot her a hooded look, his fingers tracing up her arm. "All I want is to do it again."

She could melt or play hard to get, and Lilly wasn't known for melting. "Does every woman fall at your feet when you say something like that?"

Jacob sputtered his tea, obviously not expecting that response, and earning a giggle from Lilly. "Clearly, you aren't one of those women."

Lilly's smile widened. "Clearly."

For the first time since their introduction, Lilly saw something new flash in Jacob's eyes—admiration. "Do you think we might call a truce?"

"Whatever for? I'm having too much fun with this banter to be nice to you."

Their gaze met and held, both trying to hold back their laughter. Eventually, it won, and they busted forth together.

"I can honestly say you are unlike any woman I've ever met, Lilly."

"I don't know if that's a good thing or a terrible thing."

He leaned forward again, grasping her hand. "I've known scads of women, but you have turned me on my head."

Lilly chewed her bottom lip, aware of his marked gaze, still uncertain as to the meaning of his statement. She couldn't tell if he was crazy about her or insane from being around her, and she wasn't sure which option was more dangerous. "Still a mystery."

"Let me clarify. You're an amazing woman, Lilly. Absolutely, exquisitely amazing."

Lilly's heart was in her throat; she was so screwed. He appeared to mean every word. *Fuck, it's hot in here.* Lilly tucked her hair behind her ear, an uncertain smile crossing her lips. "Let's get back to the point. What can I do for you, Jacob?"

He seemed to pick up on her discomfort and thankfully, changed topics, thrusting a box at her. "These are for you."

Lilly's nostrils were hit with the heady chocolate aroma upon opening the package. "Brownies. They look delicious, but I can't eat them. Thank you anyway, though."

"You can, they're gluten-free. I made them myself."

Lilly almost dropped the box at Jacob's words. "You...made them for me?"

"I am capable of being a nice guy."

"Are they laced with arsenic?" Lilly retorted.

"If you must know, strychnine, does it matter?"

Lilly giggled. "I suppose one poison is as good as another." She took a bite of the brownie, eyes widening at the flavor.

Jacob observed her surprised expression and helped himself to one, adding, "I can cook too. I have skills."

"Apparently. They're delicious. Thank you."

"So, do you forgive me?"

Lilly smirked, considering Jacob's proposal. "Chocolate and groveling are my favorite combination. You're forgiven."

Jacob grinned, popping another bite into his mouth. "You weren't entirely forthcoming, you know."

50

Lilly's eyes widened. "The last time I checked I told you exactly what I thought in no uncertain terms."

"No one denies your honesty is brutal, but your words were deserved. I needed to hear them. What I mean is you had me believe you were a nurse."

"I am a nurse, I'm just not a staff nurse. Dr. Torres asked that I personally supervise your sister's case."

Jacob nodded thoughtfully, his fingers drumming his leg. "Dr. Torres, a competent surgeon with questionable social motives."

Lilly smiled, choosing to ignore Jacob's barb. "Absolutely. He's very competent." A knock on the door interrupted their conversation. "Excuse me one moment." She opened the door and exchanged a few words with a co-worker before turning to Jacob. "I have to grab a file, it's right behind you." Her voice faltered as she leaned over him to snag the file, pausing to breathe him in—the perfect blend of musk and sandalwood. Memories of the other night flooded her senses and Lilly tried to look anywhere but Jacob's full mouth.

What are you doing, Lilly? You're practically draped over him! Lilly snapped from her reverie but not before their eyes met. They weren't more than six inches from each other, so close she could see every freckle and golden hair in his beard.

Flustered, she straightened her skirt and handed the file to her coworker, before shutting the door again. "Sorry about the boardinghouse reach."

Jacob appeared dazed as well, although his voice remained calm. "It's fine, small space."

With a nervous chuckle, Lilly settled back into her chair. "Janie looks fabulous; she's made tremendous strides in the last 48 hours. She'll be moving to a step-down unit later today, so you'll be rid of all us mean intensive care personnel."

"I wanted to speak to you about that, actually."

Which part, Lilly wondered, *the intensive care nurses, Janie's progress, or how after your sister transfers to another unit, I will never see your face again?* She was shocked by how the idea of never seeing him again pulled at her insides. Shaking away the feeling, she balanced her chin on the heel of her hand. "About what?"

"I want to take you to dinner."

Lilly physically started at his words, her mind reeling from his statement. "Dinner? Whatever for?"

Jacob considered her question. "Well, you do eat, as made obvious by the brownie and the hamburger the other night, but as a thank you for everything you've done for Janie."

Of course, Lilly thought, *he feels obligated.* Still, her office now felt hotter than a brick oven. "That's sweet, but it isn't necessary."

Jacob leaned forward in his chair, clasping her hand again. Holy hell, she was going to burn alive if this man kept touching her. "It might not be necessary, but it's something I'd like to do. That is if you're not opposed to the idea."

Trying to ignore the sparks sweeping up her arm from his touch, she floundered to find words. "I'm not technically allowed to fraternize with patients."

"I'm not a patient."

"Or their family members, one of those hospital rules."

"You had no issue with fraternization the other night." Jacob released Lilly's hand and leaned back in the chair, an amused smile on his face. "Well, if all goes according to plan, Janie will be discharged within the next five days, right?" When Lilly nodded, he continued. "And then she won't be a patient anymore."

Lilly smiled, fiddling with a tendril of her dark brown hair. "Fine. When Janie is released, I'll have dinner with you. Although I'm sure you'll have forgotten all about this conversation by that point."

Jacob bent down to her, his breath tickling her earlobe. "I'm sure I won't." His lips hesitated a moment on her ear before kissing her on the cheek, and Lilly felt a warmth spread through her body.

He opened the door, finding Sabina on the other side, hand poised to knock.

"Jacob, what a lovely surprise." The nurse looked anything but surprised to see them together in Lilly's office.

He smiled in return. "Hello Sabina, I was just leaving."

"I didn't mean to interrupt, but I wanted to see if my girl was going to karaoke tonight."

Both Jacob and Sabina looked at Lilly, awaiting her reply.

"I'm not certain. It's been a long few days," Lilly stated.

Sabina patted Jacob on the chest. "You could stand to blow off some steam. Why don't you join us?"

Lilly's eyes widened at Sabina's brashness. She didn't know if she was more afraid of him accepting or declining the invitation. "Sabina, I'm sure Jacob has more exciting things to do than spend time with us in a karaoke bar."

Jacob's eyes twinkled before replying. "I would love to go, Sabina, but Lilly told me it's against hospital policy for employees to socialize with family members."

Lilly covered her face with her hands, her cheeks flaming, mortified at what would come next.

Sabina shook her head as she looked back and forth between Jacob and Lilly. "Well, that's rubbish. There's no such policy. Come on, we'll have a bang-up time. I'll even buy you a drink."

Jacob's gaze pierced Lilly. She was caught. His smile to Sabina was equal parts flirtatious and devilish. "I'd love to. In fact, I'll pick the two of you up. I just need directions."

Sabina beamed at Jacob's acceptance of her invitation. "That would be lovely. What a gentleman," she said, scribbling down her address. "Eight o'clock?"

Jacob nodded, accepting the paper. "I don't have your address, Lilly."

"I'll meet you there," Lilly muttered, acting riveted by something on her computer screen. "I live just down the block from the pub. I can walk."

"Are you quite sure? I don't mind driving you."

Her cheeks couldn't burn any hotter. "I'm positive, but thank you."

"Then I'll see you tonight." He smiled at both ladies, closing the door behind him.

"Can you believe it? He's hanging out tonight! Jacob Edmonton is picking me up! Wait a second, why didn't you want him to pick you up?"

Lilly shrugged as if being asked out by Hollywood celebrities was an everyday occurrence. "Because I always walk to the bar? Besides, I'm sure something will come up with his agent or girlfriend, and he won't be able to go. You'd better have a back-up plan."

"I don't think so. The man is infatuated with you."

Lilly scoffed, ignoring the ever-present swarm of butterflies when Jacob's name was mentioned. "Don't be ridiculous. He isn't interested in me. He just feels obligated because we saved his sister and he was a total ass to me the other day."

Sabina shook her head as she turned to leave. "Fifty pounds says you're wrong and he'll kiss you again before the night is out."

"You're a whole new level of crazy."

"Is that a yes or a no? Perhaps you're too chicken to take the bet, since you know I'll win?"

Lilly grasped Sabina's hand and shook her head, smiling. "You are certifiable, but you're on, I could use fifty pounds. I'll see you tonight."

CHAPTER SIX

Jacob

As Jacob chatted with Sabina in the darkened booth, he realized how much he missed sharing a pint with friends. The pub was quaint and local enough that his presence slipped by unnoticed. He was grateful for the temporary anonymity.

He was also grateful that Sabina segued into a conversation about Lilly without him needing to broach the topic. In fact, her name came up almost immediately after they arrived at the pub. He felt oddly desperate to learn more about her, besides the lively discussion soothed his nerves. He was nervous as he awaited Lilly's arrival, not that he'd admit it, even if his life depended on it.

Jacob felt an immediate sense of comfort with Sabina and soon disclosed his family situation. "Lilly didn't approve of my extended absences from my family, and she had no issue with telling me." He raised his glass, motioning to the bartender for another whiskey.

Sabina fiddled with her swizzle stick and shrugged. "She wouldn't."

"Let me guess, she has a perfect family that never argues and spends every holiday in matching sweaters."

Sabina stopped fiddling and met his gaze. "Not even close, she doesn't have any family."

That statement hit Jacob in the gut. "I never would have guessed that."

"She keeps it close to the vest, but both her parents have passed, and she's an only child with no children of her own. She's basically alone in the world."

Jacob averted his eyes when the waitress placed the whiskey in front of him and paused for a moment, as if examining him. He waited for the inevitable question, but a call from the bartender broke the moment, and he smiled when she moved away from the table. "I pegged Lilly's situation all wrong, didn't I?"

"That's likely why she pushed you to be a bigger part of your family's life, since you still have that option."

Jacob considered Sabina's statement; despite his feelings of alienation, he was surrounded by a loving family, unlike Lilly. "She covers it well, she seems to love everybody. Except me, of course."

Sabrina grinned. "She's my tree-hugging gypsy." She sipped her drink, sending Jacob a sly smile. "And I think she likes you way more than she's letting on."

54

Sabina's statement coursed through his veins faster than the burn from a fine scotch, but he covered it with a chuckle. "A gypsy? That explains the Stevie Nicks music."

"Hey, I like Stevie Nicks too, but I'm no hippie. Lilly's quite the environmentalist, but her focus lies in protecting the animals. She's only been in London for three months and has already garnered enough funds and manpower to build a new set of dog runs at the shelter."

"I can't fault her for loving animals, my dog is my best mate. So, is Lilly this kind to people or is it reserved for the four-legged variety?"

Sabrina scoffed. "She prefers the four-legged variety, but her sarcastic exterior covers the gentlest heart. Hell, she barely knew me when I got kicked out of my flat, but she put my daughter and me up for two months until we got back on our feet. Never accepted a shilling from me. She takes care of everyone, maybe because no one ever took care of her. She's exceptional at loving people but not very good at allowing herself to be loved."

Jacob stared into his whiskey, mulling Sabina's statement. Since meeting Lilly, he felt an innate need to protect her, but couldn't put his finger on the reason why. Now he understood.

Sabina cleared her throat, smiling. "She'll kill me if I divulge any more of her secrets so let's move to a happier topic, like how fit I look in this outfit."

Jacob laughed. "Without question."

Sabina looked past him, a slow smile spreading across her face. "Of course, I don't look quite *that* good."

Jacob followed her gaze and saw Lilly walking to the bar, Dr. Torres at her side. He huffed at the sight of them together. "I see she brought a date."

Sabrina leaned further out of her side of the booth, a confused look on her face. "They're not dating. I invited him. They must have walked in at the same time." She leaned back, a knowing look on her face. "Are you not a fan of the good doctor?"

"He's a fabulous surgeon. He saved Janie's life, I'm forever grateful to him."

"That doesn't sound like a rehearsed line."

Jacob cleared his throat. "I think she could do better."

"Possibly…perhaps someone a bit more like…you?" Sabina grinned broadly.

"I didn't mean me." What a load of bollocks that was—complete crap. And judging by Sabina's smirk, she knew it too.

Jacob scanned the pub for another glimpse of Lilly. He spotted her at the end of the bar, laughing with Dr. Torres. The surgeon was hanging on her every word.

Her outfit accentuated every curve of her hourglass figure, full breasts and hips that he ached to wrap his hands around. Jacob missed women with curves—women in Hollywood either resembled toothpicks, or their curves were compliments of silicone and surgeons. But Lilly, she had curves in all the right places, and their kiss only whetted his appetite. He could spend hours exploring her body.

He stroked his beard as he watched Lilly laugh with the bartender, her pink lips curved into a smile, her long dark hair cascading down her back.

"Earth to Jacob...you all right there?"

Jacob chuckled, turning back to Sabina. "Sorry, I got distracted."

"A great ass will do that to you." Sabina nodded in Lilly's direction. "What are you sitting here for, go buy her a drink!"

Jacob hesitated, his nerves kicking in. *What is wrong with me? I'm more nervous than before my first movie audition!* "I don't want to interrupt her and Dr. Torres."

Sabina grabbed his arm across the booth, forcing Jacob to look at her. "Nothing is going on there. I get no enjoyment watching people make fools of themselves."

Jacob nodded and stood, but Sabina's grip remained firm. "But remember, I love that woman very much. Lilly is too good to be another notch on your bedpost."

"Is that what you think? I take whatever woman I want and play with them until I've had my fill?"

Sabina's eyes leveled his as she reached for her glass. "Don't you?"

The words stung, but Jacob knew she spoke the truth. He'd dated a string of Hollywood stars, but he soon tired of their wiles and left without a second look. He didn't intentionally set out to break hearts, it just worked out that way. But Jacob realized Lilly was more than a fleeting interest, no matter how much that idea terrified him. "I owe her a drink, and I promise you, I won't hurt her." His gaze held Sabina's, sober and sincere.

Sabina released his arm and knocked on the table before looking skyward with a grin. "You hear that God? He hurts her, put a lightning bolt in his ass."

Jacob grabbed his glass. "Do I have permission to approach the bar now? Do you need another?"

Sabina shook her head, laughing. "Go get her cowboy, let her know I've got our booth."

Jacob strolled to the bar, his heart beating faster as he closed in on Lilly. Dr. Torres was nowhere in sight, but a man to Lilly's left was ogling her like a dog after a juicy bone. Jacob slid between Lilly and the ogre and brushed the hair from her ear, whispering, "Glad you made it, wasn't certain how you'd feel about fraternizing with the enemy."

Lilly swiveled on the bar stool, rewarding him with a smile that outshone any starlet. "Are you the enemy now?"

"I don't want to be."

A few moments passed as they stared at each other, the air electric between them. Jacob was tempted to pull her to him for another searing kiss, but Lilly chuckled with that sexy laugh of hers, breaking the moment. "I'm glad I made it too, how are you and Sabina getting along?"

Jacob placed his hand on the bar and squeezed next to Lilly, his legs brushing against hers. She didn't move away. "We found we have something in common, which made for interesting conversation."

Lilly nodded, reaching across the bar for her glass of whiskey. Her arm brushed his, and he caught a whiff of her intoxicating scent. Leaning back, Lilly looked at him questioningly. "Do you or Sabina need a drink?"

Jacob was at a loss for words. He wanted to bury his face in her hair and breathe in her essence. Finally, he righted himself. "Two refills please, and put her drink on my tab," he muttered to the bartender before returning his focus to Lilly.

"Cheers." Lilly tipped her glass in his direction. "I saw Janie before I left the hospital, she's transferred to the step-down unit. She's a wonder, that one. Sweet as an angel."

Jacob smiled. "She has you fooled. She's not as innocent as she looks. You should have seen her as a kid. She would get into all sorts of mischief and then look at my parents with that angelic face and deny any wrongdoing."

Lilly giggled. "Maybe she was innocent."

"Not a chance! She painted the dog with watercolor paints and then blamed me! Unfortunately for Janie's four-year-old mind, she neglected to wash the paint off her hands before denying involvement in the incident."

"I must be careful with her around watercolors then."

Jacob chuckled, sinking into the now vacated barstool next to Lilly. "I believe she's progressed to oil paints, but I'll get back to you with the details." He sobered as he thought of his sister. "Janie became a wild teenager, into all manner of drugs and partying."

"And then she met Audrey, right? Janie was hiding who she really was, and when she finally opened the door to her truth, she didn't have to cover the pain anymore."

Jacob nodded, astonished how this woman understood his family dynamics. "Audrey saved her; showed her there was a better way of life. Then she had Elizabeth and Janie was complete."

Lilly leaned towards him, placing her slight hand on his arm. "Sometimes you don't realize you have holes in your heart until someone shows up to fill them."

Lilly's words tugged at Jacob. They were simple but profound, and he wondered if that someone was sitting next to him. The buzz of his phone distracted him, and he did a double take when he glanced at his caller ID. It was Victoria. Her timing was impeccable. He declined the call, but his phone vibrated again.

Rising from the bar stool, Jacob apologized. "Excuse me for a moment, I have to take this call."

Lilly nodded, a knowing expression on her face. She knew who was trying to reach him with such desperation. "Of course. I've got to find Sabina. It's almost time for her grand performance."

"I won't miss it," Jacob promised as he headed out the door.

Lilly

illy rubbed her forehead as Jacob exited the pub. *Silly Lilly, you hopeless romantic, men like Jacob are not interested in women like you.* Even though she was loath to admit it, she had looked up his ex-girlfriend Victoria online, wishing she hadn't as soon as she verified she was indeed the breathtaking blonde in the picture from the other night.

And now, Victoria was blowing up his phone, her intentions obvious. Lilly felt like an idiot for being so flirtatious, although she surmised Jacob behaved in such a manner with most women. C'est la vie.

She grabbed her whiskey and strolled to the booth where her friends had taken up residence. Enrique smiled and winked when he saw her, sliding over to make room. "Lilly, I wondered if you'd ever make it over here."

Lilly offered the handsome Spaniard a knowing smile. "Couldn't arrive empty-handed. Where's your friend tonight, Enrique?"

The pointed question hit its mark. "Emma is working late, big case in the morning."

Ben looked between Lilly and Enrique, his interest peaked. "Is Emma your girlfriend?"

Lilly almost felt bad for Enrique, cornered in enemy territory. He released his breath in a huff. "She's not my girlfriend, she's…" He struggled to find the right terminology.

"Your fuck buddy?" Sabina inquired.

"I hate that term," Enrique countered.

"So do I. Emma seems to be a lovely woman," Lilly interjected, bringing the topic to a close. She had her answer about the willowy blonde that seemed so enamored with Enrique. "Besides, it's the twenty-first century; labels are so dated."

"I disagree, I want the wife and kids," Enrique responded, his dark gaze holding Lilly captive.

"I'm trying to help you here," Lilly bit out.

"Lilly, I'm not dating her because I don't have that depth of feeling for her."

"And how does she feel about your lack of depth?" Lilly responded.

"She knows the score. I've never been anything but honest with her. I was angry with her the other night. She knew she was interrupting something—"

Sabina wasn't about to let Enrique slide. "Hey, I wasn't there the other night, so fill me in. What exactly was Emma interrupting?"

Lilly watched Enrique's jaw tense, and she swore the man blushed under his tan. "I was spending time with someone I wanted to know better; can we talk about something else?"

"But it's just getting juicy!" Sabina declared, biting her lip at Enrique's scowl.

"Sabina," Enrique growled under his breath.

"Fine." Sabina perused the bar, her gaze flitting to every corner. "Where's Jacob?"

"On the phone with his girlfriend." Lilly forced her tone to remain light. "So, what are we singing tonight?"

But Sabina wasn't letting the matter go. "Girlfriend? He said they were no longer dating."

Lilly shrugged. "It doesn't matter either way. Let's have fun, huh? Enrique, do you sing?"

Enrique rewarded her with a rich laugh. "Definitely not, I'm far better with my hands than ..." He trailed off, a flush creeping over his tanned cheeks.

Lilly and Sabina broke into a fit of giggles at his statement's connotation. "Good to know, Doc," Sabina smirked.

The house lights darkened, and the emcee appeared on the stage, announcing the karaoke contest. Sabina clapped, and Lilly beamed at her friend. What she lacked in vocal skill, she made up for in enthusiasm.

"Is there room for one more?" A low-timbred voice questioned.

Lilly glanced up, surprised by Jacob's return. "I thought you were leaving."

"Definitely not, I just had to settle something."

Lilly nodded and slid down to make room for Jacob, noticing the empty seat across the booth.

Enrique scoffed at Jacob. "Mr. Edmonton, how nice to see you again. We keep running into each other, what a coincidence."

Jacob shook hands with Enrique, his eyes piercing. "Dr. Torres, always a pleasure. Apparently, we have the same interests."

Lilly observed their brief interaction, noting the undeniable tension between the men.

Before she could consider the matter further, Sabina bounded back to the table. "The Flamenco Trees are opening with a few salsa numbers, and we get to dance!" Without hesitation, she grabbed Jacob's hand. "And you, handsome, are my dance partner."

Jacob laughed and agreed, looking at Lilly. "Will you be dancing as well?"

Before Lilly could answer, Enrique grabbed her hand, pulling her out of the booth. "She's with me. I love salsa dancing, but I haven't been able to partake in a long time."

Lilly looked at Ben, alone in the booth. "What about Ben? He needs a partner too!"

Ben chortled, stating he was fine minding the coats and purses.

Enrique led Lilly to the front of the pub. A few couples were already on the floor when the first musical notes blasted out into the pub.

Enrique wasted no time, spinning her across the floor, and Lilly shook off her momentary shock and fell into step, her hips swaying to the beat. Enrique's steps were flawless, and Lilly, although a talented dancer, struggled to keep up. She backed off a few steps to catch her breath, performing the hip shake and gyrations she perfected through hours of practice.

Lilly glanced at Sabina, twirling in Jacob's arms, and shot her a smile. Her friend was beaming. *I'd be happy too if that man had his arms wrapped around me.*

"You're quite the dancer, Enrique."

He brought Lilly close against him, their bodies inches apart. "I could say the same for you."

"I'd like to cut in," a voice stated over Lilly's shoulder.

Lilly watched Enrique's eyes narrow as he released her hand. She didn't have time to react when hands latched onto her hips, spinning her around, and she found herself pressed against Jacob, his eyes blazing with desire. He pulled her close, his lips against her neck. "You never told me you could move like that."

Fingers of electricity coursed through Lilly's body as he dipped her, his hands clutching her hips. For a moment, Lilly feared she might swoon like a character in a Jane Austen novel.

Rising up, their bodies slowed into a sexy, undulating rhythm as Lilly's lips hovered a whisper's breadth from Jacob, the people and music fading into the background.

Jacob stroked her jaw, his lips against her ear. "You're irresistible, Lilly. Don't tell me you haven't been thinking about that kiss, too."

Lilly held her breath. With her lips parted and eyes half-closed, she swore Jacob was going to kiss her again, right there in front of all the pub patrons. Instead, the noises of the bar crashed her back into reality as the song ended.

Jacob stared at Lilly, tracing her bottom lip with his thumb. She felt naked beneath his smoldering eyes, and he too seemed reluctant to surrender the moment. His hand finally released her waist, and he thanked her for the dance before turning toward the bar.

Sabina and Ben stared at her, slack-jawed when she returned to the booth.

"Girl, you two almost set the place on fire," Sabina commented.

Lilly shot her a small smile, leaning against the booth. "That's salsa for you."

Sabina shook her head. "That wasn't any salsa I've ever seen, and those sure weren't the moves Jacob used with me. Ben, is it me or is it warm in here? Damn, that was sexy."

"He's certainly got moves." Looking around the booth, Lilly asked, "Where's Enrique?"

Sabina and Ben exchanged a look. "I don't think he appreciated Jacob cutting into your dance. He muttered something about an early case and left."

"I'm sure he wasn't angry. It was *just* a dance." Lilly lifted her hair off her neck, confused by Enrique's behavior.

Ben smiled at his friend. "Enrique likes you. He doesn't want to watch you with someone else. And what you did with Jacob? That was not just a dance, that was practically sex on the dance floor."

Lilly's face flamed. Had she made a fool of herself in front of the entire pub? She could barely control her body around that man. Had she gone overboard? Was Jacob hiding at the bar because of her hedonic dance moves?

Ben picked up on her expression, giving her a quick hug. "Lilly, you didn't do anything wrong, but there's some serious chemistry between you two."

Lilly opened her mouth in protest when Jacob reappeared, four whiskeys in hand. She accepted the drink with a smile, settling into the booth.

The foursome laughed and joked over the next hour, discussing everything from houses to exotic travels. Jacob remained jovial but refrained from any overtly sexual gestures. Despite her friend's observations, there was nothing brewing between them, and Lilly would keep telling herself that lie until she believed it.

The karaoke emcee called Sabina's name, and she gulped her drink before bounding onstage. Lilly stood on her seat to get a better view as her friend belted out her slightly off-key song.

Fingers wrapped around her thigh and Lilly glanced down to see Jacob looking up at her, his hand using her leg as ballast. She was thankful for the darkness in the pub, it hid her blush as his fingers tightened their grip.

Considering what this man could do to her with an innocent touch, she could only imagine what his mouth would feel like if given free rein on her body.

The song ended, and Lilly jumped down, throwing her arms around Sabina when she returned from the stage. "You were awesome!"

A glint of sweat glossed Sabina's brow. "Thank you, you're next."

Lilly sobered instantly. "I'm not singing. I didn't request any songs."

A wicked smile crossed Sabina's lips. "You didn't request anything, so I did it for you."

Lilly paled when the emcee called her to the stage. "Next up we have our favorite Yank. Get on up here Lilly!"

Jacob pushed his body against hers. "I believe he's speaking to you."

Lilly balked as Sabina pushed her towards the stage. "I don't even know what I'm singing!"

She relented finally, taking the microphone from the emcee. Her jaw dropped when she saw Sabina's song selection—a sexy song Lilly sang regularly because it was a massive hit amongst the regulars. She could also perform the hell out of it.

I could pretend I'm sick and dart off the stage, which isn't too far a stretch, Lilly considered as she peered out at the audience. Jacob had taken up residence at the side of the stage, his eyes keen with interest. *Wonderful, he dates world-class musicians, and I'm about to make a fool of myself. At least I'm giving him fodder for his next Hollywood shindig.*

Taking a deep breath, Lilly smiled at the audience. "Evening, folks. My friend decided I need to sing a song so…let's do it."

CHAPTER SEVEN

Jacob

J acob leaned against the pub wall, the low lighting protecting his identity while still allowing a clear view of Lilly's performance. He wondered what song Lilly hadn't planned on singing and if she was as dissonant as her friend.

He noted the catcalls when she walked onstage. She had several admirers in the audience. At first, Lilly appeared shell-shocked but then offered the crowd a dazzling smile as she shed her jacket. Jacob's breath caught at the sight of her full breasts and flat stomach, visible beneath her fitted shirt. Her skin was like porcelain, a far cry from the bronzed blondes he usually dated, but he found something incredibly sexy about her dark hair and pale skin.

The audience's encouragement grew louder, increasing Jacob's curiosity. Sabina sidled up to him, grinning at the stage.

"Can she sing?" Jacob asked, his tone casual.

Sabina smirked. "Just wait."

A deep, sultry voice floated over the bar, and Jacob's jaw slackened. Not only did the song showcase Lilly's vocal talent, but it also oozed sexual overtones. A group of men crowded the stage for a better vantage point.

Lilly's body swayed to the rhythm, her come-hither voice and eyes mesmerizing men and women alike.

"I told you," Sabina whispered, amused at Jacob's apparent surprise.

"She's…wow…she's…"

"Sexy as hell? You see her fan club?"

How could Jacob miss them? He wanted to punch every bloke ogling Lilly and put an end to their lascivious gawking.

It was ludicrous. He dated countless women who posed nude, performed salacious dance numbers, and strutted the catwalk in their underwear, but Jacob felt an innate need to protect Lilly from the prying eyes and drooling mouths of the pub patrons.

His fists clenched at his sides and Sabina leaned over, commenting, "It's only a song."

Jacob nodded but said nothing, his eyes darting between Lilly and her menagerie of men at the front of the stage.

He startled when Sabina laid a hand on his arm. "I pushed her into it. Lilly has a great voice. I figured she might win the contest."

"It's fine," Jacob gritted out, his body tense as the song ended.

He took a few deep breaths as Lilly walked over; willing his jealousy down. She smiled as she approached, but after catching sight of Jacob's scowl, it faded.

Sabina hugged her friend. "You are a sex goddess. I'm going to the loo."

Lilly directed her gaze at Jacob, observing his stony features. "What did you think?"

"I think you have a lot of fans," Jacob muttered, motioning to the group of men whose eyes remained glued to Lilly's curves.

Lilly glanced over her shoulder. "They're harmless. It's part of the shtick with the song."

"The way they're drooling over you doesn't look harmless," Jacob noted the discomfort in Lilly's face and wished he wasn't so damn upset about her performance.

"Are you angry with me?"

Jacob seized that opportunity to do what he knew he shouldn't do; he played the part of the arrogant ass to a T. "No," he snapped. "Why should I be angry? You're allowed to have groupies. Although it seems many of those admirers may be more than just front-row fans. Judging by your performance, you're a consummate professional in the art of seduction."

He regretted the words the moment they left his mouth, as he watched them hit her harder than a slap. Lilly staggered backward, processing his statement.

"Ouch...you *bastard*." Lilly drew in a ragged, shaky breath. "We're done here. I'm going to say goodnight to Sabina and Ben, and you...go fuck yourself."

He couldn't let her leave like that. Somehow, he had to remove the foot permanently lodged in his mouth since their first meeting. He grabbed her arm, feeling her stiffen. "Lilly, Christ, I'm sorry. I don't know why I said that. It was abhorrent."

Lilly's eyes blazed at him. "It was a performance! You of all people should understand that. It meant nothing, it was for kicks. You strut your naked ass on television and have on-screen sex with countless starlets, and you're judging me?"

Jacob released her arm, realizing the hypocrisy of his actions. He stumbled about, trying to formulate a smart retort, but could only focus on the least important part of her statement. "I don't have on-screen sex with anyone, it's all staged."

Lilly scoffed. "Well, I didn't have sex with anyone either and that"—she said, jerking her thumb towards the karaoke stage—"was staged too. I have to go."

"Wait, wait." Jacob's voice rose, drawing outside attention, but at that moment he didn't give a rat's ass who recognized him. "I understand if you want to leave. I was an utter git, and you have every right to tell me to sod off. But please, let me drive you home first, I need to make certain you're safe. You can kick me in the balls if it makes you feel better."

Lilly turned to face him, a small smile playing about her face. "I have no desire to kick you in the balls, though you deserve it."

"It's a free shot."

"And likely one I'll regret not taking later, but I'll pass." She shook her head, a rough laugh escaping her lips. "You really are a git, you know that, right?"

Jacob grabbed her hand, kissing her fingertips. "Duly noted."

"I bring out the worst in you, don't I?" Her eyes glistened with emotion.

"No Lilly, but you affect me the way no one else does. I was so wrong for saying that before. I couldn't handle watching those men ogle you. I'm not a jealous person, but they made me see red with the way they looked at you."

"Your girlfriends, they've done far more sensual things in public—"

"They're not you."

Lilly's face softened, almost imperceptibly. "You have nothing to worry about. Those men are harmless."

Jacob wasn't convinced. "Please, let me take you home."

"It's only a few blocks, I can walk. I walk it all the time." Her gaze traveled to her hand, still pressed against his mouth.

Lilly's lips trembled and Jacob staved off his desire to grab her and kiss that beautiful mouth, surmising after his behavior it would more likely end with a slap than a reciprocation. "I insist."

Lilly pulled her hand back, relenting. "Fine, you can drive me home. Let's go say our goodbyes."

"I believe the jig is up," Sabina murmured to Jacob when they returned to the booth, nodding her head at the throng of people crowding the door. "Looks like *your* fan club has arrived."

"How do you know they're fans?" Lilly inquired.

Sabina snickered, "They're holding photos of Jacob's face, it wasn't a difficult deduction."

Jacob shook his head and sighed. He adored his fans, but tonight, he craved anonymity. "Perhaps we can sneak out the back door?"

Sabina's eyes widened. "You're leaving? Together?"

Lilly hugged her friend's shoulder. "Jacob insists on getting me home safely. He seems to doubt my ability to traverse a few city blocks."

Sabina smiled, her gaze flitting between Jacob and Lilly. "Of course, we wouldn't want Lilly getting lost in the three blocks to her cottage."

"Sabina, can I offer you a lift home as well?" Jacob offered, hoping she would decline.

Sabina shook her head. "Ben and I are staying for a bit. I'll convince him to give me a ride." She glanced at Ben, who nodded his agreement. "You two have a nice night. Call me later, Lilly."

Jacob directed Lilly towards the rear door, his hand caressing her lower back. "Hopefully, we can escape this way without anyone noticing." He realized that wasn't an option when a group of women squealed as they caught sight of him.

Within seconds, fans surrounded him, shoving papers into his face and pulling at his clothes and hair. The fans pushed Lilly to the edge of the melee, but her face showed wry amusement instead of anger.

Jacob caught her gaze and mouthed an apology in her direction. Lilly just shrugged, a strange smile playing on her lips. He signed a few autographs and glanced up to see Lilly opening the back door. His eyes widened at her in a nonverbal plea, but she blew him a kiss and waved before exiting into the night.

Jacob sighed, returning his attention to his enthusiastic fans. Within twenty minutes, he'd signed countless autographs, posed for endless photographs and hugged at least fifty well-meaning strangers. He exuded affable grace, but his thoughts focused on Lilly. He didn't know if she made it home, and that bothered the hell out of him.

He walked to his car, started the engine and immediately turned it off again. He strode back into the pub, making a beeline for Sabina and Ben.

"Didn't you two leave?" Sabina asked, scanning the bar for Lilly.

"Lilly left, I got cornered by some fans."

"She left without you?" Sabina chuckled. "That girl never makes it easy."

"I'm worried about her walking home. It's late and bitter cold."

"I'll call her and verify she's home safe." Sabina grabbed her phone and began dialing, but Jacob stayed her hand.

"I'd like to check on her in person." He fumbled over the words, like a child asking permission from a parent.

Sabina chortled. "Oh no, she'll kill me. I can't give you her address."

Jacob turned on his movie-star smile, sliding his arm around Sabina. "She won't kill you. I accept full responsibility. I just want to check on her and then I'll go straight home."

Sabina grunted, shooting him a pointed stare. "And what do I get out of this deal?"

Jacob's smile broadened, she was going to cough up the address. "What do you want? Another round? A hug? A puppy?"

"No puppies. Lilly is already bugging me to adopt from her shelter. I'll take one and two please, top shelf."

"Of course, my lady," Jacob said with an exaggerated bow. He got drinks for Ben and Sabina, setting them on the table with a flourish. "I asked the bartender to keep my tab open. I'll cover you both for the rest of the night."

Ben chuckled, exchanging a knowing look with Sabina. "You really want this address, don't you?"

Jacob said nothing, his eyes focused on Sabina.

Ben pulled out a pen and wrote the address on a napkin. "Here. It's my family's place."

"I was buttering up the wrong person the whole time?" Jacob asked, feigning horror.

Sabina giggled.

"Good night you two…and thank you," he said, shoving the paper into his pocket.

Lilly

L illy hustled the last block to the cottage, burying her face in her scarf in a futile effort to ward off the night chill. The wind wasn't helping matters. The last gust lashed her cheeks, leaving her breathless.

She sighed with relief when her porch light came into view. The cottage had been in Ben's family for generations, and he let her stay there, in exchange for her help at St. Luke.

She heaved open the oak door, greeted by her two rescue cats, who demanded attention and tuna, not necessarily in that order. Lilly lit the fire, grabbed a glass of whiskey, and peeled off her clothes.

Fifteen minutes later she crashed on the couch in yoga pants and a tank top, whiskey in hand, listening to Lenny Kravitz croon about sex. She ruminated on the evening, uncertain how to feel about Jacob Edmonton.

At times, he seemed genuinely interested in her, but then he'd cut her to the quick with a biting remark. She never knew what was going to come out of his mouth next, but she had to admit, it made for an exciting ride.

One thing was sure, Jacob oozed sensuality from every pore, but he didn't seem arrogant about it. He had to realize his effect on women. Hell, he had to know his effect on her; that kiss nearly ate her alive.

But it was their dance tonight that really got her fired up. She closed her eyes, reliving their moment on the dancefloor—lips almost touching, breath intertwining…

Lilly's reverie was shattered by the knock on her door. It was after eleven, must be Ben and Sabina stopping by for a nightcap.

"Just a second—" Lilly's voice caught when she swung open the door and found Jacob leaning against the frame.

"Hi." At least he had the grace to look uncomfortable.

"What are you doing here?"

"I wanted to be certain you got home safe."

Lilly considered his statement. "Sabina could have called me—wait, how did you get my address?"

Jacob smiled and rubbed his hands together, staving off the cold. Lilly opened the door wider, inviting him in. "I obtained it through the age-old practice of bribery."

Lilly giggled. "And what did it cost you?"

"Liquor and a hug."

"Wow. My address comes cheap. Did you stop by just to check on me or would you like to stay for a drink?"

Jacob's eyes smoldered as he raked over her form, and Lilly flushed when she remembered what she was wearing. "Crap, sorry, I wasn't expecting company." She crossed her arms across her breasts in a futile attempt to cover them through the thin material.

"You're perfect. And I would love a drink."

Lilly led him to the living room and poured him two fingers of whiskey. Jacob warmed himself by the fire, the flames casting a golden hue on his beard. "Here you go."

He thanked her and took a sip, moving towards the couch. "I hated that you left like that."

"I walk home all the time; although tonight was frigid. Besides, you need to be there for your fans."

Jacob stared into his whiskey. "I wanted to be there for you."

Lilly plopped down on the opposite side of the couch, smiling at his statement. "I'm still mad at you." She giggled when he groaned and leaned back against the sofa cushion.

"It was such bad form, I was a total wanker." His face grew somber as he held her gaze. "I'm sorry, Lilly."

Lilly pretended to mull over his apology but broke off laughing when a sofa pillow flew in her direction. "Don't make me spill my drink, that's alcohol abuse." Their laughter dissipated any remaining tension. "Tell me, what's it like?"

Jacob's face scrunched in confusion. "What's what like?"

"Being famous, being a sex god—"

"You think I'm a sex god?" His mouth twitched with amusement.

"I'm not saying *I* think that—" Lilly faltered, her cheeks growing red.

"Then why are you blushing?" Jacob was enjoying this line of questioning far too much.

"I blush at everything. I'm white as a ghost, it's an unfair trait. Now, what was I saying before I was so *rudely* interrupted? What's it like, having people hound you everywhere you go?"

Jacob sighed. "My fans are amazing, but it gets exhausting. My career doesn't allow me privacy, and the tabloids write all sorts of—"

"Garbage?"

"I hate to admit it, but tabloids are often spot on with their stories, they just don't wait for approval before publishing."

Lilly pulled a pillow in front of her, leaning on it with her elbows. "I don't read tabloids."

Jacob's gaze warmed her insides as his fingers brushed up her forearm. "I didn't figure you did. You're different from the women I know."

Lilly leaned back, uncertain of how to interpret his statement. "I'm not surprised. How many hippie tree-huggers do you know in Hollywood?"

"Not enough."

Now, what in the hell does that mean? Lilly wondered. She opted to shrug it off and return to the conversation, which flowed effortlessly over the next hour.

Jacob seemed intrigued by her pre-London life, as Lilly described her childhood in New York and the loss of her family. She tried to downplay everything, but her emotions bubbled beneath the surface when she delved into her past.

Jacob regaled her with stories of his English upbringing, his childhood spent at boarding school and how his life changed when he discovered theater.

He regarded her with a look that was both curious and apprehensive. "Have you seen any of my films?"

Lilly nodded but said nothing further.

"What was your opinion?"

Lilly chose her next question carefully. "My opinion on the movies or your acting?"

Jacob scoffed at the question. "Both, I suppose."

Lilly chewed her lip before answering. "I think you have an air of Gene Kelly about you, but you seem to prefer darker roles. I adore those lighthearted movies that make me smile. I've had enough darkness in my life."

Jacob sighed, and Lilly realized he had no idea how to interpret her statement. After a few moments, he replied, "The roles are dark, but that's what gives them depth and realism."

"Perhaps, but darkness doesn't always equal depth. One doesn't have to dwell in the shadows to be enigmatic or profound. And people often watch films strictly for the happily ever after. It so rarely exists in this world. It always gave me hope to know that although my life might be a total disaster, those characters on the screen figure it all out in the end. So, there's a chance for all of us. I guess I'm sentimental."

Jacob nodded, his azure eyes intently focused on the fire.

Time to backpedal. "I'm sorry, I rambled too much. You know better than me, I'm just some twit moviegoer."

Lilly waited, prepared for Jacob to launch into a diatribe about her lack of taste in film or get up and stalk out, but he did neither. He ruminated on her words as if he had never given upbeat movies a thought before that moment. "My agent presented me with a romantic comedy. I didn't think it was a good fit, so I passed. Now I'm wondering if I should reconsider."

Lilly's next statement hit the bullseye. "You're an actor, Jacob, can't you make any role fit?"

His jaw dropped, and he wrinkled his brow. "No one's ever put it quite that way before."

"I think you possess amazing talent. I'd just like to see your softer side."

Jacob raised his eyebrows, followed by that sexy smile that turned Lilly's insides to molten lava. "My softer side? Now that's a very interesting topic."

Lilly hid her flaming cheeks behind her whiskey glass, unable to think of a single comeback, entirely out of character for someone with her grasp of sarcasm.

Jacob thankfully changed topics. "You're a talented singer. Do you sing professionally?"

Lilly chuckled. "Not unless karaoke bars count, but it makes me happy."

"It makes many people happy."

"Don't start," Lilly huffed.

Jacob grinned. "Trust me, it's not an insult. I enjoyed tonight. It's tricky living a normal life in my profession. I'm grateful for all the opportunities I've been given, but most people can't comprehend what it's like to have your good days—and bad days—publicized to the world..." His voice trailed off as he gazed at the rug.

"I suppose that's why Hollywood people stick together. They understand that way of life. People like me, we don't get it, which has to be exhausting for you, too. It explains why you've dated all the starlets in Hollywood."

"I haven't dated quite *all* of them," Jacob responded dryly.

"You mean you missed one?" Lilly joked, earning a side-eye from Jacob.

"I'm not quite the playboy you think."

Lilly raised her eyebrows.

"Fine, I suppose I do have a bit of a reputation—"

Lilly sputtered her whiskey, receiving an incredulous look from Jacob. "Can I finish?"

Lilly cleared her throat, a smile curving her lips. "By all means."

"Do you know why I dated those women? It was easy, I met them on set or through connections. I never get the opportunity to meet someone the old-fashioned way and let things progress naturally. But those starlets are only concerned with advancing their career and upping their notoriety. They didn't give a damn about me, and I didn't care about them." Jacob poured himself another finger of whiskey before turning the tables on Lilly. "I'm done with the hot seat; it's your turn. What type of blokes do you date?"

"I don't have a type."

"Everyone has a type."

"It has to be someone who gives me butterflies, which is a rarity."

Jacob leaned against the cushion, regarding her. "Butterflies, huh?"

Lilly felt her cheeks fire up. "I know it likely sounds trite for someone of your experience, but I believe you know the moment you kiss someone—" She broke off the sentence, wishing she could crawl under the couch.

Jacob inched closer, running his fingers along her jaw. "You were saying?"

Lilly's lower lip quivered. How in the world could she talk her way out of that statement? "You know as soon as you kiss someone if there's chemistry."

His eyes scanned her face as if considering her words, before sitting back and taking a swig of whiskey. "Butterflies are a rarity indeed. Nine times out of ten, it's just hormones."

Fuck, I've made the biggest fool of myself. Lilly stood up, determined to get the conversation back on track. If she acted casual, then he might not think she felt anything when they kissed. "I've dated within the medical field, because it's easy, like you date within the Hollywood set."

Her return to the previous topic caught him off guard, but he recovered quickly. "Do you only date within the medical field?"

"No, but I don't date actors or musicians." Lilly paused, surprised by her bluntness.

Her statement also piqued Jacob's interest. "You've never dated an actor or musician? I find that surprising."

"I've dated my share of musicians, dated one for five years. Unfortunately, they have issues keeping it in their pants, and I'm not one to look the other way. That, and you're expendable if you're not helping them build their empire and fame."

A muscle twitched in Jacob's jaw. He looked contrite at her statement. "Anyone who treats you like garbage is an idiot, you're fabulous. But you can't hold it against all of us."

Lilly blushed, sipping her whiskey. "He was an idiot, but so was I for believing in him."

"So, no more musicians? What about actors, you said you don't date them either?"

"I've never dated an actor. I don't think I could."

Jacob leaned on his hand. "I don't know what to say to that statement, except it's very unfortunate for me. Can you tell me why? You think we're abhorrent liars or playing a part?"

Lilly barely heard his last question, her mind spinning around his first statement. She snapped to and giggled. "It's a stupid reason, but I stick by it."

"Now I demand to know what this reason is for casting aside the thespian world."

Lilly's New York heritage took center stage as she paced the carpet, waving her hands around. "It's the whole sex scene thing, kissing other women, rolling around naked with gorgeous starlets, it feels like cheating—why are you laughing?"

Jacob tried to stop, but it only increased his amusement. "I'm not laughing."

"Okay, now you're lying."

Jacob grabbed Lilly's hands, settling her on the couch. "First, I don't have sex on-screen with anyone, *ever.* And the kissing isn't real kissing; it's a screen kiss."

"But it looks real…like, really real."

Jacob's smile broadened, and Lilly felt her entire body pulsate. "But it's not real." He stood, grabbing the whiskey bottle and filling her glass. "Picture this, your lips press together, but there is no tongue involved, it's imagined—" He returned to her side. "Let me show you."

Lilly blinked, her eyes widening. "Excuse me?"

"It's too difficult to explain, it's easier if I show you."

"I have no idea how to screen kiss someone," Lilly stammered.

A fire smoldered in Jacob's eyes. "I do."

"I don't think this is a good idea—"

"I do. Consider it educational, if you will. Besides, we've kissed before, and it wasn't a screen kiss."

Lilly scrambled for a witty retort, but her mind blanked at the idea of Jacob's lips on hers again. *Calm down Lilly, it's a fake kiss. Actors do it all the time. Tonight, you'll be an actor.* "You're not going to let this go, are you?"

Jacob shook his head, his eyes riveted on her face. "Not a chance."

Lilly licked her lips, a nervous habit, aware of Jacob's focus on her mouth. "Fine, what do I do?"

"Have a seat."

She giggled as he slid closer. "Even I can handle that." Within seconds his face was inches from hers, and Lilly bit her lip, trying to slow her racing heart.

Jacob cupped her face in his hands, his thumbs stroking her cheeks. "Relax."

Lilly took a deep breath. "No problem."

"Close your eyes."

Lilly's eyes closed and she felt his lips brush against hers; a tingle moving through her body from his touch. Their previous kiss had been fierce and angry. This time his lips were soft and yielding against hers. His tongue tickled her lips, and without thinking, she opened her mouth, melding her tongue against his.

Jacob groaned and pulled her closer as he deepened their kiss, his hand tangling in her hair. Lilly felt his breath hitch when she wrapped her arms around his neck, twining her fingers in his curls. Within moments, she was straddling his lap, his hands caressing her back and hips.

Reality crept into Lilly's brain, and she jerked to a standing position, mortified by her impetuous actions. "I'm sorry!"

Jacob sat back, his chest heaving. "Why in hell are you apologizing?"

"You wanted to demonstrate a screen kiss, but it felt so real I responded. Damn, did I respond."

Jacob grabbed her hands, pulling her on top of him again. Chuckling, he traced her lips with his finger. "That *was* real. That was not a screen kiss."

Lilly smacked his chest, grinning. "You're a horrible teacher! I know no more about screen kissing than I did before!"

"Horrible, huh?" Jacob's lips nuzzled her neck as his fingers traced the length of her spine, while Lilly struggled to form a clear thought.

"Hardly, but I pity the women who aren't getting that variety of screen kiss, they'd line up around the block."

Jacob kissed the corner of her mouth. "They'll have to stay lined up around the block because there's only one woman I want to kiss. One whose lips I've been craving since the other night."

The last vestige of Lilly's common sense departed at that moment. She grabbed the back of his head, sliding her tongue into his mouth with a fervent ardor as her hips pressed against him.

Jacob eased her back on the sofa, careful not to break the kiss. A small moan escaped Lilly's lips as her hands slid under his shirt, caressing his muscled back.

Jacob suckled her neck, one hand cupping her breast, the other tracing up her thigh. Lilly's common sense pitched a last-ditch appeal. At this rate, they would be naked within ten minutes, and she would be another name in his black book within twenty. With tremendous effort, she pushed against his chest, licking her swollen lips.

Jacob's lids were heavy with lust as he met her gaze. "We don't have to go any further."

Lilly smiled, grateful for his mental telepathy. "I don't…I don't do this."

Jacob shushed her with a soft kiss. "I'm happy just kissing you for the rest of the night. Everything else can wait until you're ready."

"Is this where I'm supposed to say how wonderful it is that you understand and now, we can sleep together?"

Jacob chuckled, sitting up with a grunt. "Absolutely not. Some women, Lilly, are worth the wait."

CHAPTER EIGHT

Jacob

J acob meant every word, not that he wasn't mentally stripping Lilly naked and devouring every inch of her body.

It was refreshing to meet a woman who didn't throw herself at him. It was a nonexistent trait in the dog-eat-dog world of Hollywood, sleeping your way to the top was a practiced artform.

"It's getting late, and I have an early yoga class in the morning." Lilly glanced at the clock, her lips swollen from his kisses.

Jacob smiled, embarrassed he'd overstayed his welcome. "I'm sorry, I'll leave immediately."

Lilly stopped him. "You don't have to leave. You've had several drinks, and it's after midnight. I don't think it's safe for you to drive."

Jacob smiled at her innuendo. "Are you asking me to stay the night?"

Lilly's cheeks flamed, a trait Jacob found adorable. "Not in that way. You can have the bed, and I'll sleep on the couch."

"You're not sleeping on the couch, but you're probably right about driving. Let me make a quick phone call and check on Charlie."

Lilly's head cocked inquisitively. "Who's Charlie? Your son?"

Jacob laughed, shaking his head. "I suppose in a way, he's actually my golden retriever."

"You're an animal lover."

Jacob pressed his lips to Lilly's forehead. "And he's a rescue, you'd be proud."

Lilly's brow furrowed. "How do you know about my animal rescue? Never mind, she has a name, and it's Sabina."

"It's wonderful you're so committed to them. Most people look the other way."

"They don't have a voice, so you'll never stop hearing mine. That's a quote I saw and adopted immediately. We're building a new wing onto the current shelter that includes dog runs. It will increase shelter capacity by ten, and that's more lives saved."

Jacob was enamored watching Lilly speak about the shelter, her face glowing with passion. She could rally troops like a general if needed, her enthusiasm was contagious. "When are you building the dog runs?"

"This weekend."

"I have interviews Saturday morning."

Lilly nodded absently as if unsure how his statement related.

"I could head over there in the afternoon and help."

Lilly's face lit up at his offer, and she threw her arms around his neck. "That would be wonderful, thank you!" Her lips pressed against his, and he felt the fire reignite in his belly. She was making it damnably tricky to keep his libido in check.

"I hope you don't convince everyone this way," Jacob murmured, his hands wrapping around her hips. "It would be an honor to help you."

Lilly backed away, blushing at her impulsive gesture. "Sorry, but your presence would bring so much attention to the shelter. You're a huge star, and people would flock there to catch a glimpse of you."

Jacob slumped his shoulders in disappointment. "I was doing it for you and the dogs, not as a public relations spot."

Lilly's brow furrowed with concern. "I didn't mean it that way. You're an important person, and people respect you. I'm thrilled if you can assist in any way. It means the world to me."

Jacob chuckled, pulling out his phone. "Let me call my house and check on Charlie."

Jacob stepped into the other room. When he returned a few minutes later, Lilly's face was cloaked in uncertainty.

"Did I miss something important in the last three minutes?" Jacob inquired.

"I don't want you to be in a bad spot with your girlfriend because of me and too much whiskey. Never mind the fact I've kissed you several times—"

"My girlfriend? That was Hannah, my housekeeper. Although lovely, she's a bit too married for my taste. She lives with her husband in a cottage on the property."

Lilly smiled, her hand on her hip. "Of course, your housekeeper! My live-in help is away for the week…and the week after that…"

They shared a laugh, and the mood returned to its levity. Jacob settled next to Lilly on the couch, his hand idly stroking her legs as the fire died down.

"You're very dedicated to your yoga class. I don't know if I would make an early morning after a night of whiskey and debauchery."

Lilly giggled and stretched. "I don't know how much debauchery I'll be involved in tonight, but they depend on me. I can't let them down."

"They can't survive without one participant?"

"Not when I'm the instructor."

Jacob's thoughts shot to the gutter. Lilly must be extremely flexible to hold those yoga poses. "You teach yoga, too? What else do you do on the side—competitive archery?"

"Every Thursday," Lilly smirked at his look of reproach. "Yes, I'm a yoga instructor and a healing touch practitioner."

Jacob's eyes widened. "You're a what? What's healing touch?"

"Energy medicine, clearing your auric field."

"That new age mumbo jumbo?" Jacob lacked experience with alternative methods of healing, most were too off-the-wall for his liking. "But you're a nurse."

"I use an integration of Western and holistic principles. There are many paths to healing, and it's not new age mumbo jumbo." Lilly shot him a look of reproach.

"Why would someone need healing touch?"

"Anyone can benefit from a session, people with all manner of disease, and those with unresolved issues of sadness, betrayal, anger…" Lilly trailed off, her eyes locked on his face. "I completed a session with Janie this afternoon."

Jacob started, surprised his straight-laced sister permitted such a strange practice. "I didn't know doctors would allow that in the hospital."

Lilly chuckled. "It's not like I'm doing a session and then not administering her medication. It's complementary. She said she felt immensely better afterward."

"Would it benefit someone like me?"

Lilly nodded, and Jacob stood up, unbuttoning his shirt. "Let's do it then."

Lilly's eyes widened at his sudden striptease. "Now?"

"Is there a problem? Am I not a candidate?" Jacob wasn't going to lie, the idea of this woman putting her hands all over his body made him hard as a rock. Hopefully, he could keep it together throughout the session.

"Anyone is a candidate, but I don't normally practice after I've imbibed whiskey. If you really want a session, I can accommodate you, but it won't work if you don't have faith in the process, or in me as the practitioner." Her eyes darted toward another room. "It would be easier on the bed."

Jacob smiled wickedly, receiving a scathing glare in return. He liked where this was headed. "I'll meet you in there."

Lilly

N o one will believe Jacob Edmonton is half-naked in my bed right *now,* Lilly thought as she walked into her room. Jacob laid across the bed, looking so delectable she had to stop herself from jumping on him. No one should be that attractive. He resembled a chiseled marble statue—absolutely delicious.

His eyes tracked her every move as she lit some candles. Lilly tried to ignore the hammering of her heart as she directed him to a comfortable position, her hands resting on his arm.

Lilly explained the process and Jacob smiled, a wry smirk. "Are you going to be serious about this? I need you to trust me."

His fingertips reached up to trace her lips, sending tingles down her body. "I do trust you. I've always trusted you."

Lilly saw something flash in his eyes at his statement, another glimpse of the wounded heart laying beneath the playboy facade.

"I'm beginning with an energy assessment, so I'll be running my hands down your body."

He quirked his brows at her, offering a smile. "God give me strength in resisting you."

Lilly remained silent, trying to rein in her emotions before beginning the session. As her hands flowed along his body, she tried not to focus on the muscles rippling under his smooth skin or the intense heat emanating from him.

Within a few minutes, any naughty preoccupations were replaced by thoughts of healing as she cleared each chakra systematically. His breath caught a few times, and by the end of the session, Jacob appeared infinitely more relaxed.

After she was finished, Lilly turned on the stereo and smiled. The song playing was one of her favorites.

Before considering her statement, Lilly blurted, "This song is what love feels like, an all-encompassing adoration. The world is better with that person by your side, and you'd walk through hell to protect them and give up everything just to see them smile." She blushed, embarrassed she had spoken the words aloud. "You probably think that's an absurd thought."

Jacob shook his head, studying her face. "I'd like to believe in a love so powerful I would sacrifice everything, but I've never felt that way. Maybe some people aren't born with that emotion."

Lilly shrugged, squelching the feeling of disappointment that moved through her body at his words. "Perhaps you haven't met that person yet, or perhaps you have to take down that wall around your heart. Otherwise, you'll never know when that person is right in front of you." *Shit, why in the world would I make that statement?*

Jacob's eyes widened, and Lilly stammered out her explanation. "I didn't mean me, it came out wrong—"

Jacob clasped her hand, a slow smile crossing his features. "I think it came out perfectly."

Great, now he thinks I'm pining for him and likely planning our damn wedding.

Lilly drew her hand back, offering up an embarrassed chuckle. "What I mean is, I believe there's hope for everyone, including you. You'll know it when you feel it. Love can't be ignored."

"Have you been in love?"

"I love everyone."

"Don't avoid the question. Have you ever felt the emotions described in that song?" His eyes burned into hers, as if they could see straight into her heart.

Lilly shook her head. "I know no one's ever felt that way about me, but I choose to believe in that kind of love, regardless." She had said too much, been too intimate. She couldn't expect a man like Jacob to understand her romanticized viewpoint. He had his pick of lovers and would never need to sacrifice himself for a woman. "I'm babbling."

She leaned over him to snuff out the candle, gasping when his fingertips danced over her stomach and hip. Her body was on fire, and it took every ounce of courage she had to look at him.

"Have you ever felt butterflies, Lilly?"

"Yes," Lilly breathed, tilting her cheek into his palm as his other hand twisted in her hair, pulling her to his waiting lips.

"If I kiss you, will you feel butterflies?"

She should lie, but her heart wouldn't let her. "Yes."

"Good." His mouth pressed against hers, his hands tangling in her hair.

This time, Lilly didn't hesitate. She moaned softly into Jacob's mouth as he turned her over onto the bed. This was no run-of-the-mill kiss. This was a mind-blowing, fireworks exploding, panties on the floor kind of kiss. His tongue laved into her mouth as his hands tugged her tank over her head, tossing it over his shoulder. He pulled back, his breath catching as he gazed at her before lowering his head, his tongue tracing from her collarbone to her breasts.

Jacob brought his mouth back up to hers. "You're so lovely." Before she could respond, his lips claimed her mouth again, and at that moment, she believed him without reservation.

Their tongues danced for a few minutes, until Jacob pulled back, a rueful smile on his face. "You're making it very hard to keep my promise." With those words, he stood, pulling on his shirt.

Lilly propped herself up in the bed, bewildered by his sudden turnabout. Realizing she was nude on top, she reached for her tank, yanking it over her head. "I hope the session was helpful."

"I feel amazing." He perched on the edge of the bed, his blue eyes searching her face. "What is it about you?"

"It's not me, it's a clearing of stagnant energy."

His lips claimed hers, soft and tender. "No, it's you." He stood and pulled on his pants, and Lilly realized he was leaving.

"Is it safe for you to drive?" She was mortified, uncertain of what she'd done to cause this sudden change.

Jacob nodded. "I feel great, and the whiskey has worn off. You need to sleep. You've got your class tomorrow." He kissed her cheek before turning toward the door. "I'll call you. Thank you for tonight." And with that, he walked out.

Lilly sat motionless for a few minutes, feeling like a complete moron. *What the fuck just happened?* She paced the bedroom, before finally picking up her phone.

Sabina and Ben arrived fifteen minutes later, demanding every sordid detail. Lilly provided an overview, focusing on his sudden departure.

Ben spoke first. "You did mention that his ex-girlfriend called him earlier. Maybe they're in the process of reconciling?"

"Are you kidding?" Lilly shrieked. "I asked him if his girlfriend would mind him staying and he said it was his housekeeper."

"So," Ben hedged, "he never said he didn't have a girlfriend."

Lilly paused, uncertain if he had negated her statement. "I...I don't think so. Ugh, I'm such an idiot."

"I don't know, he was persistent about coming here tonight," Sabina said, stroking her chin thoughtfully.

"Yeah, he thought he would get laid." Lilly flounced down on the sofa, sipping her whiskey. She would be a mess for class tomorrow, but that was beside the point. "Hell, even I figured we would sleep together by the end of the night, especially after our last kiss."

"So, Jacob got up and left after you told him you wouldn't sleep with him?" Ben inquired.

"I didn't tell him anything. He pulled away and said I was making it very hard for him to keep his promise. Then he got dressed and left. He practically ran out the damn door." Lilly shook her head, angry for behaving so foolishly. "He even parted with the classic 'I'll call you' line. I guarantee I'll never hear from him again."

"I wouldn't be so certain," Sabina replied, "and you owe me fifty pounds."

Lilly shot her friend a death glare before shaking her head. "Back to life as I know it. Maybe the whole alternative healing session and my discussion about love were too outside the box for him."

Ben and Sabina gathered Lilly into a human sandwich, and soon they were all laughing. "You did get to see him naked," Ben remarked slyly.

"Not entirely naked…"

"What I would give to see that man naked," Ben quipped, making Lilly giggle.

"You and half the world. Jacob *is* beautiful. It's an interesting deposit for my memory bank. Okay, besties, I need to sleep. Time for you to either cuddle in or get out."

Sabina and Ben left a few minutes later, and Lilly crawled into bed, scolding herself for her naivety and forgiving herself for it in the next moment. She wasn't the first person to fall for Jacob Edmonton's charms, and she certainly wouldn't be the last.

CHAPTER NINE

Jacob

Jacob strolled into the hotel suite, weaving his way through the throng of reporters gathering for the interview. He made a beeline for Roger, pulling his best friend into a fierce hug.

"There you are. I was shocked that I arrived first. You're always early to these things."

Jacob grunted in reply, sipping his tea. "I had a few things to take care of this morning, took a bit longer than expected." He stroked his beard as he gazed out the window at the bustling London street, recalling his earlier conversation with Sabina.

Leaving Lilly that night was torturous, and he knew his abrupt departure upset her. Jacob tried to track her down at the hospital, but she was always out of the office. He found her once with Dr. Torres, but she only nodded in his direction before walking away.

Her theory about love lingered as much as her scent; this woman intoxicated him. There was something fragile about Lilly, and Jacob knew she was unlike anyone he'd ever met. She willingly opened herself to people and offered her heart while asking nothing in return, Jacob wished he was that brave.

Roger tapped Jacob on the shoulder. "Are you okay?"

"What?" Jacob snapped from his reverie. "Yeah, I'm good."

Roger raised his eyebrows in disbelief but changed the topic to his daughter's upcoming birthday when Jacob cut him off.

"I hung out with Lilly the other night."

Roger shook his head as if to clear it, surprised by the sudden turn in the conversation. "The nurse who took care of Janie?" When Jacob nodded, Roger smiled. "Good for you, Janie adores her. It's about time you found a good woman."

"Then I buggered it completely." Jacob's eyes focused out the window, avoiding his friend's gaze.

"How did you manage that? Did you sleep with her?"

"No! She didn't want to have sex, and I respected that, but I took off at the end because I knew if I didn't leave immediately, we would've slept together."

"I'm confused. How exactly did you fuck it up?" Roger looked thoughtfully at his friend.

"One minute we're fooling around and the next I'm throwing on my clothes and running out the door. And I told Lilly I'd call her—"

"But you didn't. Well, if you don't like her, you don't like her."

Jacob slammed his cup down, splashing tea onto the table. "That's just it. I do like her, I like her too much. I can't stop thinking about her, and I have to see her later today."

"You have lost me, mate. I thought you fucked it up. How are you seeing her later?"

"Lilly volunteers at an animal rescue, and they're building new dog runs. I offered to help this afternoon."

Roger regarded Jacob. "Is she aware you're coming?"

Jacob shook his head. "I never got her number, so I had to speak to her best friend who read me the riot act for ten minutes before finally giving me the address of the shelter." He ran his hand through his curls. "I'm going there when the interviews are finished."

Roger chuckled, and Jacob glared at his friend. "Sorry mate, it's funny."

"I'm glad you're amused."

"Some people get under your skin and work their way into your heart. Before you know it, you're married with kids and only accepting local roles to avoid leaving your family." He leaned into his friend and whispered, "Welcome to the club."

Jacob scoffed at Roger's words. Acting was his true love. He'd lost friendships, relationships, and even family over the years as he consistently chose his career over everything else. And now, the juiciest acting role in decades was being cast, and if he landed that gig, Jacob's place in Hollywood history was secured.

"Absolutely not, I have too much on the line, and they're casting soon for Milieu of Madness. I will not let anyone derail me from that, no matter how adorable they may be. I have a plan for my life."

Roger shook his head. "Sometimes life makes other plans for you. Speaking of Milieu of Madness, I found out that Victoria is close friends with the director."

Jacob's eyes widened. His ex-girlfriend's reach within the entertainment industry seemed limitless, and now her claws were sunk into his movie's director. "That's what she was talking about on the phone the other night. How do you know?"

"I saw her at a network function. She attended with the director and droned on about their friendship, following it up with questions about you and why you weren't there."

"Really, where was her latest lover, one of those nameless faces she slept with while we were together?" Jacob's blood boiled at the notion of Victoria worming her way back into his life. A few weeks ago, he would have been thrilled, now she was an unnecessary aggravation.

"They're 'taking a break', whatever that means. Victoria was far more focused on you and your current status. I'm advising you once again to be careful, no role is worth reconciling with that piranha."

"I see you love her as much as ever," Jacob scoffed.

"I hate the bitch. I hate her for what she did to you. And I don't want to see her screw up your life again. She's not worth it."

A few hours later, Jacob slid his sunglasses over his eyes and unlocked the door of his Aston Martin. He texted Sabina when he arrived at the shelter twenty minutes later, per her insistence.

He was scrolling through his phone when someone tapped on his window. He looked up to see Sabina glaring at him.

"I wondered if you'd show." Her arms crossed over her chest, making no secret of her annoyance. "Aren't you a little overdressed?"

Jacob got out of the car, gym bag in hand. "I hoped there was a bathroom where I could change." He shifted nervously. "Does Lilly know I'm coming?"

"Hell no, I wasn't going to say anything when I didn't know if you'd show up."

"Is she angry?"

"Lilly doesn't get angry, but you hurt her feelings. She has no clue what she did to make you behave in such a manner."

"You didn't tell her what we discussed?"

"It's not my place Jacob, that's your business to tell her…and for the record, I think you should. Anyway, let's get inside."

"Just a moment. I got Lilly something; I don't know if she'll like it."

Sabina raised her eyebrows. "You got her a gift?"

"Lilly gave my sister her necklace, she called it her talisman, I wanted to replace it." He pulled a small box out of his gym bag and thrust it at Sabina.

Sabina let out a low whistle when she opened the box. "Impressive, but Lilly's not one to be bought."

"I'm not trying to buy her forgiveness, I just wanted to do something nice for her."

"Stop hurting her feelings, that's the easiest way to be nice." Sabina's face softened when she caught Jacob's crestfallen expression. "I'm sure she'll love the necklace. She never gets gifts. It will be a treat."

Jacob nodded and took a deep breath, trying to squelch his nerves as he followed Sabina into the animal shelter. He stopped in his tracks when he caught sight of Lilly, holding a length of fencing on the dog lot. Her arms were well defined, and her long hair was pulled back with a bandana. She looked hot, sweaty and more beautiful than ever. *God, I'm in so much trouble, what if Roger is right?*

He felt Sabina nudging him. "You have to actually enter the premises, you know." She smiled. "You'll be okay, just tell her the truth. Lilly will appreciate you being here even if she doesn't act that way at first."

Jacob nodded but wondered if Lilly wouldn't rather smack him than accept his help.

Lilly

L illy's arms burned as she held the section of fencing off the ground, Enrique was far savvier with a scalpel than a drill.

She scanned the parking lot for the local media, set to arrive at any moment. She wasn't prepared for an interview, but she'd winged it before, and this time would be no different.

"Sorry, Lilly," Enrique murmured as the drill slipped off the bolt for what seemed like the hundredth time.

"No problem. Thanks again for giving up your day off."

Enrique sighed, shooting her a rueful smile. "I'd do anything for you, Lilly, but I stuck my foot right in it the other night."

Lilly raised her eyebrows. "Well, if the shoe fits…" She noted his look of dismay and stifled a giggle. "I'm joking, Enrique. I think you're a great guy. You're becoming a dear friend to me."

"Friends, terrific," he muttered, his face suddenly darkening.

"What's wrong?"

"What's he doing here?" He motioned over her shoulder, towards the parking lot.

Lilly turned and spotted Sabina walking into the shelter with Jacob. *Oh Jesus!* She got so flustered she dropped the fence section, eliciting a string of profanities when it landed on her toe. "Can we take a quick break?"

Enrique nodded, his jaw twitching. "I could use some water. You want some?"

Lilly shook her head, distracted by Jacob's presence. *He disappears after kissing me, doesn't make contact for three days and then reappears at the shelter?*

Lilly walked over to the blueprints spread across two sawhorses and examined their progress, trying to calm her heartbeat. "It will be Christmas by the time this gets done," she mumbled under her breath.

"Let's be optimistic, maybe by Halloween." Sabina was right behind her, but Lilly kept her focus on the blueprints, wanting to throttle her friend for consorting with the enemy. "Before you get mad, hear him out. Jacob really wants to help."

"Of course he does, a chance for media exposure so he can look like the quintessential good guy."

"Not at all, actually," Jacob's smooth voice replied.

Lilly blushed, glad she could blame the warm day and physical labor for the flush of color. Swallowing hard, she peered up at him. "Then why are you here?"

"I told you I'd be here. Do you want me to leave?" His voice wavered at the end of the statement, his eyes searching her face.

Lilly hung her head and sighed. It would be foolish to let Jacob leave—he was physically strong and a huge celebrity. It would benefit the shelter if he stayed. She needed to push her feelings aside. "No, I'm happy you came to help."

"What can I do?"

"The media just arrived. It would be monumental for the shelter if you spoke up in support of it. You could raise awareness about the fundraising ball on Friday and hopefully attract some big donors." She watched Jacob shift uncomfortably. "But you don't have to. It was only an idea."

He cleared his throat, his eyes still focused on her face. "Whatever you want, Lilly, but I'll need a wing-woman to discuss the particulars, and it is your project."

"Okay, I'll take the lead, and you jump in when you want. Fair enough?" Lilly was startled as he pushed a lock of hair out of her face. "Thank—thank you." She knew she was sweaty, dirty and without a stitch of makeup, but she adjusted her bandana and turned toward the journalists.

The reporters flew into a tizzy when they spotted Jacob, he was perfect catnip. After their excited coos settled, the reporters shifted their focus to the interview.

Lilly felt Jacob's gaze on her as she described the shelter, the plans, and the upcoming fundraising ball. It was ironic, the reporters stared at Jacob, but his eyes never left her face. After her interview, the reporters thanked her and giddily turned to Jacob, asking about his involvement.

Jacob answered their questions with his famous charm, giving Lilly and the volunteers kudos for their hard work and dedication. The reporter asked if he would be at the ball and he said if someone extended an invitation, he would happily attend.

"There you have it, folks. The biggest draw in town next Friday is this fundraising ball, now that they have worldwide acting sensation Jacob Edmonton in attendance." The reporter ended the segment and began gushing over Jacob, pouring compliments over him like water through a fountain.

Lilly excused herself, not that any of the reporters noticed, and returned to the runs. She couldn't imagine living with that level of adoration. In fact, she'd never felt adoration from anyone, much less the world at large.

She busied herself tightening up fence sections when a hand grasped her elbow. The wrench slipped and hit her finger, letting slip a curse as she shook her throbbing hand.

"You deserted me." Jacob's tone was joking, but there was an undercurrent of seriousness. He held her hand, massaging the area where she was injured.

"You handled yourself fine." She extricated her hand, mumbling a word of thanks before returning to the task at hand.

"I went by your house, twice actually," Jacob blurted.

Lilly stopped and turned to him. "You did?"

Jacob nodded. "You weren't home. I was going to leave a note but…and I didn't have your number to call you."

Lilly nodded. She wasn't sure where this conversation was headed, but she assumed it was his way of apologizing for the events of the other night.

"Can you say something, please?"

Lilly sighed before answering. "It's fine, really. It's over and done with. Let's blame it on too much whiskey and bad karaoke."

Jacob leaned back as if slapped. "I don't regret anything from that night, except the way I rushed out on you. I didn't think I could stay there and keep my promise to you."

Lilly's brow furrowed. "What promise?"

His eyes held such longing that any vestiges of anger washed out of Lilly. "To not make love to you." He turned, gripping the section of fence with white knuckles. "I wanted you so badly, but I had to respect your wishes. I can't stop thinking about you, you and those damn butterflies."

Speaking of butterflies, they whipped into a frenzy at Jacob's words. Lilly's jaw slackened, but before she could respond, Enrique marched up, drill in hand. "Lilly, I need some help, can you give me a hand?" His gaze hardened on Jacob. It was clear he didn't appreciate his presence.

Lilly nodded. "Of course." She extended her hand to Jacob. "I'm sorry I was boorish before. Friends?" She saw the hesitation in his face before he grasped her hand. "Sabina could use some help inside." She backed away, her gaze locked on his face. "Thanks again for being here." With that, she turned, walking to the other side of the shelter.

A few hours later, the volunteers were famished and sweaty, but the runs were complete. Lilly smiled at the finished product, excited for the pups that would enjoy the sunshine and fresh air.

It was a pleasant afternoon, and the group worked well together, except for Enrique's pointed questions toward Jacob about his girlfriend and their reconciliation. Jacob dodged and denied any involvement, but after each answer, Enrique caught Lilly's eyes as if to drive home the point that this man was not someone she should get involved with.

She shrugged off the situation although it hurt her heart to think of Jacob reconciling with that gorgeous vixen. *How can you believe you were ever his type—short, brunette, ordinary—compared to a blonde goddess who owns half the world?*

Lilly returned her focus to the dog runs and stepped back to admire their handiwork, her boot snagging a piece of lumber on the ground. She tumbled backward but Jacob scooped her up, and Lilly wasn't sure if her pounding heart was from the near fall or staring into his eyes. His scent washed over her—a mixture of musk, cologne, and sweat—it was a heady aroma. "Thank you," she tittered. "No one ever accused me of being graceful."

His eyes searched her face. "Are you okay?"

"Right as rain, thanks to your quick maneuver." She wiggled, but Jacob seemed content to hold her in his arms.

"Do you want me to put you down?" He shot her a sexy smirk as his grip tightened around her, sending a flash of longing through her body.

Lilly cleared her throat. "I'm sweaty and sticky, so, yes, that would be wonderful." Her voice caught as his hand caressed the side of her breast, she was reasonably sure it wasn't an accident.

Jacob set her down on a nearby picnic table, and Lilly rubbed her hands on her jeans, aware of his eyes observing her every move. Feeling the all too familiar flush creep up her cheeks, Lilly pushed the hair from her face, wishing he would direct his piercing gaze elsewhere.

Sabina and Ben interrupted his attention, strolling over with keys in hand. "Well folks, are we ready to go?"

Lilly nodded and stood, seeing a muscle twitch in Jacob's jaw. Unsure how to behave, she opted for gratitude, wrapping her arms around his waist. "Thank you so much for today."

His arms enveloped her, and she inhaled his scent again, feeling his hesitation when she pulled away.

Sabina stepped in, smiling at Jacob. "Will we see you at the fundraiser?"

Jacob nodded, but his eyes remained on Lilly. "Absolutely. I wouldn't miss it."

Lilly smiled at him. "People will swarm the place, hoping for a glimpse of you."

"I'm only looking to attract one person. Ben, if you don't mind, I'd like to drive Lilly home."

Ben shrugged as he looked from Jacob to Lilly. "I suppose that's up to Lilly."

Lilly, surprised by the offer, shook her head. "I'm sure it's out of your way, Jacob. I couldn't ask you to do that."

Jacob's eyes locked with hers. "You didn't ask, I offered."

She bit her lip. "How can I turn down a ride in a car that costs more than my house? Just give me a moment to say goodbye to everyone." She watched Jacob head to his car before turning to her friends.

Sabina laughed. "That boy has got it bad."

"What are you talking about? He admitted he's back with his ex-girlfriend," Lilly replied, shaking her head at her friend.

Ben shot Lilly a questioning look. "When did he admit that?"

"When Enrique mentioned the articles in the tabloids."

Sabina shook her head. "He didn't admit anything. Truth is, Enrique was trying to make Jacob look bad in front of you."

"Why would he do that? Jacob and I are friends."

Sabina and Ben broke out laughing as Lilly glared at them. "Whatever you say, dear heart, you two are definitely just friends. By the way, did you get any kind of present?"

"Present? Besides the dog runs being finished? No, no gift."

Sabina furrowed her brow. "Hmmm, that's odd."

Now it was Lilly's turn to look confused. "Was I supposed to get a gift?"

Sabina shrugged it off. "I must be mistaken. I guess Ben is saving the gift for next week."

Lilly caught Ben's bewildered look to Sabina and surmised her friend's last vestiges of sanity had snapped. Laughing, she headed to Jacob's Aston Martin. Waving over her shoulder, she smiled, "We'll just have to figure out that situation later."

CHAPTER TEN

Jacob

acob pulled up to the entrance of the shelter and watched Lilly walk out. She stopped to tie her shoe, gifting him with a fantastic view of her ass and legs when she bent over. He hopped out of the car and opened her door.

Lilly slid in, the surprise on her face was undeniable. "Wow, thank you, most guys don't do that anymore."

Jacob returned to the driver's, grabbing her hand and kissing her inner wrist. "I'm not most men."

With a radiant smile, she ran her hand along the dash. "It's a beautiful machine. She's got more than five hundred horses under the hood, right?"

Jacob chuckled. "563, to be exact. Why do I suspect you know more about it than I do?"

"I've always been a tomboy, more interested in cars than dolls."

He came to the on-ramp for the highway and headed north, garnering a look of confusion from Lilly.

"I'm no expert with London roads, but I think my cottage is that way." She jerked her thumb over her shoulder, pointing southward.

Jacob nodded his eyes on the road. "I know."

Lilly licked her lips and Jacob fought the urge to park the car, pull her into his seat and kiss her until neither of them could see straight.

"Are you going to tell me where we're going or is this when you drive me into the woods to murder me?"

Jacob smiled. "I'll keep you alive a little longer."

"Gee, thanks."

He chuckled. "I wanted to stop by my house if that's okay with you."

"Do I have a choice?" Lilly grinned.

"Not really."

A lilting song about love lost came over the speakers, and Jacob saw Lilly's face light up with recognition.

"We played this at my father's funeral; a reminder of the sunshine when the skies were cloudy."

Jacob turned up the volume as Lilly's eyes focused somewhere past the window. The song was hauntingly beautiful, a memorial to days and people long gone. Jacob realized all Lilly had left of her family were memories. She looked so fragile in the passenger seat, and he felt an inherent desire to protect her from all harm in this world.

The song ended, and Lilly sighed, her eyes glassy with unshed tears. "Thank you."

He looped his fingers through hers. "You are ridiculously easy to please."

Lilly gazed out the windshield, her mind still replaying memories. "I guess that's how it is when you're not heaped in expectations. I appreciate the little things because that's what you remember down the road. You forget the fights and remember the laughter instead."

Jacob couldn't comprehend her pain. He kept people and emotions at arms' length, focusing solely on his career. He could play the role of the brokenhearted, downtrodden man, but he never experienced the loss that Lilly endured.

"Do you miss them?"

Lilly nodded, continuing to gaze out the windshield. "Every day. But I know they're somewhere beautiful." When she looked at him, a tear slipped down her cheek. "And I have the memories, so many memories."

Jacob wiped his thumb across her cheek, keeping one eye on the road, his heart tightening at the sight of her tears.

Lilly looked down, embarrassed. "You must think I'm so silly, all this from a song. Me and my damn music." She rubbed her eyes and rolled her shoulders, composing herself.

"Don't do that."

"Do what?"

"You don't have to pretend you're fine, or that your tears are silly. You have an amazing capacity to love. I've never met anyone like you before." Lilly shifted uncomfortably as Jacob continued. "How do you do it? How do you keep giving out love even when it can't be returned?"

Lilly's smile was wise beyond her years. "Because," she whispered, "love is a gift, it's supposed to be given freely. It doesn't come with attachments or requisites, and it's all I have to offer the people and creatures in my life."

Jacob wanted to respond with some profound, philosophical statement, but her brutal, biting honesty left him wondering if he had wasted the first 37 years of his life. Here was a woman who gave more of herself than anyone he ever met in Hollywood and expected nothing in return. Life wasn't like that in his circles. People only gave of their time and money when they stood to earn something in return. "Anyone who receives your love is lucky indeed."

"Why do you say that?"

"Is there any greater gift than to be loved by an angel?"

Her eyes brightened at his words. "I'm no angel."

His fingers slid along her jaw. "You are to me."

He watched that beloved flush take hold of her face. God, she was beautiful. "I'm a big sap, still believing in fairy tales. And I know that when you meet someone extraordinary, Jacob, you'll give them love you didn't realize your heart contained. Wow, now *this* is a house." Her eyes widened as the car stopped at the stone wall surrounding his home, and he punched in the access code at the gate.

Jacob pulled up the drive to his Tudor home and helped Lilly out of the car. She gazed around the mansion grounds, walking over to a small stone wall surrounding one of the gardens. That particular wall was due for repair, the stones had loosened, and the structure lurched precariously.

Lilly knelt by the wall, placing her hands on the stones. "This is original from when the house was built, isn't it?"

Jacob nodded, and Lilly smiled, gazing up at the oak tree next to the wall. "I'll bet this tree was only a few feet tall at that time. The dreams they had as they watched their home grow." She placed her hands on the tree's trunk, staring up at the leaves as if seeing the memories the tree witnessed firsthand.

Jacob realized he was falling in love with Lilly at that moment. It hit him like a lightning bolt, leaving him breathless.

He entertained many guests at the house in the past year, but they were only concerned with his liquor cabinet or interior designer. This remarkable woman gravitated towards the original pieces of the house and instead of commenting on the state of dilapidation, focused on the passage of time and the realization of dreams. She expressed the reason he loved this manor house but was never able to put into words.

Lilly walked to his side, an otherworldly smile on her face. "It's lovely. Thank you for bringing me here."

Jacob wanted to lay her down on the grass and make love to her, but instead, he lifted her chin, depositing a soft kiss on her lips. Lilly looked surprised at his gesture, and he cupped her face in his hands. "It always just felt like a house until you arrived, you make it feel like home." He meant every word, and she rewarded him with another kiss. "I wanted to know if you had a date for the fundraising ball. I know it's last minute, but I did only find out today."

Lilly shook her head. "I was going to meet up with friends once I arrived."

"Would you be open to an escort?" He realized he was holding his breath, unsure of her answer. It surprised him he even wanted to be so public with someone.

Lilly considered for a moment, biting her lower lip in that manner that drove him crazy. After what seemed an eternity, she nodded. "I'd like that."

Jacob grinned like a fool, but he didn't care. He swept her into his arms and twirled her around, eliciting a laugh from them both. Setting her back down, he pressed his lips against her hair, loving the feel of her slight frame in his arms.

Lilly pulled back, smiling up at him. "Not to disrupt this amazing moment, but do I get a grand tour of this fabulous home or does it end with the wall?"

Jacob slipped an arm around her shoulder, chuckling. "What kind of host would I be if I didn't show you the highlights? I thought we might relax in the hot tub for a bit?"

Before Lilly could answer, a plump woman in her late fifties with a golden retriever appeared in the garden, and Jacob greeted her with a warm hug. "I'd like you to meet Lilly."

The woman smiled at Jacob before turning to Lilly, clasping her hands. "It's so nice to meet you. I've heard so much about you."

Lilly returned the smile, kissing her on the cheek. "You must be Hannah."

"Guilty. I apologize, I wasn't aware you two were coming, or I would have made supper."

"I wouldn't want to trouble you, it was a last-minute decision. And this must be Charlie." Lilly squatted next to the dog, where he rewarded her with a slobbery kiss. She fell backward, laughing.

Hannah laughed at the duo before shifting her attention to Jacob. "There's another matter."

"And what's that?" Jacob asked, his eyes locked on Lilly and Charlie.

"Victoria is here."

Lilly

Hannah's words knocked the breath out of Lilly, but she maintained her focus on Charlie. It appeared Enrique's comment about Jacob reconciling with his ex-girlfriend was correct, and once again, she looked like an utter fool.

Jacob's face paled, his words guarded. "When did Victoria get here? Why didn't you call me?"

Hannah ushered them into the foyer. "She arrived a couple hours ago, and said you were expecting her."

"I was *not* expecting her."

Hannah nodded, patting his arm. "I didn't think so, but I couldn't reach you on your phone, and she insisted on staying."

Jacob ran his hand through his hair, his frustration evident.

"I'll take a taxi home," Lilly stammered, her stomach flipping.

"No," Jacob barked. "Don't go. I'll take you home. Give me a moment to get this sorted."

Lilly watched him climb the stairs, presumably towards Victoria and the bedroom they shared. Swallowing, she turned to Hannah. "I can call a cab. It's not a big deal."

Hannah offered her a seat, giving her a rueful smile. "That situation," she waved her hand toward the stairs, "is not at all what it appears."

Lilly forced a smile as fake as a three dollar bill.

"You look exactly how I pictured you." Hannah's head cocked, studying her.

"Sweaty and dirty?" Lilly scoffed.

"Hardly. Naturally beautiful and absolutely tiny."

"How did you even know I existed?"

Hannah smiled. "You've been a consistent topic of conversation."

Lilly felt the blood rush to her face. Hannah's statement was so unexpected, especially considering current circumstances. She was about to retort when Jacob reappeared in the room, shooting Lilly a look of resignation. He looked so dejected that she pitied his situation, whatever it was with Victoria.

"I'm so sorry, I—" Jacob was cut off by heels clacking on the floor, and Lilly found herself face to face with Jacob's golden goddess.

97

Victoria towered over Lilly, she was well over six feet tall in her stilettos. She wore a white dress that showcased her tanned, mile-long legs. Her white blonde hair fell down her back, and her green eyes regarded Lilly with cool indifference.

Lilly wanted to climb into a hole and never emerge. Now that she saw firsthand the type of woman Jacob considered a romantic interest, and she knew she was the opposite of Victoria in every way. She prayed the floor would open and swallow her dirty, sweaty body.

Lilly's internal demon beat against her fragile ego. *Stupid woman, here you go again, falling for a man who will never love you. You're a world class idiot. This is his type, a singing unicorn and you're a dwarf in comparison.*

Drawing upon all her resources, Lilly took a deep breath and extended her hand in Victoria's direction, ignoring the look of resigned horror that crossed Jacob's face. "You need no introduction. A pleasure to meet you, Victoria. Jacob was kind enough to assist my charity today and offer me a ride home."

Victoria's long fingers enveloped Lilly's slight hand. "And you are?"

Lilly grimaced at her faux pas. "Lilly. My name is Lilly."

Victoria's grip tightened. "The nurse?"

Lilly's New York upbringing got the best of her manners. "Do I have a sign on my forehead that lists my occupation?" She was at a loss why her name would ever come up in the conversations of A-list Hollywood stars and their hired help.

Victoria laughed at her outburst. "You're a Yank! My sister-in-law mentioned you when I visited."

Lilly's pulse raced, but she maintained a stoic exterior. "Do I know her?"

"Janie, of course!" Victoria moved over to Jacob, tangling one hand in his curls while the other laid across his forearm.

Jacob visibly tensed at Victoria's words and touch, and he wouldn't even look in Lilly's direction. "Victoria, that topic of conversation is best left for later."

Victoria rolled her eyes as though the outcome was already decided in her favor. "How rude of us. Lilly, would you like a drink?" Charlie ambled over to Victoria, but she shooed him away with her foot. He found solace next to Lilly.

Lilly shook her head. "No thanks, Victoria. I really need to be going."

Victoria's huff was as artificial as her breasts. "Pooh. Tell me, before you leave, what charity work?"

Lilly provided Victoria with a brief rundown of the shelter's work, ending with Friday's fundraising ball. The singer's eyes sparkled, and she glared at Jacob, feigning anger. "Jacob, you know I adore animals, why didn't you tell me?" Turning back to Lilly, she clasped her hand. "What if Jacob and I attend the ball together to bring in some additional media coverage? Get the real big fish to open their wallets."

Lilly bit back the tears that sprang to her eyes, she wouldn't let anyone see how deeply she was hurt. She might be a fool, but she would play the part of a stoic warrior. Nodding, she forced her best smile. "That would be wonderful." She saw Jacob close his eyes and look away, breathing hard. "It would attract a whole different caliber of people with a couple of your renown in attendance. I hope it isn't too much trouble."

Victoria shook her head. "Jacob and I would be thrilled to attend, wouldn't we, sweetie?" She kissed Jacob firmly on the mouth before turning her million-dollar smile back to Lilly.

Kill me now, Lilly thought, wondering what karmic debt she was paying off to be in this hell. "Great. I really have to go, but it was a pleasure meeting you." Swallowing hard, she extended her hand to Jacob. "Thanks again for all your help today."

Jacob's blue eyes revealed a man drowning. "I'll take you home."

Lilly shook her head, but his grip tightened significantly.

"I said, I'm taking you home."

He apparently wasn't taking no for an answer, and Lilly resigned herself to his decision.

This time Lilly slipped into the passenger side before he could open her door. Once inside, silence reigned as he backed out of the driveway.

After a few miles, Jacob pulled to the side of the road. He threw the car in park and clutched the steering wheel like a lifeline. His breathing was ragged, and when Lilly looked into his face, he seemed to be holding back tears.

"Jacob? Are you okay?" Lilly knew her question was ridiculous considering the love triangle she was now firmly ensconced in, but her nurturing nature won out.

"What must you think of me?" He looked skyward, releasing a resigned sigh.

Lilly placed her hand over his. "I think you're a good man. A man who loved a woman very much, got his heart broken, and is unsure whether he should give that person a second chance."

Jacob nodded his head. "That's the exact truth—"

Lilly's breath caught.

"—until a week ago."

Lilly nodded. "Janie's situation *would* be life-changing for you."

"Janie's surgery changed my perspective, but you're the one who changed everything." He slammed the steering wheel. "Now my past is pushing back into my life without my permission and mucking up any chance I have with someone remarkable."

Lilly's heart raced at his words, but she remained calm. "You have a lot to consider. You've been through tremendous upheaval in the last few weeks. Maybe you need time to yourself to think things through."

Jacob put his head in his hands. "I know what I want, but I also know Victoria has a lead on a movie role, and I've waited almost a decade for this opportunity. She's got the leverage to blacklist me if I don't play by her rules. I won't reconcile with her, but I can't have her as an enemy either."

Lilly nodded, swallowing around the lump in her throat. "Your decision makes sense. You've dedicated your life to your craft. This could be life-changing, in every sense of the word. Let's get me home so you can get back. The rain is about to set in."

Jacob pulled back onto the road, shaking his head. "Rain, perfect."

The rest of the drive passed without a word. Lilly exited the vehicle and saw he was holding his head in his hands, unable to look at her. "Thank you for everything Jacob, I mean that. You've helped so many with your time. I'll see you and Victoria at the fundraiser. Get home safe."

The door was almost closed when she heard his voice. "Lilly."

"Yes?"

His blue eyes were murky as a swamp at dusk, swirling with untapped emotions. "I wanted to take you to the ball, I wanted to dance with you again."

She entered her house and leaned against the wall, tears in her eyes. She had always heard there were the haves and the have-nots, and this evening made it apparent that she'd never be part of their world. It was time she accepted the truth, fireworks or no.

CHAPTER ELEVEN

Jacob

Victoria was lounging in the living room when Jacob returned home, her legs hooked over the arm of the sofa, wearing only a sheer white bra and g-string. She flashed him a seductive smile as she walked over to him and wrapped her arms around his neck. "Hello handsome, I've been waiting for you."

Jacob removed Victoria's arms, sighing. "Stop."

Her eyes grew wide and incredulous. "Stop? Don't pretend you don't want me, I saw you watching me at the awards dinner. I've missed you so much." She pressed her lips to his neck, right on the spot that always drove him wild.

Jacob stepped back, his blue eyes steely. "I said no, go put on some clothes."

"Why?"

"Are you serious? Perhaps you've forgotten the last month or your many lovers while we dated?"

Victoria perched on the arm of the sofa, crossing her arms over her chest. "We discussed all of that."

"We never talked about it, not once. One day you're in my bed with another man, and the next day, you're gone. You made your choice, it wasn't me, and I'm fine with that."

Victoria wrapped her arms around him again, her red lips pouting. "Aren't I allowed to make a mistake? I'm only human."

Jacob shook his head, extricating himself one last time. "Why are you here? What is this, showing up here with no call, no notice, nothing?"

"I left you a message saying I was coming to London. I assumed you wanted to see me as much as I wanted to see you."

He watched her stretch and realized her every move was calculated. There was an ulterior motive behind her sudden reappearance. "I didn't get the message. I've been busy."

"I know, I wish I could have been there when Janie had her surgery."

Jacob flashed a fake smile. "Janie's doing great. Going home in a few days, as a matter of fact." He walked to his liquor cabinet and poured a finger of whiskey, not bothering to offer Victoria a drink. "What are you *really* doing here?"

Victoria huffed, laying aside her sex kitten act. "Let's just say I have a proposition that will benefit us both."

A muscle twitched in Jacob's jaw as he waited for her 'deal.'

"I happen to be friends with the director of that upcoming movie. You know the one? The one role you'd do anything for? I can make certain you're the forerunner for the lead, but I'll only do that if you help restore my reputation."

Jacob's jaw dropped. "Why the hell should I help restore your reputation? I didn't damage it. You bedded half of Hollywood on your own." He slammed his drink down, sloshing whiskey out of the glass.

"I screwed up, okay? But these men threw themselves at me, they worshipped at my feet—"

Jacob guffawed. "I do not want to hear this crap."

"Right," Victoria sighed. "My behavior has put me in a compromising position, and I can't have that with my album release in a couple months. Plus, my fans love you; they loved *us* together. I thought if we reconciled, just until the press forgot about my recent indiscretions, I would speak with the director of Milieu of Madness, and your lead would be guaranteed." She walked over to the bar, taking the last swallow from his glass. "And," she whispered, grabbing his crotch, "we do work so well together."

Jacob looked skyward, laughing bitterly. "So, to get the role of a lifetime, I have to dance with the devil? Wonderful."

Victoria's eyes darkened. "There's a price to pay for everything we want, Jacob. You've always known that. It's a win-win situation."

The words resonated with Jacob. There was truth in them, but the idea of reuniting with Victoria made him physically ill. The flip side was not playing her game, but would that cost him the lead in Milieu of Madness? Would he regret that decision forever?

His thoughts drifted to Lilly, a woman who in a few short days had mesmerized his every thought. *But how can I pass on the most significant role of my life?*

Jacob swallowed hard, pouring himself another drink. "I'll help restore your reputation, but we aren't reconciling. I'll act as your public escort, but you are not staying here. This is an act, and when the act is finished, we return to our real lives."

Victoria rolled her eyes and nodded. "Whatever you want, just remember that publicly, you're mine." She cupped his cock again, causing him to wince. "And soon, it won't be an act." She grabbed her coat, flouncing toward the door. "I'll be at The Lanesborough, in the penthouse suite." She paused, her hand on the door. "If I didn't know better, I would swear you've developed feelings for someone, like that little scamp who was here earlier?"

Jacob said nothing but his glare spoke volumes.

After a moment, her cold laugh echoed into the room. "How silly of me, you would never fall for someone who couldn't help you with your master plan."

Jacob heard the front door close, sinking into the sofa as he gulped down his whiskey. He had just prostituted himself to the devil, leaving an angel stranded at the bus stop.

Jacob wondered how long he could remain drunk and still function. It might be the only way he could tolerate his arrangement with Victoria. Thankfully, he hadn't seen his ex-girlfriend since Saturday, a blessed two days without her in his life. But it was also forty-eight hours since he dropped off Lilly, and her absence was a whole new form of torture, one with which he was totally unfamiliar.

He picked up his phone and dialed Sabina, he wouldn't make another forty-eight hours.

"To what do I owe this unexpected phone call?" Sabina sounded anything *but* surprised to hear from Jacob.

"Can you give me Lilly's phone number? I'd really like to speak with her."

Sabina cleared her throat. "I don't think that's a good idea, Jacob. I don't know your current girlfriend situation, but I love my friend too much to let you hurt her. Perhaps, if you show up at the fundraising ball, you can speak to her then."

Not a good enough option. Not by a long shot. "I need to fix this bloody mess. Can you please help me? Meet me for dinner? My treat."

He tapped his fingers against his leg as he awaited her reply. How damn long did it take to accept a free offer of dinner?

Finally, she let out a huff of resignation. "What time are you picking me up?"

"Is this restaurant acceptable? The food is phenomenal, and you said you like Japanese."

Sabina glanced around the five-star restaurant, nodding her approval. "Certainly opulent, well worth hiring a babysitter."

"I appreciate you coming out tonight."

They ordered a bottle of sake before Sabina cut straight to the chase. "What are you doing, Jacob?"

"With what, specifically?" Jacob adjusted his blazer, then ran his hand over his beard.

"With the stock market...what the bloody hell do you think I mean? With Lilly, you git. I don't get it—or you! You buy her this fantastic present and then sic your ex-girlfriend on her! Who does that?"

"I had no idea Victoria was at my house. I was as shocked as Lilly when I found out."

Sabina scoffed, tasting her sake. "Somehow, I doubt that."

Jacob sighed and flopped back against the chair. "How did everything get so buggered? All I want is to spend time with Lilly. I'm crazy about her, and that's driving me certifiably insane. I'm also acting as Victoria's escort, which is the equivalent of the ninth circle of hell. Thank God for alcohol." He swigged down his first glass of sake, pouring another.

Sabina remained silent for a few beats, observing Jacob. "You really fancy Lilly, don't you?"

Jacob leaned forward, his arms on the table. "More than you can possibly imagine, and it's scaring the hell out of me."

"Will you excuse me for a moment?" Sabina stood up, glancing around the restaurant.

"Planning your escape already?"

"Only to the loo, this is too fine a restaurant to leave early. I'm taking full advantage of your deep pockets."

Jacob snorted, the woman was certainly candid. "Fair enough."

Sabina returned a few minutes later and settled into her chair. "How about we start at the beginning? Tell me your situation with Victoria, and that way I'll know if I should tell Lilly to forgive you or run for the hills."

Jacob let out a compliant huff and filled Sabina in on the details, covering all the highlights of his relationship with Victoria. He then segued onto the topic of Lilly, and how the woman had turned his world upside down in a matter of days.

"There you have it, my last six months, the abridged version. You're likely right to tell Lilly to avoid me at all costs."

Sabina smirked, taking another swallow of sake. "Is that what you want?"

Jacob's eyes widened. Hadn't this woman listened to a word he said? "Of course not!"

"You'd like the opportunity to spend some time with her, get to know her more...intimately?"

Jacob huffed, downing another glass of sake. "This isn't about sex, not that I wouldn't be interested. *Very* interested."

"And you're not sleeping with Victoria? That doesn't play into your business arrangement?"

"God, no way in hell."

Sabina stood again. "Excuse me one more moment."

Jacob watched Sabina walk to the front of the restaurant, wondering if she was either going to vomit or had a bladder the size of a hamster. Two minutes later his phone buzzed. It was Sabina.

"Could you meet me out front?"

"What are you doing out front?"

"Just walk out here."

The line disconnected and Jacob ran an exasperated hand through his curls. This woman was off her rocker. He strolled to the entrance and stopped in his tracks. Lilly stood beside Sabina, wearing a red dress that accentuated her delectable figure.

Sabina sent him a knowing smile when he walked out. "Look who I ran into, what a coincidence."

Jacob walked up to Lilly, grasping her hand and pressing it to his lips. He couldn't hold back the shit-eating grin crossing his face. "You look amazing."

"I'm not certain what I'm doing here. Sabina insisted I get her straight away. Some sort of Japanese cuisine emergency, apparently." Lilly bit her bottom lip and Jacob leaned in, stealing a quick kiss from her beautiful mouth.

Lilly blushed. "It's wonderful to see you, too."

"You can thank me later, both of you." Sabina waved as a taxi pulled up to the valet booth. "Thanks for the sake. Lilly, I ordered your favorite meal. Enjoy." With those words, Sabina ducked into the cab and was gone.

"I smell a setup," Lilly stated, smiling up at Jacob.

Jacob chuckled, wrapping an arm around her waist. "I hope you're hungry."

"You're lucky, I'm famished."

Jacob leaned into her, her scent feeling more and more like home. "I am lucky. I'm spending the evening with you."

He wished he could frame the smile that crossed her face, the way she lit up under his gaze. Then she smirked, giving him a slight hip bump. "Damn straight."

They chuckled as they walked back into the restaurant, hand in hand.

Lilly

L illy tried to maintain a calm facade, but she feared she might melt into a puddle being this close to Jacob. He led her to the table, pulling out her chair. "Thank you. This is quite a swanky establishment. When Sabina told me to meet her here, I figured she'd met a crown prince who was footing the bill."

Jacob smiled at her, grasping her hand across the table. "It's pricey, but the food is delicious."

Lilly pulled her hand from his grasp. "What are we doing, Jacob? Are we two friends having dinner? Is this a gentle way of giving me a kiss off?" Jacob's eyebrows raised at her last question. "Saturday was a bit too surreal for me. I'm not certain how I'm supposed to act."

He leaned back in his chair, his eyes studying her face.

After several silent moments, Lilly spoke. "This wasn't a good idea—"

Jacob grasped her hands again, pressing her palm against his lips. "After Victoria, I swore I would never let another woman close to my heart—"

"Numerous romps and meaningless sex, I remember." Lilly bit her lip, her stomach in knots. "That's not really my scene, even for a man of your caliber."

"It's not mine either. Can we consider this our first date?"

The noise of the restaurant faded away as Lilly gaped at Jacob. "I thought you didn't want to date anyone."

Another kiss, this time to her fingertips. "You changed my mind."

If I don't calm these butterflies, I might vomit. "Since I'm so all-fired powerful, can I make one request?"

Jacob's sultry smile made Lilly want to climb across the table and rip the clothes from his body. "Anything your heart desires."

A dangerous proposition. I'll let him slide...this time. "Can we get this food to go?"

His smile broadened, his fingers trailing up and down her forearm, his gaze locked on her face. "That's the best idea I've heard in a long time."

They arrived at Jacob's house thirty minutes later with two bags of food and a bottle of sake. He led her into his kitchen and started laying out a myriad of containers, while Lilly attempted to look casual surrounded by his priceless furnishings.

"You're not going to break anything."

Lilly smirked. "Don't count on that, I'm not known for my grace. Remember the dog run incident?"

His smile was pure, unadulterated sex. "I remember catching you in my arms. It was the highlight of my day."

Damn me and my fair skin, I spend all of my time around Jacob blushing as red as a lobster.

He handed her a glass of sake, turning on some old school jazz. "I'd like to propose a toast."

"Actually," Lilly interjected, "would you mind if I did it?"

"Not at all. Should I be scared?"

Lilly giggled, raising her glass. "I think you're safe. I'm borrowing a quote from one of the greats, Oscar Wilde." She noted Jacob's look of surprise. "We are all in the gutter, but some of us are looking at the stars. To the man who came into my life in the most unexpected fashion and reminded me to look up. Thank you for bringing the stars back into my life." She teared up, her words and emotions laid bare. "To you."

She raised her glass to toast, but Jacob grabbed it from her hands, pulling her to him in a kiss that spoke volumes, holding nothing back. His fingers tangled in her hair as his embrace set fire to her body.

Lilly released a low moan into his mouth, his arms wrapped around her like a vise, lifting her off the ground and enveloping her in the warmth of his affection.

Jacob offered her a smile that reeked not of Hollywood, but of humility. "I pray to one day be the man you believe me to be."

Lilly stroked his jaw, pressing kisses to the corner of his mouth. "You already are, Jacob."

He set her back to the ground, his hands sliding to her waist. "How did you know about Oscar Wilde?"

"Umm...I'm not the only person familiar with his works—"

Jacob chuckled. "And there's the smart ass I know and love—"

"Had to make an appearance," Lilly giggled.

"His plays set me on my course as an actor. He inspired me to strive for a life of creativity. The fact that of all the writers in the world, you chose the man who changed my life is beyond serendipitous." He kissed her fingers, massaging her hands. "But then again, so are you, Lilly."

"Do you have a favorite Oscar Wilde quote that might fit the evening?"

Lilly sipped her sake, resting her hands on the counter to keep them from trembling.

Jacob nodded, moving around behind her. He hugged her from behind, pressing his chest to her back. "You don't love someone for their looks, or their clothes, or for their fancy car, but because they sing a song only you can hear." His lips nuzzled her neck, dropping kisses along her shoulder. "I hear the music with you."

Lilly's body couldn't contain the emotions stirred up from his words, and she bit her lip in a futile attempt to hold them back. "I hear it too, Jacob."

"Thank God," Jacob whispered, smiling against her skin, and Lilly lost her grip on reason or reality. "Let me get you fed. I have plans for us this evening." Jacob moved to the counter, setting up their plates.

"Really? What plans?" *Are you going to strip me naked and kiss every inch of my body? Please say yes.*

His blue eyes twinkled, his long curls falling into his eyes. "You'll see."

Lilly pushed the curls back, pressing her lips to his jaw. "Fair enough."

The food was scrumptious, the presentation for takeout was beyond anything Lilly had ever seen. However, her focus throughout the meal was torn between not dropping sushi onto her lap and shooting glances at the man who was stealing her heart with the ease of a master thief.

She assumed their dinner chat would focus on trivial topics—the weather and day jobs—but nothing about Jacob was trivial. Even his more mundane questions held a deeper meaning.

"What was your favorite movie as a child? What one did you enjoy watching with your father?"

"No, you'll laugh."

"Never."

Lilly flushed, drinking her sake. "It's a Wonderful Life. I know it's cheesy and sentimental—"

"It's an amazing film."

Lilly beamed at him, grateful for his understanding, contrived or not. "We watched it every Christmas. Last year was the first year I missed watching it."

"How come?"

"I was so busy with moving, and I was alone, so it didn't really feel like Christmas."

She expected a 'keep your chin up' retort, but Jacob only nodded thoughtfully as he chewed his food.

He continued with his probing questions about her childhood, listening with intensity. It seemed he wanted to learn all Lilly's inner workings.

"You're not one for small talk, are you?" Lilly inquired, popping some sashimi in her mouth.

Jacob smiled, picking up her hand and pressing his lips to her fingers. "Not where you're concerned. I hate that I've missed this much of your life. I want to learn all the details, everything that makes you...you."

Damn butterflies were back—with reinforcements—it felt like an entire tribe of swallowtails had moved into her body.

"What about you, sir? You've lived such an interesting life—traveling the globe, being celebrated for your works—and your looks. You've experienced more in your first three decades than most people do in their entire lives."

He nodded, but the smile faded from his face as he stared into his glass of sake. "I guess to most people I have a perfect life."

"I didn't say perfect, I said interesting." Lilly leaned forward, her hand stroking his arm. "Where do you go from here? How do you top all the excitement that has been constant in your world?"

His gaze held hers, speaking volumes even before he opened his mouth. "I want to share all those experiences with someone, show her all the beauty I've seen around the globe."

"Won't it be trite for you, reliving the same cities and memories?" Lilly couldn't look away if she wanted to, she was riveted by him.

Jacob leaned forward, stroking his hand along her jaw. "It would be like seeing it all over again for the first time. We would create our own world together."

Holy hell, there's no way I'm not falling head over heels for this man... even if he's not referring to me.

"I think that would be beautiful." *Christ Lilly, there you go again, planning the wedding.*

Jacob stood, pouring them both some more sake. "Tell me, Lilly, where would you like to go?"

"Paris," Lilly blurted without pause. "I've always wanted to see Paris."

He smiled, leaning against the counter. "Paris is beautiful. There's an otherworldly feel to the city; a leisurely pace despite the bustle. And the smells from the patisseries are enough to make your mouth water." He turned on the stereo, turning to Lilly and extending his hand. "May I have this dance?"

"La Vie en Rose" played through the speakers and Lilly hid a smile behind her hand. She was right, this man was no Hollywood playboy but a romantic whose heart had been closed off by a world that didn't appreciate sentimentality.

He pulled her close as they swayed to the music in his kitchen. Lilly lost herself in his gaze, and the walls of the kitchen faded. She could almost hear the sounds of a Parisian street in the background.

He twirled her, bringing her back to the comfort of his embrace, his lips pressing against hers. "I'll take you to Paris, Lilly."

For once, her heart didn't allow her mind to over analyze his words. This moment belonged to the ideals of love and romance. "What would we do there?"

Jacob grinned, leaning down to press a kiss to the curve of her neck. "I would have to take you to the top of the Eiffel Tower—tourist trap though it may be—it's still a requirement. But we would also stand below and see her light up in the evening. It's magical, watching the city come alive. It's as if time stands still for just a moment and all the lovers that ever walked the Parisian streets are together."

Lilly willed her heart to stop fluttering but soon gave up, this evening was worthy of some palpitations. "Their love returns to the one place where it was always understood."

His jaw twitched, his eyes lit with a fire she hadn't seen there before. She sensed he wanted to say something, a response so intimate his body could barely contain it, but at the last minute he held back. "The Pont des Arts no longer allows the locks, but I would take you there regardless. Sneak a lock when no one is looking."

"I thought the locks were for lovers."

He closed the small space between them, framing her face with his hands. "The locks are for people *in* love, Lilly."

Before she could stumble her way through a response, his mouth claimed hers in an unspoken promise, pushing the mundane reality she'd always known before further away. She lost all sense of time as the kiss continued on, unbroken, the only sound the faint strains of French music and the rain on the windows.

"Jacob, the landscape architect called—" A female voice broke their moment, wrenching them back to reality. "Oh goodness, I'm sorry."

Jacob looked up, holding Lilly against his chest. "Hi, Hannah."

Lilly turned the color of her dress, her ears burning with embarrassment. She stepped away from Jacob, walking over to his housekeeper. "Hannah, it's so good to see you."

Hannah smiled warmly. "Lilly, I'm so glad you're here. Jacob isn't the same without you."

Lilly glanced at Jacob, smiling at the flush that crept up his neck. "I'm glad I'm here too."

"French music, very nice," Hannah murmured.

"Lilly wants to visit Paris, I figured this was the closest I could get tonight."

Hannah squeezed Lilly around the shoulders. "You should take her, Jacob. It truly is the city of lovers."

His bright blue eyes held Lilly's, a seductive smile on his lips. "I plan on it."

Hannah cleared her throat, chuckling. "I apologize for breaking the moment. I didn't realize you were here."

"It's fine, Hannah," Lilly replied, offering a warm smile.

"May I borrow this fine gentleman for a few moments? Just some boring business talk about house repairs."

Lilly giggled. "Of course, steal away."

Jacob squeezed Lilly's shoulders as he walked past, dropping a kiss on the back of her neck. "I'll be right back."

Hannah and Jacob left the room, and Lilly fanned herself, willing her heart rate and temperature down. Her fingers pressed against her lips, smiling at how his mouth felt against hers. That kiss was one for the record books. A giggle escaped. She had experienced a full array of the kisses in Jacob's arsenal—from angry to raw to sweet to...loving. Their kiss tonight radiated love. She couldn't be the only one who felt it.

She stood at the kitchen counter, taking the time to admire his home without appearing like an ogling idiot. It was immaculately decorated yet it didn't reek of pretension. It felt comfortable despite Lilly's knowledge that the vase was likely a Ming and the painting was probably not a reproduction Rembrandt.

"So long as I don't touch anything, we should be safe," Lilly murmured to herself.

"Having a good conversation?" Jacob asked, stepping back into the kitchen.

Lilly released a self-conscious laugh, feeling her damn ears flame again. Christ, she could fill in for Rudolph at this rate. "Just telling myself not to get too close to anything. Don't want to break a priceless artifact."

Jacob chuckled. "I told you before, you won't break anything. And even if you do, it's replaceable."

"Ah, you see, that's not entirely true with some of these pieces."

Another chuckle as he raked his fingers through his golden curls. God he was gorgeous. "I think the stereo is safe. Do you want to find us some music?"

"Sure, what's your pleasure?" Lilly asked, scanning through his collection of digital music.

Her breath caught when his arms wrapped around her waist, his lips nipping at her ear. "You're my pleasure, Lilly."

Lilly turned in his arms, running her hands over his shoulders. "How would you know? We haven't done anything yet."

Jacob's hands slid along her sides, grasping her ass and pulling her against him; her body hummed when she realized he was rock-hard, and it was all for her. "Yet would be the operative word."

"So that's what all the romance was about? I knew there was an ulterior motive to the French music and dancing." She smiled up at him, enjoying the warmth in his embrace.

Jacob chuckled, nipping her neck. "You've discovered my secret. I figured one dance should entitle me to several hours exploring your curves. My mouth has waited long enough."

Lilly arched an eyebrow at him, although his statement made her body quiver with anticipation. Just the thought of his mouth on her body made her clench with desire. "Aren't we presumptuous? I think I can withstand you, even if you do resemble a Grecian God."

There was that familiar smirk. The man loved a challenge.

His mouth nuzzled her neck as his hand wound into her hair. "What about now?" Jacob breathed against her skin.

Stay cool, Lilly. Don't show all your cards. She released a throaty laugh. "Getting warmer."

His hands slid up her legs, under her skirt, until he cupped her mound, his thumb circling her clit. "And now?"

Lilly's breath caught, her body moving against his hand. "Definitely moving in the right direction."

A fire lit in Jacob's eyes, an intense desire sprang to life as he backed her against the wall, his fingers unzipping her dress, letting it slide to the floor. She heard his breath hitch as he looked at her body. "Fuck Lilly, you're gorgeous."

Lilly's niggling self-loathing crept into her brain as she recalled how Victoria looked draped over Jacob's tanned body. She moved her arms to cover herself, but Jacob held them at her side, shaking his head.

"Don't ever hide this beautiful body from me."

"I'm certainly not your usual type."

"Thank God. Hold onto me." Jacob lifted Lilly into his arms, her dress now a useless rag on the floor.

Lilly blushed, aware of his piercing gaze on her body, but she wrapped her legs around his waist, his erection pulsing against her and sending shock waves through her body.

"Keep your eyes on me, Lilly." Jacob carried her to the kitchen counter, laying her back on the cold marble. His hands descended the curves of her body, his breath coming in short huffs as he positioned himself between her legs.

She closed her eyes and fell into the moment, fell into the sultry song playing on the radio, fell into the feeling of his hands working over her body. "You feel so good, Jacob," Lilly murmured.

"Open your eyes, I want you to see what I'm doing to you, see how much I want you." His mouth pressed a kiss to her left hip before he tongued his way across her abdomen to press a second kiss on her right hip. "I've dreamt about touching you like this. I wanted to kiss every inch of you the other day. It took everything I had not to strip you down and have my way with you."

It was getting hard to breathe, her thoughts messy and jumbled. "Which day?"

He smiled against her skin, his mouth deftly opening her bra clasp. "Since before we met, the moment I heard you laugh. You laugh is the sexiest damn sound all wrapped up in this exquisite package." He stood back, his hooded gaze lasered on the gentle rise and fall of her breasts. "Just look at you, Lilly."

Lilly moaned when his hands cupped her breasts, sucking her nipple into his mouth. His tongue flicked over the sensitive tip, blowing softly on her skin before moving to her other breast. She tangled her hands in his curls and pressed his head against her body, earning a low growl of appreciation.

Jacob ran his hands down her rib cage and over her hips, his fingers latching onto her silk thong and pulling it down her legs. His eyes widened, and Lilly traced his lips with her thumb, a breathless whimper escaping her when he caught it between his teeth.

He lowered his head, placing a kiss against her mound. "You're beautiful, Lilly. Every inch of you is beautiful." His fingers teased her open, sliding inside her and Lilly bucked her hips instinctively at his touch.

Am I ready for this? Lilly contemplated, knowing her body was screaming in the affirmative. "Aren't I supposed to be resisting you?"

"How's that working out for you?" Jacob smiled, pressing a kiss to her inner thigh.

Her only response was a purr as his fingers took turns tracing her folds, then diving deep inside her. Damn this man had talented hands.

He claimed her mouth again, and Lilly propped herself on her elbows,

113

wrapping her hand around the nape of his neck. She wouldn't let him escape this kiss, but it was apparent he had no plans of abandoning the moment. His tongue waged a sensual war on her, his mouth commanding her body to obey, and Lilly wasn't about to fight a direct order.

Jacob pulled back, his finger tracing her lips. Lilly sucked the tip into her mouth, her tongue running up and down the length and swirling over the top. His breath hitched as Lilly played with him, driving him as crazy as he was driving her.

She sat up and unfastened his belt and trousers, never breaking contact with his lips, her tongue twirling around his in the same fashion it had worked over his finger.

Her hand moved along his shaft, and she smiled against his mouth when he pulsed against her.

Lilly dropped off the counter, her hands sliding his pants down as she dropped to her knees. It was a bold move, but she wanted him crazy with desire—for her.

"Lilly—"

Her gaze wandered up his muscled frame, and she shot him a seductive smile as her lips closed around him. Jacob released a grunt as she tongued along his length.

"Oh, Fuck. Christ, Lilly—"

His guttural groans spurred her on as her mouth massaged him, and she moaned when his hand grasped her hair, directing her movements. She ran her hands along his sculpted legs and up around his ass, feeling his body clench with each thrust.

"Lilly, I'm going to—"

She already knew, and she sure as hell wasn't stopping. She had him right where she wanted him, and she was enjoying every second of having this larger than life man at her mercy. She hummed in the back of her throat as her movements intensified until his hands wound tight in her hair and he growled out his release.

She gazed into his face as she bit her lip and shot him an innocent smile. "I couldn't let you have all the fun."

A surprised squeal escaped Lilly as Jacob picked her up off the floor and carried her to the living room, laying her on the couch. His eyes were alight with a raging fire, his breathing ragged, his skin flushed. He knelt between her legs, hooking them over his shoulders and without ceremony, buried his tongue deep inside her. The intensity nearly caused Lilly to levitate off the couch as she grabbed his head, sensation ripping through her body.

His tongue worked her over, circling her clit and teasing along her folds. Her back arched in response as his hands held her firmly against him. He nipped her thigh while his fingers worked her into a frenzy. "You are so sexy, Lilly. You have no idea what you're doing to me. Tell me you want me, angel."

It was a demand, not a question, and she had no trouble supplying the answer. "Fuck yes, I want you."

"I want to watch you come." Jacob nibbled her clit as he curved his fingers, hitting the spot deep inside her and Lilly's entire body shook. She felt herself unravel as she writhed against him. Lilly's brain was no longer able to form sentences as his fingers and mouth continued their magic quest. All she could manage was a low moan, her hips moving of their own accord as she came down from her orgasm.

Jacob slid his fingers from between Lilly's legs and slipped them into his mouth, a low growl rising from his chest. His mouth claimed hers again, the kiss demanding and fiery. "You have no idea how delicious you taste. I could feast on you for hours."

Lilly had never been one for dirty talk, always feeling as if she was engaged in some private porn, but damn, Jacob's lascivious statements only got her more heated. She wrapped her hands around his neck, tonguing circles on his shoulder. "I know how delicious you taste."

"Temptress. God, you're beautiful." Jacob's eyes searched her face, a small smile on his lips.

Their gazes held as a palpable current of energy passed between them, and Lilly knew she would never be the same. She released a satisfied moan and leaned back on the couch, noting Jacob's intense stare. "What?"

He leaned over her, placing a soft kiss on her lips. "I'm just picturing us in Paris. There are so many things I want to show you, experience with you."

Lilly's heart caught, she could see it—basking in his adoration beneath the Parisian lights, making love under the stars, belonging wholly and utterly to Jacob Edmonton. "It will be beyond my wildest dreams to experience Paris with you."

He was so close their breath mingled, but it was the feeling of their hearts intertwining that gave Lilly chills. He pressed a kiss to her ear, his hand cupping the nape of her neck. "I'm not just talking about Paris, Lilly." Another kiss, as soft as butterfly wings danced across her lips. "Don't you realize? You *are* my wildest dreams."

CHAPTER TWELVE

Jacob

Jacob watched Lilly's eyes brighten with emotion, felt her pulse quicken and damn near spilled his guts and heart right there. He was overcome with feelings, and he knew it wasn't just the afterglow from his orgasm. Although, fucking hell, Lilly had the most talented tongue he'd ever encountered.

He was falling in love with her, and he wasn't even sure when it happened, everything moved so quickly. He looked at her, lounging on the couch, a sated expression on her face. The woman unhinged him at every level, and it felt amazing.

But then the thought crept back into his brain, the idea that kept him on a one-way track throughout his adult life. *Don't forget what's important. Don't let a beautiful woman throw your life off kilter.*

He shook away the thought, content to enjoy the moment. He told himself he would come back to rights soon enough. The glitter would fade, and he would bore of Lilly, like every other woman in his past.

What a load of bullshit. You aren't going to bore of her, she's become your favorite addiction. One you never want to recover from.

Her body was incredible, and Jacob yearned to lay her back and bury himself inside her until she screamed his name. Yet he hesitated because deep down, he knew the truth. Once he made love to Lilly, there would be no coming back—his heart and soul would be lost forever to this petite beauty.

Sliding his hands under her hips, he hoisted her into his arms.

"Where are we going?" Lilly inquired, wrapping her arms around his neck.

"Let's go get comfortable. How do you feel about a shower and a movie? The caveat is you have to let me snuggle you the entire film."

Her laugh washed over him. "Sounds wonderful."

Jacob carried her to the bathroom, walking them under the warm spray of the showerhead.

He massaged every inch of her body, willing his erection down as his hands slid between her legs. Her moans weren't helping matters.

"You have the most spectacular body," Jacob murmured, pressing open-mouthed kisses to Lilly's back.

"Oh please," Lilly guffawed. "I've seen the women you've dated. I'm not

116

even in the same sport, much less the same league."

His hands slid up her abdomen, cupping her breasts. Christ, the woman had amazing tits—and they were real. He'd almost forgotten the feel of natural breasts. "You're right."

She stiffened, and he smiled against her neck, gently squeezing her nipples. "You're far superior to any of them."

Lilly turned in his arms, standing on tiptoe and offering him a chaste kiss. "You'd better be careful."

Jacob's brows knitted. "Why?"

"If you're not, I'll fall head over heels in love with you, and then where will we be?"

Jacob's world stopped when he heard her words. Her smirk indicated she was joking, but something in her eyes told him she meant every word. He took a deep, fortifying breath when he realized the idea of her not falling for him was far worse than her becoming utterly besotted.

His biggest fear realized—what if she didn't love him back?

Jacob offered a well-practiced smile, wrapping his arms around her ass and giving those luscious cheeks a squeeze. "A fate worse than death, huh? Falling in love with me?"

Lilly's joking smirk faded as she gazed at him. It was as if she could read the fear beneath his polished facade. "No, falling in love alone. Falling in love with you would be exquisitely easy."

His heart raced as his brain sought the right response. Instead he opted to back her against the shower stall and kiss the living daylights out of her. His hand held her chin as his tongue traced the contours of her mouth. The kiss was wild with reckless abandon, a sentiment Jacob had become well-acquainted with since meeting Lilly.

"Am I still tempting?" Lilly teased, her fingers tracing along the lines of his shoulders.

"Even more so since I've had a taste of you. And the day I make love to you, I'll be completely lost."

"Don't worry, I'll find you," she whispered, and Jacob damn near took her right there, burying himself inside her and caving to these overwhelming emotions.

"You hold a power over me unlike anyone before."

"I'm as much under your spell as you are under mine."

His lips crashed against hers in an unspoken promise of future moments and experiences. "Darling Lilly..."

Lilly turned off the water, pulling a towel off the heater and handing it to him. Her eyes shone brightly, but her smile was guarded. "Be gentle Jacob, I'm not built like you."

Her quiet plea snapped him from his reverie. It was there, glimmering faintly—her fear that she was nothing more than a notch on his bedpost.

He extended his hand to her, wanting to scream in protest when she wrapped the towel around her, blocking her body from his view. "Let's go find you some comfortable clothes."

Fifteen minutes later she snuggled under a blanket on the couch, the fire chasing away the evening chill. She looked bloody adorable in his clothes, especially since they were about ten sizes too large for her diminutive frame.

"I look ridiculous," Lilly complained, holding the shirt from her body. There was enough room for another person to crawl in there with her...tempting idea, really.

"You might start a trend."

She let out a harrumph before settling back against the cushions.

Jacob grabbed them both a glass of wine and dimmed the lights before slipping under the blanket. Lilly promptly positioned herself against him, leaning her head against his chest. He dropped a kiss on her hair before starting the movie, chuckling at her excited intake of breath.

"It's a Wonderful Life?"

"You missed it last Christmas."

She raised her huge doe brown eyes to him, and Jacob realized he would be happy looking into them for the rest of his life. "You were listening. Thank you." She nuzzled his nose, peppering his face with kisses.

"I'll make certain we watch it this Christmas, Lilly. You won't be alone this year." *Holy fuck, where did that come from?* Jacob never intimated a future with any of the women he dated, especially not one that was ten months away.

But the smile that lit up her face chased any uncertainties from his mind. He made the statement, and he was standing by it.

She ran her hand along his jaw, her mouth nipping at his neck. "I told you to be careful."

"What do you mean?"

A coy smile played on her face. "You know exactly what I mean." With that, she nestled in his arms and turned her focus to the movie.

Jacob considered her words, and when he realized their connotation, a smile split his face. He didn't want her to stop falling for him, not by a long shot.

Jacob glanced down at Lilly as the movie played—she dozed off fifteen minutes in, and he took the opportunity to really examine her while she slept.

He ran his fingers along her cheek, she had the softest skin. Her lips were slightly parted, and her long lashes fluttered occasionally. She was entirely natural, which was so unnatural in his world of silicone, fake lashes, lip injections, and Botox. She was real, and she was the most beautiful woman he had ever seen.

Granted, he'd slept with scads of women world renowned for their beauty, but it was only skin deep. These women caked on makeup like plasticine, surviving on a steady diet of caffeine, nicotine, and vomiting. Any allure ended the moment they opened their mouths. They were beautiful, but only on stage, on the catwalk or on television. And Victoria was their ringleader.

But Lilly's beauty permeated to her core. Her heart was pure, and her soul was kind, and Jacob knew he would never be the same without her in his life.

He pressed a kiss to the corner of her eye, chuckling when she grumbled and snuggled closer against him. He had to say it, even if she couldn't hear him—especially if she couldn't hear him, because right now, it was the only way he could vocalize the words.

"I'm falling in love with you, Lilly," Jacob confided, his lips grazing her forehead, his breathing ragged. "That's not true either. I'm already there."

His phone startled him, breaking the moment. He snatched it from the table, careful not to jostle Lilly. The pleasure of this woman cocooned in his arms was beyond compare.

Jacob's eyes widened at the barrage of messages and missed calls—all from Victoria. She was dogged when she wanted something.

Juggling the phone, he shifted Lilly to his right arm and began scrolling through the texts. She wanted—no demanded—to have dinner the following evening, complete with the requisite media entourage tailing their every move.

Jacob released a sigh; he was in no mood to deal with Victoria's antics. Sliding out from under Lilly, he opted to phone his ex, much easier than communicating through text messages.

"I was wondering when you were going to return my calls. I assume there's something more pressing than your film role?" Her tone dripped a warning like a bag of morphine—cooperate or the outcome could be lethal.

"I was busy. I didn't have my phone. What's this dinner tomorrow night?"

"I made our reservation at the Chiltern Firehouse tomorrow at seven. Will you pick me up or should arrange a limo for us—"

"Whoa, hold on a second. I never agreed to dinner tomorrow night." Jacob drummed his fingers against the counter, his aggravation rising with every syllable out of Victoria's mouth.

"Dar-ling, you agreed when we made our deal."

"To be your public escort to events. Private dinners are not part of the deal."

"Fine."

That was too easy. No way was she letting him off the hook with that response. "Fine? That's it?"

"Yes, fine. I'll be sure to let Albert know your intentions regarding the film role."

What a fucking bitch. Jacob groaned audibly, gripping the phone with one white-knuckled hand. "Look, things are a bit complicated—"

"I don't give a shit. Seven o'clock tomorrow or we're done...I mean, *you're* done."

God give me strength. Another audible sigh, he was going to need a paper bag soon—either to prevent hyperventilation or to catch vomit—either one a possibility at the moment. "Since this is your circus, and I'll need alcohol to play the part of your dancing bear, send a limousine. But, remember, it's just dinner."

"Whatever you say, darling. See you tomorrow. Oh, and do you think you can manage a shave and haircut? I much prefer the clean-cut look."

"No."

"Fine. Just remember to have your adoration turned on high by the time the limo arrives." The phone clicked dead, and Jacob was tempted to hurl it across the kitchen.

"Is everything okay?"

Jacob jumped and turned to see Lilly standing in the doorway, a sleepy smile on her face. "Yeah, just business. Did I wake you?"

"I missed your warmth."

His heartbeat quickened as he crossed the room and wrapped his arms around her, wondering if he should tell her about his dinner with Victoria the following night. "Better?"

Lilly snuggled against his chest, pressing kisses against his skin. "Much."

After a few moments, she gazed up at him, her chin on his chest, adoration in her eyes. Jacob decided to shelve any talk of Victoria—no point in ruining their amazing evening. After all, it didn't mean anything to him, it truly was a business dinner.

"I have to go home," Lilly stated.

"You can't stay?"

Lilly shook her head. "I have to take care of my cats."

Jacob narrowed his eyes in mock anger. "They won't be able to survive until the morning? I'll drop you off early."

Lilly groaned. "I'm off tomorrow, so I don't want to do anything early."

"Fine, but I'm protesting this decision."

"Let me get dressed. Should I call a cab—"

"Don't be ridiculous Lilly. I'll take you."

She walked back to the living room and slipped on her dress and shoes. Jacob stood in the doorway watching her. It took everything in his power to not yank the clothes from her body and spend the rest of the night making love to her.

"Are you going like that? Not that I'm complaining, it's a hell of a view." Lilly's eyes roved over Jacob's form, clad only in a pair of boxer briefs.

Jacob chuckled and shook his head. "What? Am I overdressed?"

"In my opinion? Definitely."

"Give me a minute. I'll be right back." He ran upstairs and threw on a pair of sweats, sneakers and a t-shirt. He caught a glimpse of his reflection, running his hand through his mop of curls. Maybe Victoria was right, perhaps he did resemble a wooly booger.

"Let me take Charlie out before I go—"

"You know, you could bring Charlie...and stay over at my house."

Jacob couldn't hold back the smile crossing his face. She didn't want the night to end either. "We'll have a sleepover?"

"Complete with ghost stories and hot chocolate."

Her smile would be the end of him. "How about I take Charlie out, ask Hannah to walk him in the morning and then we have our sleepover? Just the adults."

Lilly giggled and nodded. "Deal."

Jacob grabbed his keys, wrapping his arm around Lilly. "Question."

"Answer."

"Do you hate the beard and long hair?"

Lilly's eyes widened in surprise. "No, not at all. Have I been acting like I do?"

"I was just curious." *Fuck you, Victoria.*

Lilly wrapped her arms around his neck, tangling her fingers in his curls. "I actually have a distinct weakness for men with long hair and beards."

"Lucky for me." Jacob pressed his lips to hers, feeling the tingling building in his body again. Every time he was close to Lilly, he felt less and less in control over his emotions.

"I think lucky for me," Lilly retorted as they walked out the door.

121

Lilly

illy stirred from her sleep, opening her eyes to smile at Jacob—and finding the other side of the bed empty. He was gone.

Did I dream last night?

Lilly shook off the last vestiges of sleep and padded into the bathroom to splash her face, noting a small mark on her neck, a parting gift from Jacob.

"Vampire," she grumbled, smirking at her reflection.

"I can give you a few more if you like."

Lilly whirled to see Jacob in the doorway, an amused grin on his face, clad only in his underwear. Christ, the man looked good enough to eat. "I thought you were gone."

"I made us breakfast."

"You cook too? Any other superpowers I should know about?" Lilly marveled.

"I told you, I have skills...and maybe I can show you another superpower after breakfast." His lips nipped her neck, and Lilly almost swooned in his arms.

"Well, if it's anything like the powers you displayed last night, I'm all in."

They exchanged a chuckle before his lips met hers. The kiss was slow and easy, but it still made Lilly's ever-present butterflies flutter into a frenzy.

Jacob dropped kisses along her shoulder. "How would you feel about starting our journey of the world someplace other than Paris?"

Lilly shot him a surprised smile. She didn't realize Paris was something Jacob was seriously considering. "Where were you thinking?"

"I start filming in Santorini in two weeks."

Lilly's eyes widened. "Greece?"

He nodded, his fingers tracing along the line of her collarbone. "Have you ever been?"

"No. I've heard it's beautiful—the sea is so blue, and the sun sparkles off the buildings. Lucky man, what a location." Her heart clenched at the idea of him leaving her for such an extended period, but that was the nature of his job...of his life. And he wasn't hers to hold onto, as much as she hated that connotation.

"I've never been there either, that's why I thought it would be perfect.

We would experience it together."

Lilly let out a nervous giggle. What exactly was he saying? "I'm pretty busy with work, but I'm sure I could find time to visit at some point."

His sapphire blues pinned her as his fingers became more presumptuous, stroking the curve of her breasts. "Maybe you could take a leave of absence..." Jacob stammered, running his hand self-consciously through his hair.

"You want me to leave my job?" She didn't hear him correctly. She couldn't have.

"I want you, and I want you with me. I'll be filming during the day, but we could spend our evenings together, and you could visit the set whenever you wanted."

Lilly drew in a deep breath. This was unexpected—and quick. She waited for her mind to provide a million and one reasons why Greece was a bad idea, but the only sound she heard was her heart, telling her to take the chance.

"I'm sorry. I pushed too hard," Jacob murmured, running his hand reassuringly down her back. "I didn't mean to put you on the spot."

Lilly offered him a dazzling smile. "What's the weather like in Greece?"

"Beautiful. Why?"

"I'd need to know what to pack—"

Jacob's mouth was against hers, claiming her before she even finished the sentence, his kisses hot and fervent as if her statement had awakened some deep-seated need within him. He leaned her against the wall, his hands running along the sides of her body, a deep moan of satisfaction rising from his chest.

Lilly pulled back an inch, releasing a giggle. "I guess you approve of my decision."

Her answer was another kiss, as deep and passionate as the first. "Does that answer your question?"

"More than."

"I'll get you all the details. We're going to love Santorini."

"How do you know? We've never been."

"How can I not love it? I'll be with you." He offered a final peck on the lips, a broad smile splitting his face. "Come on, let's eat." Jacob led her to the kitchen where the man had put his cooking abilities on full display—eggs, bacon, toast, coffee, and tea all laid out on the counter.

"Wow," Lilly breathed, grabbing a sliced strawberry from the plate. "This is amazing. How long have you been awake?"

Jacob chuckled, preparing a plate for Lilly. "Not too long. I went for a run and then came back and watched you sleep for a while—"

"You did what now?"

"I watched you sleep."

Lilly flushed bright red—she wasn't used to this level of intimacy. "God, was I drooling?"

Now his laugh was full-fledged. "Not too bad." He smiled when she smacked his chest with a playful swat. "You were beautiful. You are beautiful. It's amazing how gorgeous you are when you wake up."

Lilly stared at this man, adored by millions, and listened to him worshipping her. She was at a complete loss for words.

Sensing her discomfort, Jacob handed her a mug of coffee. "I'm assuming you want coffee?"

Lilly nodded, her jaw still slack from his earlier comment. "Where did you come from?"

He leaned in, his lips grazing her cheek. "I was waiting for you." He handed her a plate and a smile. "Eat up."

"Eat up? After that statement? All I want to do is jump you right here in the kitchen."

Jacob's signature smirk crossed his face while Lilly's turned beet red. "Really? Is that a fact?"

"Oh shit, I said it out loud," Lilly breathed, burying her face in her hands.

Jacob's arms grabbed her waist, his mouth tickling her ear. "I promised I would show you that superpower after breakfast. Why do you think I want you to eat? You'll need your strength. I plan on making love to you for hours."

Lilly whimpered as his hand slid down her body and slipped inside her panties to stroke her, teasing every cell into a frenzy.

"You want me, Lilly?" His gruff whisper danced over her skin like fingers as his mouth moved to bite her shoulder.

Screw waiting, I need this man—now.

Thankfully for the remaining bit of Lilly's modesty, Jacob's phone rang, and he grimaced when he glanced at the caller ID.

"I need to take this; I'll be right back." He stepped into the back bedroom and shut the door while Lilly tried to ignore the seed of doubt twirling in the pit of her stomach.

He's entitled to privacy Lilly. You're not his wife. Hell, you're not even his girlfriend.

She returned her focus to her breakfast, her stomach thanking her for the rare—and appreciated—treat. Breakfast most mornings consisted of a protein shake as she ran out the door.

She had finished off most of the plate when Jacob reemerged, a forced smile on his face.

"I'm going to have to leave," Jacob glowered, his gaze focused over her shoulder.

Lilly's heart—and libido—sank to her now full stomach. *So much for my illicit plans for the day.*

"Is everything okay? You look upset."

"A meeting this evening. Pointless business crap, always getting in the way."

Lilly sipped her coffee, trying to gauge his mood. "I thought you lived for your business."

Jacob nodded, his blue eyes finding hers. "I did, but things change."

His tone was kind, but something in his voice asked her not to question him further, and Lilly wasn't one to pry. "I am sorry I won't get to experience your last superpower."

That did it. Now his smile was genuine—and heated. "Not as sorry as I am." He walked behind her, pushing her hair over one shoulder and wrapping his arms around her waist. "I'd like nothing more than to lay you down and kiss every inch of your body until you scream my name."

He didn't have to kiss every inch of her, Lilly almost came from just his words and the feel of his breath on her shoulder. "Another time?" She forced out the whispered words.

"Many, many times in the future. I will make love to you everywhere, every day and in every imaginable way." He tongued the hollow of her neck, and Lilly clung to her last hold on sanity. Her body pulsated for Jacob, in a way she had never experienced before. She knew falling in love with him was foolish, but she also knew it was too late. Her descent into the inconceivable began from the moment they met.

Lilly was enjoying her day off, and her cats had forgiven her absence after she let them outside to enjoy the sunshine.

Her phone rang, and she glanced down, hoping it was Jacob, then realized they hadn't exchanged numbers.

How odd. I'll have to rectify that the next time I see him. God, it's only been a few hours and I miss him.

Ben was calling, likely under the guise of confirming their dinner date that evening but mostly to glean all the juicy details about the night before. Sabina was not known for her discretion.

"Good morning, gorgeous."

"Don't you sound chipper and sexually satisfied this morning."

Lilly snorted. Subtlety wasn't one of Ben's strengths. "Are you digging?"

"Me? Never. I'm shocked that you would even think such a thing."

"Uh-huh."

"I'm simply verifying that you are still attending the medical dinner this evening."

"Of course, I have my dress picked out and everything. Where is this fancy schmancy dinner?"

"The Chiltern Firehouse. I've never eaten there, but it's supposed to be divine. The best part is the surgeons are footing the bill, so you and I can eat like pigs and drink like fish."

Lilly giggled. "A regular farmhouse romp. Sounds like a dazzling and smart plan, sir."

"I'll pick you up around six? The reservation is for six-thirty."

"Great. Will Sabina be there?"

"No darling, it's only for us terribly important people," Ben replied with a faux haughty air. "She couldn't get a sitter until after eight, so she's meeting us at the pub once we're done. That's if you're not too tired from gallivanting with a certain fair-haired God last night."

"And there it is. I give you credit. You made it two minutes without asking."

Ben chortled. "A new world record. I've wanted to call you since six this morning, but I figured I might interrupt you swinging from the chandeliers."

"Sadly, no chandelier swinging…at least not today. Maybe tonight…I might have to leave the dinner early if I develop a sudden headache."

"And Jacob Edmonton holds the only cure. Am I right?"

"Dead on."

"Is he wonderful?"

Lilly couldn't hold back the smile that crossed her face. "He's so far beyond wonderful, Ben. The way he makes me feel, the way he looks at me, the way he touches me—"

"Enough! Christ, you're making me green with envy. So basically, he's perfect."

"More than perfect." Lilly shocked herself, oozing happiness like a waterfall.

"Wow, sounds like someone's in love."

Lilly searched for an appropriate response, but her silence was more than enough answer for her close friend.

"Good for you, Lilly. I hope he realizes what an amazing woman you are."

"He wants to take me to Paris."

"Sounds like Jacob's in love too. You'll have to fill me in on all the details this evening, luv."

"All the details?"

Ben scoffed. "Obviously. Don't you dare leave anything out, particularly about that man's anatomy."

"You mean his chiseled, delectable anatomy?"

"I think I hate you."

Lilly guffawed. "Nope. You have to love me, part of the contract. See you at six."

Two five-star restaurants in two days, Lilly bemused as she looked around the Chiltern Firehouse.

The interior of the restaurant glowed in the mood lighting while servers, all resembling fashion models, buzzed around the patrons. There was an air of importance to the restaurant, the place radiated with grandeur and sophistication.

Lilly waited for Ben in the lobby, smoothing her deep blue chiffon dress and patting her hair nervously. She glanced at her phone again—a bad habit—hoping that she would hear from Jacob. Hoping that somehow, he procured her number and was as desperate to see her again as she was to see him.

But something felt off, the air crackled with a nervous energy. Lilly couldn't understand the knot in the pit of her stomach, she felt as if she were treading on a razor's edge that could slice her open at any moment.

"Lilly, you look exquisite!"

Lilly turned to see Enrique, cutting a striking form in a fitted gray suit, his dark eyes tracing over her body.

"You look wonderful, Dr. Torres."

"Enrique," He replied with a mock scowl.

Lilly giggled as he kissed her cheek. "Gotcha. What a treat! Thank you for doing all this. I've never been here before, but the reviews are fantastic."

"The food is divine; I think you'll enjoy yourself. Where's Ben run off to?"

"In the ladies' room," Lilly joked, earning a chuckle from the surgeon.

"Any chance he might make an appearance in the next hour or so?"

"One can hope." Lilly couldn't wipe the smile from her face. She was positively giddy.

127

"Did I hear my name?" Ben asked, clapping Enrique on the shoulder.

"I was afraid you fell in," Lilly quipped.

"It takes an effort to look this good. And," Ben whispered, "Enrique tells me one of the surgeons just broke up with his boyfriend. He's devastated. "

Lilly kissed Ben on the cheek, embracing her friend. "Are you planning to help him through his mourning?"

Ben snapped his fingers with attitude. "You know it."

"I'll put in a good word then."

"You'd better, Lilly. Otherwise, what do I keep you around for?"

"Comic relief?"

Ben hugged Lilly around the shoulders. "Most definitely, luv."

Enrique was right. The food—appetizers at least—was terrific, and the alcohol flowed as if from a river. You no more than took a sip and someone was refilling your glass.

The dinner was held under the guise of a business meeting but the only business being discussed was squash games and golf scores.

"Too bad Jacob couldn't accompany you," Ben murmured. "How is our—I mean your—resident Hollywood hunk?"

Lilly blushed. "He's wonderful. He had a business meeting this evening, so he's engaged elsewhere."

"Are you still speaking to that man?" Enrique inquired, a frown marring his face.

Lilly checked her anger at his obvious irritation. "Yes, I'm very interested in him. I think he's interested in me too."

A flurry of activity floated through the room at the same time Enrique spoke. "Are you certain, Lilly?"

"About what? Enrique, I really don't appreciate you bashing Jacob all the time. He's done nothing to you, and the man has been amazing to me—"

Her tirade was cut short by Enrique's finger pointing towards the right side of the restaurant. Lilly followed his gaze and felt her stomach flip, her appetizers threatening to make another appearance.

Victoria stood in the center of the dining area, looking as though she had walked straight off the catwalks of Milan in a skin-tight cream-colored dress that barely covered her ass. Her perfect, shapely ass.

There beside her, gorgeous as ever in a navy suit, stood Jacob, his arm around her waist.

"Holy shit," Ben breathed, staring at the Hollywood golden couple.

"Wow." It was all Lilly could manage, even that single word hurt passing through her lips.

"Maybe they're just friends. Don't read too much into it."

As if on cue, Victoria curled her hands in Jacob's hair and pressed a kiss to the corner of his mouth. Unless they were kissing cousins, this wasn't a 'just friends' scenario.

"Jesus Christ, what are the chances?" Ben snarled, squeezing Lilly's clammy and shaking hand. "Fuck him, Lilly. He's an asshole. The prick doesn't deserve you."

Enrique grabbed her other hand, murmuring words of reassurance, but Lilly couldn't hear anything except the pounding of blood in her ears. She wanted to look away, but she was riveted. It was like watching the carnage of a car wreck, only it was the tortured, twisted remains of her heart.

She watched their personal maître de settle them into a booth. *Of course, they're in my direct line of sight.*

When Victoria wrapped her arm around Jacob and pulled him to her for another kiss, it took everything Lilly had not to pitch her wine glass in their direction.

Lilly sucked in oxygen, followed by a long swig of wine, wishing she had the whole bottle in her hands. She stared down at her lap, her entire body trembling with embarrassment and anger.

All those things he told her the night before, all those moments, it was all an act. It was all for show. It meant nothing. She meant nothing.

"Ma'am, what would you like as your entree?" The server shot her a concerned glance. Obviously, she had been repeating herself a few times.

"Umm," Lilly stammered, trying to focus on the menu through her tear-filled eyes. "I'll take the chicken please."

"Deep breaths, luv. Keep it together. Don't let that bastard see you upset." Ben continued to hold her hand, and Lilly grasped it like a lifeline.

"Ms. Staver, are you quite all right?" One of the surgeons inquired, and Lilly forced a smile and nod.

High-pitched tinkling laughter carried across the room—apparently Victoria and Jacob were having a fantastic time together.

"I can't stay here, Ben." Lilly blotted her eyes, sniffling. She swung her gaze to Enrique. "It's really a beautiful dinner, and the restaurant is wonderful, but I can't stay—" Christ she was pathetic, blubbering like a fool over a self-proclaimed playboy. What a cliché.

"Fuck this," Enrique muttered, standing suddenly. Lilly watched wide-eyed as he walked to Jacob and Victoria's booth. She couldn't hear his words from across the room, but she watched Jacob pale, his jaw slacken...and his eyes lock on hers.

Jacob started to rise but whatever Enrique said made him take his seat. Then Enrique turned, fixed the lapel of his jacket and walked back to their table.

"What—"

"I didn't say anything to embarrass you, Lilly. I simply let him know he didn't get away with his little game, and that he's an idiot for passing on a woman such as yourself."

"You're my hero," Lilly choked out, swigging down more wine and trying not to notice Jacob's intent azure stare fixated on her. "Screw this, I need whiskey, not wine. And a bathroom. I'll be back."

"I'll walk you, Lilly." She would usually argue Ben's offer but didn't want to be forced into a conversation with Jacob.

Too late.

"Lilly, may I please speak with you a moment?" Jacob stood over the table, his fingers lightly drumming the edge.

Lilly took a moment and dug deep, finding every last drop of her strength. "I'm busy Jacob. As are you. I suggest you return to your *business meeting* and leave me to enjoy my dinner." Her gaze swung up to his, her jaw set and her stare steely.

Jacob's tongue flicked over his lips and Lilly cursed her body for reacting to the innocent move. "Lilly, please. This isn't what it seems—" He reached out his hand to grab hers, but Enrique stopped him dead in his tracks.

"The lady said no. Now, if you'll excuse us."

Jacob's blue eyes shot daggers at Enrique. "I'm speaking to Lilly. So, if you don't mind, stay out of our personal business."

"When your behavior causes my friend to shed a tear, it becomes my business." Enrique's dark eyes lobbed grenades right back at Jacob.

Jacob's face fell at Enrique's statement. "Please don't cry, angel."

That did it. Lilly could handle only so much and his use of such an intimate pet name broke her last defense. To make matters worse, the surgeons at their table were now focused entirely on their exchange…as was Victoria across the room.

"I can't speak to you now," she said, and with that looked away, picking up her glass and offering a toast to the surgeons at the table, effectively shutting out Jacob—and his excuses.

She heard his whispered expletive before he turned and walked away, and although her jaw trembled, she held her head high. Fuck Jacob Edmonton.

The next hour passed by so slowly Lilly swore the clock must be moving backward. She did her best to ignore the table with the two golden-haired celebrities, but her eyes kept moving in that direction, and every time her eyes locked with Jacob's fiery gaze.

She darted her gaze away every time, but they both knew the truth—her face was incapable of deception. Her mouth could tell a lie, but her face would never back it up. Jacob would be able to read the heartache etched on her features from a mile away.

Lilly closed her eyes and flashes from the night before flew through her mind—his mouth worshipping every inch of her body, his whispered promises that she was unlike any woman before her. Lies, all lies, spouted by one hell of an actor.

After an hour, her bladder was begging for mercy, but as luck would have it—and luck is such a fickle bitch—she had to walk right past Jacob's table to reach the lavatory.

Holding her head high, she walked past the table at a fast clip, her eyes focused straight ahead. She sure as hell didn't want to see the radiant and statuesque Victoria draped all over Jacob, her mouth caressing the same body parts Lilly kissed the night before.

She was washing her hands when the door swung open, and someone moved to the sink beside her. "Quite the little scene your surgeon friend pulled earlier."

Lilly groaned inwardly. It was Victoria, towering over her in five-inch heels.

"I'm sorry if it ruined your dinner." What the hell else could she say? *Sorry but seeing you two together destroyed my appetite as well?*

She dried her hands and turned toward the door, but Victoria caught her arm.

"What ruined my dinner was Jacob's incessant puppy dog stare towards your table. Do you want to tell me what the nature of your relationship is with my boyfriend?"

Lilly swallowed around the nausea threatening to erupt all over Victoria's insanely expensive dress. Her boyfriend? "We don't have any sort of relationship. I took care of his sister, remember?"

Her green eyes pinned Lilly. "You're a bad liar. Now I know that Jacob is hung up on someone and I'm guessing that someone is you. But he has much more on the line than just his heart, Ms...Lilly, is it?"

"Yes."

"He's in contention for a huge movie role. One that will ensure he goes down in history as one of the greats—like Humphrey Bogart great. You are a distraction to that goal, a goal which Jacob and I have spent years building."

Lilly focused her stern brown gaze on Victoria. She was tired of being a shrinking violet—fuck Jacob and his blonde bombshell. "You think my presence in his life is affecting his choices?"

"Yes, I do. And I would appreciate it if you would back off and let him focus on his real priorities—me and the movie."

Victoria's words stuck in Lilly's craw. Real priorities, which Lilly was not. It sounded like a page taken directly from the playbook of her earlier relationship.

"Do I make myself clear?" Victoria dabbed her lips before meeting Lilly's gaze in the mirror.

"Crystal. I just find it amusing that you consider me such a threat to your little world." Lilly wasn't sticking around for more veiled threats; she had heard enough. She turned and walked out of the bathroom.

She hadn't taken three steps out of the loo when arms wrapped around her waist, pulling her to an empty closet. She initially freaked, thinking an attack was imminent, but Jacob's familiar scent wafted to her nostrils.

But despite knowing the identity of the man holding her flush against his body, she wasn't going to allow his advances. She struggled to escape his grasp, but his grip only tightened.

"Let me go, Jacob."

"Give me thirty seconds, Lilly," Jacob pleaded, his usually confident voice shaking with emotion. "I'm so sorry. Please angel, say something."

Lilly wanted to hurl insults or throw something at him, but instead, she did the one thing she didn't want to do—she cried. "Why, Jacob? Why did you say all those things—"

"Because I meant them, dammit!" His voice was a fierce whisper in her ear. "I meant every bloody word that I said to you."

"Liar," Lilly hissed.

"*Never*. Never where you're concerned. I meant everything I said to you. Even the things I told you when you were sleeping in my arms. *Especially* those things."

Lilly's breath caught—what had he said? Her mind told her not to care, to blow it off, but her heart demanded more information. "What did you say?"

His lips pressed against her neck. "Your heart knows what I said…and I *mean*t it. I mean it."

She shouldn't believe him, but she did. Stupid love, stupid heart. "She requested I stay away from you, that you need to focus on your priorities—"

"That bitch—"

"I agreed."

"What?"

Lilly turned in his arms, reaching past him and fumbling on the light. "You need to focus on your priorities."

"Lilly, my priorities have changed."

And with that final falsehood, Lilly was able to don her emotional armor. She'd heard enough crap from both of them. They deserved each other, and she would keep telling her heart that until the stupid organ believed her.

"Clearly, they haven't. You and Victoria make sense. I don't know what illusion I was living under thinking that we had a future."

"I want us to have a future—"

"In between dates with your other girlfriends? I told you already, that's not my scene, and fuck you for letting me believe it wasn't yours." Jacob opened his mouth to speak but Lilly wasn't finished. "It's funny, looking at you now. I can't remember why I ever wanted to make you mine."

Her words hit him like a train, and he took a step back, shaking his head, his jaw clenched.

The distance opened up a space for her slip past him. She was too good to hide in the close. Any man worth her time would show her off, not hide her away. "Goodbye Jacob."

She stormed out the front door, ignoring his pleas to return, so angry she opted to forget about dinner, marching instead to the coat check.

She looked over her shoulder and saw Jacob no more than ten feet away, his eyes speaking volumes, begging her to talk to him. But just as she felt her resistance waning, Victoria sidled up to him, shooting Lilly a look of pure venom.

This was ridiculous. It was time to go. Turning around, Lilly took a deep breath and walked out of the restaurant. Jacob didn't deserve her tears.

Lilly left the restaurant and called Sabina. "Are you up for a drink?"

"You're done with dinner? That was one quick meal. Did you have time to chew?"

"They're still eating. I left."

"What the hell happened?" Sabina puzzled.

"Jacob fucking Edmonton happened."

"Oh boy, this sounds interesting."

"Meet you at the pub?"

"Good thing the babysitter arrived early. Are Ben and Enrique meeting us after dinner?"

133

"No penises tonight. I've had enough to last me a lifetime."

"Spill it, what happened?" Sabina slipped onto the barstool, shooting her friend a questioning look.

"Jacob Edmonton is an asshole," Lilly bit out, her jaw clenched.

"Care to elaborate or is that the whole story?"

Lilly scratched at the surface of the bar, her favorite nervous habit. "Alcohol first, story after."

Their whiskey arrived, and Lilly slugged back half the glass, the burn a painful but beautiful feeling. She knew after the burn came the numbness. Numbness was good. Numbness made the heart hurt less.

"Lilly, the man has called me fifteen times in the last ten minutes. If you don't want me to answer him, you'd better tell me what the hell is happening."

"Why does he keep calling you?"

He's looking for you. He's sick with worry, wondering where you are. You told me earlier today that you had the most amazing night with him. What in the world could he have done in less than twenty-four hours to earn this level of animosity?"

A single tear slid down Lilly's cheek, and she wiped it away. "He made me feel and look like an utter fool. Apparently, he fit in sex with me between appointments."

Sabina grasped her arm. "You slept with Jacob? I thought you said you hadn't—"

Lilly shook her head. "Not quite, it's my only saving grace in this situation, not putting out for the infamous playboy." She looked at her friend. "Why were you having dinner with him last night, anyway? Has he put you in the rotation, too?"

Sabina smirked at her friend's comment. "Not hardly. He felt awful about Victoria showing up at his house uninvited on Saturday. He hoped I could shed some light on your mindset, and how you felt about him. I know he's crazy about you—"

"Oh bullshit," Lilly bellowed, taking another swig of whiskey.

"Lilly, the man is head over heels for you."

"No, he's an out of this world actor. You know, I actually believed all the lies he told me last night."

"What lies were those?"

Lilly blinked back tears—stupid, stupid heart. "That he'd never felt this way before, that I was different from any woman he'd ever met…but it was all a load of crap. And that man's tongue should be outlawed—"

"That bad?"

Lilly groaned, resting her head on the bar. "No, that damn good."

"You demanded I meet you here, now you're not saying anything, except that he's an asshole." Sabina put her finger under Lilly's chin, forcing her face up. "I can't help you if I don't know what happened to cause this reaction."

"We had this amazing night together—off the charts romantic. I slept curled in his arms all night. But then he rushed off this morning, claiming he had some business to attend to—what a crock. Then I run into him with Victoria at the Chiltern Firehouse."

Sabina's face fell. "Fuck. Did he explain his situation with Victoria?"

Lilly took another swig of whiskey. "Nope and I don't care about his reasons. I don't ever want to see that man again."

"So, you didn't let him explain anything?"

"Why should I? I think it's pretty apparent what happened. I was played for a fool by Jacob bloody Edmonton. You know Victoria demanded I leave him alone? She claimed I was distracting her boyfriend from his priorities."

Sabina gasped. "She said that? What a conniving bitch." She heaved herself from the stool, sliding a bowl of peanuts in front of Lilly. "I'll be right back. Eat something before you puke."

"I'm not going to puke, and don't go call Jacob." Lilly shot her friend a stern glare.

"I would never. I'm calling the babysitter," Sabina muttered as she walked outside.

Lilly lost track of time as she downed another drink, but she felt sufficiently numbed and a tad bit silly.

Sabina slid a glass of water down the bar, shooting her a sympathetic look. "Let's switch it up, shall we?"

Lilly shook her head, feeling like a bratty teenager. "I don't want to be sober. I want to be inebriated. I also want to dance."

Sabina smirked. "You sure you can stand upright?"

"No guarantees," Lilly admitted with a giggle, swigging down some water. "I also want popcorn."

"How many has she had?" A deep voice asked behind her and Lilly spun on the stool, her whiskey glass in hand.

"What the fuck are you doing here?"

CHAPTER THIRTEEN

Jacob

J acob let out a deep sigh, this was going to be a long night. He drove immediately to the bar after Sabina disclosed their location, uncertain what he might face at the hands of a drunken Lilly. His brain replayed memories of Victoria when she was soused, and he would rather face a firing squad than his ex-girlfriend when she'd thrown back one too many. He only prayed Lilly was a kinder, gentler drunk.

"Why are you here, Jacob?" Lilly's dark eyes perused his face, but he didn't denote any malice in her tone. Belligerence, sure, but no open hostility.

"I'm saving you from alcohol poisoning, apparently." His hands curled around the glass, but Lilly held firm. "Give me the whiskey, Lilly."

"No." She glared at him, smacking his hand as he tried to take the glass.

Jacob moved closer, trying not to chuckle as her fingers tightened around the glass—as if that would stop him. "You've had enough tonight. Come on, the last thing you want is a hangover. I'm not worth the headache."

Lilly's eyes moved between Jacob and her glass of alcohol, and he wondered which path she would choose. His question was answered when she took another sip of her drink, shooting him a snarky look. "You're not the boss of me."

"Clearly."

The barkeep approached with a fresh drink, and Jacob sent him a scathing glare. "No, take it back."

"Sorry sir, the man down at the end of the bar wanted to buy the lady a drink."

All three of them swung their heads to the right, observing the handsome man in the dark suit. Sabina looked amused at the turn of events, Lilly offered a sweet smile and Jacob wanted to pound the bloke's head into the wooden bar.

Lilly raised her glass in the man's direction and smiled. "Thank you, sir."

Jacob snatched the fresh drink and marched to the end of the bar, slamming the glass down in front of the surprised man. "Here's your drink."

"I bought it for the lady."

"That lady is with me. I don't want you to look at her or even think about her. You read me?"

The man leaned back on the stool, a smirk crossing his face. "She seemed pretty grateful, you certain she knows she's with you?"

"Stay away from her." Jacob stomped back to where Lilly and Sabina sat regarding him.

"Down killer," Sabina stated, her smile fading when his blue gaze pinned her.

"You took my drink." Lilly took another sip from the glass in front of her. "A drink that nice—and handsome—man bought for me."

Jacob swallowed against his rising temper. Lilly was drunk and angry—rightfully so, he had to tread lightly. "Would you like me to go introduce you?"

He immediately felt terrible for the snappish reply, especially when her gaze moved from his to the bar. "I'm sorry. You know how I am when another man looks at you." He stroked her hair, biting back a smile when she swatted his fingers like an annoying wasp.

"How did you know I was here? And where's your girlfriend? You know the one, she's like twelve feet tall…however many meters that is…she's *really* tall."

Jacob laughed, Lilly was adorable when she was inebriated. "I've been worried sick about you since you ran out of the restaurant. Ben and Enrique didn't know where the hell you were, so I called Sabina, and she gave me the low down."

Lilly turned her glare on her best friend. "Traitor. Red Coat."

Sabina snickered, Lilly was not an intimidating figure, drunk or sober. "I am a Red Coat. You're in England."

Lilly waved her hand, spilling whiskey on her leg. "That's a technicality. You're still a traitor. T-R-A-I-something-something."

He wanted to be cross with Lilly, but she was too cute, and he was too damnably in love with her to be anything but glad to be near her. Jacob laughed again and wrenched the glass from Lilly's hand before scooping her into his arms. "Come on, silly one, let's go home."

Lilly struggled in his arms. "I don't need you to take me home. I can get home myself."

"Love to see you try," Jacob stated as he carried her to his car, settling her into the passenger seat.

"This isn't your car," Lilly exclaimed. "You're stealing cars now?"

"At least you're an amusing drunk. I own more than one vehicle, Lilly."

"Of course, you do. You're a huge movie star who fucks huge movie stars," Lilly grumbled, more to herself than the other occupants of the car.

Sabina slid into the back seat, patting Lilly on the shoulder. "Glad you got here when you did, Jacob, she was threatening to shave her head, get a tattoo, and join a motorcycle club. Her gang name was going to Yank Ninja Express."

Jacob and Sabina exchanged a glance, both fighting back laughter at Lilly's ridiculous drunken escapades.

"Don't laugh. I'll do it," Lilly pouted.

Jacob cupped Lilly's chin, forcing her to look at him. "Am I going to have to remove all the scissors from your house?"

Lilly smacked his hand away again, huffing in his general direction. "My hair, I can cut it if I want."

"Yes, you can. But I'm going to recommend a professional stylist instead of going GI Jane on me." Jacob slid the car into gear and rested his hand on Lilly's leg, grasping it tighter each time she tried to flick him off.

The drive was quiet, and Jacob dropped Sabina off first. "Thanks for rescuing her. Goodnight, my darling friend." Sabina leaned over, kissing Lilly on the cheek.

"Goodnight Benedict Arnold," Lilly grunted.

Jacob pulled back onto the highway, shooting looks at the slightly slumped woman in the seat next to him. The evening certainly hadn't played out how he hoped, but it gave him an odd sense of satisfaction that she was so upset she had gone out to get drunk, over him.

"It smells like burgers in here," Lilly muttered, her finger tracing the dash.

"That's because there are burgers in the backseat."

"Did you have to leave your date to rescue me? Did you have to get a doggy bag?"

"I wasn't on a date."

"Oh, bull cock."

Jacob sputtered on his laugh. "What?"

"I'm trying to curse less…it's not working out so well. Why are there burgers in the back?"

"I know you didn't eat your dinner, and I could barely choke down mine, so I thought we could eat some takeout at your house."

"You probably poisoned it."

"Of course, with strychnine, remember? My poison of choice."

That did it, Lilly tried to hide her face, but he caught the smile flit across her gorgeous mouth.

"What you saw with me and Victoria wasn't a date—"

"I don't want to talk about it."

"Lilly, please. You deserve an explanation."

138

Lilly turned in the seat, inebriated enough she didn't notice her skirt hiked way up her thighs. "I deserve all sorts of things."

Her statement likely wasn't sexual, but no one sent that memo to his dick. Jacob tried to look away, it wouldn't do to take advantage of someone drunk, but her body truly was luscious. The memory of her taste and scent came wafting back to him. She was delicious, and all he wanted was to spend the rest of the night exploring her curves.

"I'll give you anything you want. Just name it, and it's yours."

Lilly narrowed her eyes at him. "I wanted you, but you're with Victoria."

"I am not with Victoria and...what did you say?"

But Lilly had already moved on to new topics. She ran her fingers through her hair, examining it closely. "I'm going to dye my hair blonde, then all the men will want me. Why do men prefer blondes?"

Jacob chuckled. "Not all men prefer blondes."

"You do."

"I do not, actually. I discovered a great attraction to brunettes, one in particular." His attempt to sweet talk her failed miserably.

"Then I'm definitely dying it." Her chin jutted out in a petulant scowl.

He snorted back a laugh as he pulled into her driveway and shut off the car.

Lilly opened the car door, sucking in a lungful of fresh air. "Thanks for the ride, sorry I ruined your date with Victoria."

Jacob rushed around the car, grabbing her by the waist, but it was too late, and Lilly lost her balance and fell onto the grass, dragging Jacob down with her. He was about to check her over for breaks and bruises when Lilly giggled, then snorted. Even in her worst drunken state, she was far kinder than Victoria sober. He nuzzled her nose with his own, smiling at the inebriated woman with whom he was fast falling in love. "Are you okay?"

Lilly bit her lip, letting out a half-laugh, half-cry. "No." She blinked back tears.

Jacob pulled back, studying her. "Are you hurt?"

Lilly shook her head. "I don't want to like you, Jacob, but I do. I like you too much, and you're going to break my heart."

Her drunken admission floored Jacob. The truth comes out when you're drunk, and the truth was she cared about him, perhaps even loved him.

"Who says I'm going to break your heart? You won't even let me in, Lilly."

Lilly wrapped a finger around one of his curls, a rueful expression on her face. "I already have, Jacob."

Jacob held his breath. It wasn't quite an admission of love, but it was close, and the scary part wasn't her admission, but the fact that he felt the same way. He stroked her hair from her face, peppering her face with kisses.

Lilly pushed him away, pulling herself to a seated position. "We can't do this anymore. We're too different. What I want and what you want are so far apart." She threw her arms open, signifying the distance between them.

Jacob cupped her face, his mouth against her cheek. "You don't know what I want, you've never asked."

"I know you don't want me like you want Victoria." She stood up, a bit wobbly as she slipped off her heels and headed to the door.

Jacob hurried after her, afraid she might take another tumble. He took her keys and unlocked the door, helping her to the couch while he lit a fire and brought in the hamburgers he ordered.

He smiled as she scarfed down the burger, oblivious to the ketchup in the corner of her mouth. He moved closer to her, his mouth licking away the red dollop and earning a gasp from Lilly.

"You had ketchup, right here." His thumb traced along her lower lip, and he had to move back before his libido took control.

Lilly bit her lip again and sucked down the rest of the water. "I need to take a shower."

"How about a bath?"

Lilly shrugged.

"Give me a few minutes." Jacob walked into her bathroom and turned on the warm water, adding a few drops of lavender oil. He never took care of the women in his life, but he loved taking care of Lilly. He'd gladly handle her every need if she'd let him.

A slightly more cognizant Lilly walked into the bathroom, giving him a smirk. "I've got it from here. Thanks for the ride…and the burger. You can head on home now. I'm sure your girlfriend is waiting for you."

"The only one waiting for me at home is Charlie, and he'll understand. Truth is, he'd want to be here with you too. So be quiet and come over here." Jacob pulled down the zipper on her dress, letting the material slide off her body to the floor. His fingers popped open her bra and Jacob had to state the alphabet backward in his mind to avoid a raging hard-on. When she shed her panties, it was all over.

Jacob wanted her so badly he ached. He should look away—that was the polite thing to do—but to hell with manners. His gaze roved over every curve and plane on Lilly's body, itching to kiss every inch of her until she screamed his name so loudly everyone in London heard.

But Lilly seemed blissfully unaware of his hedonistic ogling as she stepped into the tub and leaned back, her fingers moving through the water. "It feels good. Relaxing. Be honest, did I ruin your night, Jacob? Victoria looked really beautiful."

"*You* looked really beautiful. She looked like she was craving attention, which is what she does."

"Isn't that what you all do?"

"That's not fair, Lilly." Her words cut him because they *were* true...at one point. But not anymore. One Yank Ninja Express wannabe gangster had changed his outlook on everything.

"Not fair is saying what you said to me, making me feel those things—"

"I meant every word. Every word."

Lilly shook her head, running her hands up her legs. Jacob grabbed her foot and began massaging it, his thumbs sliding across her slick skin. "Give me my foot back—"

"No. You're going to have lay there and endure this foot massage."

"You never answered my question."

"What's that, angel?" Jacob's hands froze on her foot as their eyes locked on that last word. He never referred to women by anything other than their names, he never let them stick around long enough to receive anything more. Yet he'd been referring to Lilly as angel practically since day one.

Lilly swallowed hard, her eyes lasered on him. "Why do you call me that?"

Time to bare *his* soul. "Because you are."

"Am what?"

Jacob felt his heart rate increase. "My angel."

Lilly's eyes filled with tears and she shook her head, snatching back her foot. "You can't say things like that and then act like you do."

"I've *never* said anything like that to another woman. Just you. Only you. Why didn't you let me explain what was going on with Victoria?"

"There's nothing to explain, I saw you two having dinner. I saw her touching you." Her voice broke with emotion. "I saw you letting her."

"It's not what you think—"

"Was it a date?"

How the fuck was he supposed to explain this situation? "Yes, but—"

Jacob regretted the words the instant they left his mouth. Bugger he was an idiot. He knew he should have come clean and told Lilly the situation as soon as he agreed to Victoria's ridiculous demands.

But he hadn't. He instead tried to toe the line, keep his Hollywood life

141

separate from his personal life, and now they collided like two cars in a high-speed crash.

He watched Lilly's sweet face turn to steel, her eyes glazing over as she donned her emotional mask. He realized how the situation sounded like she was another girl in a long line of conquests. There was no way he could explain the situation with her as drunk as she was. Hell, he might not be able to convince her if she was stone cold sober.

Lilly focused her gaze downward, her hands clenching and unclenching, and he worried she might take a well-deserved swing at him. Instead, a tear slid down her face, and he realized he would rather take a punch than see her cry. "It's time for you to leave, Jacob."

"That came out wrong—"

Lilly held up her hand. "Please, just go, I'm begging you."

Jacob gripped the side of the tub, wishing he had kept his big mouth shut. "Lilly, you don't understand—"

Lilly nodded. "You're right, and I don't want to. Please leave. And please leave me alone, Jacob. I told you to be careful with my heart. It isn't like yours, mine will break. And that's what you're doing right now."

Christ, she was killing him. Jacob wanted to spill his guts, tell her how he felt, but he didn't know how to describe it. He'd never felt anything remotely like this before, and his situation with Victoria only made things messier. He smacked his lips nervously. "Lilly—"

"No, Jacob."

He grabbed her chin, forcing her to look at him. "You have no idea how I feel about you, what you're doing to me, to my life. I had everything planned, a plan to get on track and back on top of my career. Then I meet you, and I'm upside down."

Lilly's tears fell in earnest now, god he was making a mess of this situation. "I'm sorry I knocked you off course. It won't happen again."

Her crestfallen expression broke his resolve, and his lips crashed against hers, desperate for her to feel anything but this pain. His tongue laved into her mouth as his hands tangled in her hair, holding her to him. He kissed her with a ferocity he didn't know he possessed. She might be drunk from alcohol, but Jacob was drunk on love. He was bloody in love with Lilly, and she was pushing him away.

Her hands pushed at his chest, her mouth breaking free from his embrace. "Goodnight Jacob. I won't be your runner-up, no matter how much my heart wants you."

"Lilly," Jacob groaned against her hair, wishing he had the courage to tell her how he felt.

"Goodnight, Jacob," Lilly repeated firmly.

Jacob stood, hating the idea of leaving this woman as much as he hated the idea of never acting again. "I need to see you again. I'm going to see you again."

"I'll see you and Victoria at the ball on Friday."

"I don't have to take Victoria—"

"Jacob, please. Let me save what little dignity I have left." When the tears started falling again, it was time to leave her alone. He'd inflicted enough pain tonight.

Janie stood to hug her brother when he walked through the hospital door, and Jacob marveled at her progress in only a week after surgery. "I'm so glad you could drive me home. I was shocked when you picked up your phone. You're always so busy."

"I'm never too busy for you." He noticed a tabloid sticking out of her bag, his face gracing the cover. Snatching it, he read the headline 'Jacob and Victoria headed for a reconciliation? Victoria visits Jacob's London home.' He groaned, tossing the magazine into the trash bin.

Janie shot him a stern look. "Audrey found it in the gift shop."

"I'm sure she got a kick out of it. She relishes when they make me look like a cad."

"Hey," Janie snapped, "don't get mad at Audrey, this isn't about her. You make yourself look like a cad."

"Don't I know it."

"I thought you were past Victoria and all her games. It shocked me when she visited the other day, then I see this magazine and realize there might be truth to the rumor. Why in God's name have you two reconciled?"

Jacob sighed, sinking onto the hospital bed. "We didn't. She made me a proposition; she can get me the lead role in Milieu of Madness if I help restore her public reputation. Apparently, sleeping with half of Hollywood doesn't enamor her fans. This," he motioned at the trash bucket, "is part of her public relations scheme. Funny thing, she must have leaked the information before I even agreed to this debacle."

"Apparently she knew your answer before she asked. I thought you were interested in Lilly, especially after our last phone call. I've never heard you speak about a woman in that manner. Hell, I told Audrey it sounded like you were in love. My mistake."

His little sister's words cut through him. Was he that transparent? He couldn't go a couple hours without thinking about Lilly, wondering where she was, how she was doing, wishing she was naked in his bed—the list went on.

Jacob ran his hands through his hair and groaned. "I'm crazy about Lilly, but I can't get too close. I already feel like I'm losing all my power to withstand her. Soon I'll be wrapped around her little finger, bending to her every whim." Christ, he sounded like an asshole.

His sister agreed with his mental evaluation. "Stop being such a git. And stop comparing Lilly to any of the useless harlots you dated—I mean fucked— in the past. She's nothing like them, and you know it. And she would have you wrapped around her little finger, but she's not the type to ever take advantage. All she would do is love the hell out of you. And trust me, big brother, you could use it."

Jacob was reaching, searching for any reason why keeping his distance from Lilly was in his best interests. The truth was he was trying to convince his heart he was okay with Lilly's request that he maintain his distance. "What about the film role that Victoria has lined up? I can't risk losing this role for something that may or may not pan out. How often does an opportunity like this come along?"

"I don't know, Jacob, how often does an opportunity with a woman like Lilly come along?" Janie crossed her arms and glared at Jacob. "It probably wouldn't have worked out, anyway."

"And why is that?" His body tensed at Janie's words, his temper rising at her insinuation. Deep down, he knew he wanted someone to kick him out of his comfort zone and pursue Lilly's love with reckless abandon.

But Janie wasn't handing him a permission slip on a silver platter. "Because that would mean having to love something more than your career. It's better for Lilly, she's got too kind a heart. She'd be railroaded by you and your quaint conception of love. Besides, I'm sure she's seen the tabloid by now so it wouldn't make any difference, regardless." Janie cleared her throat. "I'm sick of being in the hospital. Let's get out of here, shall we?"

Jacob paused, his sister's words hitting him like a punch in the gut.

"Jacob? Are you ready?"

Jacob nodded, giving his sister a smile as the orderly helped her into the waiting wheelchair.

An icy rain was falling, the perfect match for the coldness in his heart. As he pulled the car to the entrance, his heart jumped into his throat.

Lilly was chatting with Janie, a smile illuminating her features, but it faded when she caught sight of him. "Jacob, I'm surprised to see you. I

144

expected Audrey would take Janie home."

Jacob nodded, his mouth dry as he looked at her, his hands itching to take her into his arms and kiss her until she believed he loved her the way she loved him.

Janie squeezed Lilly's hand. "You have my number. You better stay in touch with me."

Lilly squatted by Janie's wheelchair. "Wild horses couldn't keep me away."

Janie's eyes teared, and she pulled Lilly in for a hug. "Thank God for you, Lilly." Her hand went to the talisman around her neck. "You saved me. How can I ever repay you?"

Lilly's smile lit up her face. "Live an extraordinary life and enjoy every minute." She peered around the car park. "Where's the orderly?"

Janie waved her hand. "I can manage."

"Nonsense," Lilly replied, setting down her briefcase. "I'm happy to help." She glanced at Jacob, her expression guarded. "Will you help her balance, please?"

Jacob realized he was standing there like a dolt until he snapped from his reverie, hurrying to Janie's side as Lilly helped her stand. Within a minute, Janie was seated and comfortable, but she shot her brother a look before grabbing Lilly's hand again.

Jacob realized Janie was stalling and he rushed to where Lilly was standing. Lilly said a final goodbye and straightened, looking at him. "Get home safe." She had taken a few steps away when Jacob grabbed her arm.

"It's not what you think. I'm not with Victoria."

"You don't need to explain anything to me." Lilly's jaw was tight, and it was all Jacob could do to not grab her and kiss her until she softened.

"But I want to explain it to you, I want to explain everything to you." He closed the gap between them, taking her hands and pressing his forehead against hers. She stiffened, and he massaged her hands with his thumbs in a futile attempt to relax her. "You won't give me a chance?"

Lilly pushed back from him, her eyes glistening. "No need. I'll see you and your girlfriend at the fundraiser."

"Lilly…we need to talk about the other night. Things were said—"

She bit her lip, gazing at the concrete. "I was drunk. I don't have a clue what I said."

But Jacob wouldn't release his grip, not yet. "Yes, you do, Lilly. I know you remember. I want to talk about what you said that night, and what I need to tell you—"

She snatched her hands back, her eyes brimming with tears. "I told you, I was drunk. Nothing I said meant anything."

The saying by Jean-Jacques Rousseau floated through Jacob's mind—'a drunk mind speaks a sober heart'—but he opted to keep it to himself. She was clearly embarrassed, which meant she remembered every word she spoke that night. "It meant something to me."

Lilly whirled on her heel; her expression as cloudy as the storm-ridden London sky. "Goodbye, Jacob."

And with that, she disappeared into the hospital.

Jacob got back into his car, slamming the door. He turned to Janie and muttered, "Don't say it, I know I've screwed up."

Janie grabbed his hand, whispering, "Then fix it. It's obvious you two care about each other."

Jacob nodded, realizing he cared too much about this woman and he wasn't sure what that meant for anything anymore.

Lilly

P eople milled about the fundraiser, dressed in their finery and downing champagne like water. The guests discussed a variety of high-brow issues, ranging from butlers to polo. Lilly stifled a laugh when she overheard a middle-aged woman groaning about an escargot fiasco. *Oh, the problems of the wealthy.*

The ballroom was decorated to the hilt, and the turnout already surpassed estimates, but if the event weren't for her charity, Lilly would have skipped it in favor of a movie marathon and pint—no a gallon of ice cream.

She realized how foolish she appeared to anyone who saw her with Jacob, a schoolgirl with a crush on the unattainable teacher. Worse, she believed he reciprocated those feelings. She usually kept men at arm's length, but Jacob broke through her defenses as if they were constructed of marshmallows.

Lilly heard her name being called and turned to see Sabina hurrying over. "My God woman, you look fantastic!"

Lilly smiled, sweeping thoughts of Jacob from her mind. "Thank you, and ditto for you!" Her friend twirled in a circle, and Lilly laughed for the first time that day.

"Obviously, I look amazing, don't I always?" Sabina's eyes twinkled as they linked arms. "I've discovered the location of the closest bar."

Lilly giggled. "Now I know why I love you, lead onward." They crossed the room, a sea of tuxedos and ballgowns. Lilly opted for a floral gown in black and white, her hair swept into a French twist. She felt beautiful and judging from the salacious looks of the men around the ballroom, she wasn't the only one with that opinion.

Lilly had just placed their drink order when she felt eyes boring into her. Peering to her right, she saw Jacob, debonair in his fitted tux, his eyes transfixed.

Sabina nodded in his direction. "He hasn't stopped staring since you walked in."

"I didn't realize he was already here, I don't see his girlfriend." Lilly tried to sound nonchalant, but she choked out the words.

Sabina sipped her wine. "Jacob and I had a little chat about that situation."

"How is reconciling with your ex-girlfriend a situation?"

"He hasn't reconciled with her, it's all a public relations ruse. He was supposed to escort Victoria tonight, but he arrived alone."

Lilly's eyes widened, but her voice remained steady. "Why would he do that?"

"Because," a deep voice rolled like honey over her shoulder, "I wanted to dance with someone else."

Lilly turned to Jacob, inhaling his scent as he kissed her hand. His beard was newly trimmed, his eyes as blue as the spring sky. He was grace personified.

Lilly smiled in spite of herself. "Is that a fact?"

He turned her hand over and kissed her wrist, his eyes never leaving her face. "That is a fact, but she's no ordinary woman, she's absolutely captivating."

The electricity sparked between them, and Lilly was sure they would catch fire. His smile unhinged her, and her eyes fluttered closed when his thumb traced her lips. She should resist him, push him away, but it was pointless. Where Jacob was concerned, she was all heart and no head.

His mouth brushed her ear as he whispered, "Dance with me, angel."

Lilly nodded, and Jacob escorted her to the dance floor. The guests stepped back to allow them room, eager to observe the Hollywood star in action.

The song ended as they reached the center of the floor and Lilly gave a self-conscious giggle. "So bad they stopped the music entirely."

Jacob wrapped his arms around her, whispering, "Not quite."

The first strains of the song rang out, and Lilly's heart leapt. It was the same music that played their first night together. "My favorite song."

He replied with a small smile as he tightened his embrace.

Lilly noted the growing group of onlookers, but they faded into the periphery as she gazed at Jacob. He twirled her, drawing her body to him.

"You're exquisite, Lilly. I've missed you."

"It's only been a few days. It hasn't been long enough for you to miss me," Lilly retorted, although her statement was a lie. A minute away from him seemed an eternity.

"Every moment away from you is too long."

Lilly sighed. Damn, but he knew how to say all the right things, and her foolish heart believed his words every time. "Jacob—"

He pressed his lips to her hair, a bold move in such a high-profile, crowded locale. "Will you stop fighting me on this? I know how I feel."

"I'm supposed to be mad at you." God, she sounded like a five-year-old throwing a tantrum.

She felt him smile against her skin. "How's that working out for you?"

She looked away, feeling that familiar flush creep into her face. Jacob's fingers lifted her chin to meet his gaze. "No hiding that beautiful smile from me tonight. You can be angry with me, but it's not going to stop me from showering you with adoration. So get used to it, angel."

And just like that, her mind was locked into a cupboard and her heart took back full control. As she met his sapphire gaze, a smile crossed her face and all remnants of anger slipped away.

"Ready for one more twirl?"

Lilly nodded as he spun her for the end of the song.

As the last notes rang out, his lips grazed the inside of her wrist, his eyes making love to her. "Thank you."

Lilly smiled, suddenly shy in front of this man. "For what? I'm hardly the consummate dance partner."

His fingers traced down her arm. "For being you."

Lilly's heart fluttered in her chest. Against every good judgement she possessed, she had fallen—head over heels—for Jacob Edmonton.

A group of wealthy patrons greeted them as they left the dance floor, eager to mingle with the Hollywood actor. Jacob smiled and shook hands but then directed their attention to Lilly, detailing her tireless efforts to work against a society that didn't place any value on an animal's life.

"You have quite the cheerleader, young lady." The elderly gentleman's eyes twinkled as he looked at them.

Lilly blushed. "I'm so grateful for his support. This cause is precious to me, and to the animals that the shelter saves."

"What are your long-term plans beyond this shelter?" A small crowd had gathered, ogling Jacob.

Lilly had her platform, now she needed to find her voice. Taking a deep breath, she spoke, surprised at the strength of her words. "To rally parliament so that animals are recognized as companions and not belongings. We must institute harsher punishments for those found guilty of animal abuse and neglect. From there, form a database of abusers that can be utilized should they attempt to purchase another animal, and—" she looked at Jacob, who appeared utterly entranced by her words, "—to establish sanctuaries throughout the UK for domestic, livestock, racing and circus animals who would otherwise be euthanized since they're no longer considered useful."

The elderly man stroked his mustache, considering her words. "So, a zoo for domestics and livestock?"

"No, a zoo would keep them in cages. They've lived all their lives in cages. A sanctuary would provide hundreds of acres where the animals could run, graze and rest, safely." Lilly's eyes grew misty as she pictured the sanctuary, a place where unwanted creatures finally belonged. "But it would cost a fortune. I'm grateful we increased the space in our current shelter. It will save many lives in the long run, and we have all of you to thank for that benchmark."

The patrons nodded, losing themselves in tales of animal companions.

Jacob pulled her from the group, guiding her to a quiet corner. His face was a mixture of amazement and surprise as he gazed at her.

Lilly flushed. "God, did I babble on and bore everyone?"

"Hardly, your passion is riveting, you're riveting." His fingers traced the lines of her arms. "I believe your dreams will become a reality when you visualize them and communicate them with such eloquence." He looked down, releasing a frustrated huff.

"What's wrong?"

"Celebrities have long been associated with all manner of charities, they write checks or appear at charity balls," his arms sweeping the hall, "but they don't usually dirty their hands. The real work falls to the true heroes of the causes, and those people remain nameless and uncelebrated. I've been celebrated for my work with charities, but I've never gotten hands-on like you do every day, and yet no one knows your name. It's a loss to the world, not to know an amazing woman like you."

"Us nameless faces don't do this work for personal recognition. It's a calling. Trust me when I say those animals save us as much as we save them." Lilly placed her hand on his arm. "We're not here for the accolades."

Jacob shook his head, a smile playing on his face. "How did I get so lucky?"

"I don't understand."

"To be in the company of the most incredible woman I've ever met."

At that moment, an earthquake could level the building, but Lilly would scarcely notice. She felt loved and admired for being unabashedly herself, a feeling with which she had little experience. Her ex-boyfriend always cajoled her to play a part and not make waves. Her opinions might contradict those of someone truly important to his musical career, and where would that lead?

But tonight, Jacob celebrated her for that same passion and determination.

Lilly smiled, attempting to lighten the mood. "You're not so bad yourself."

He grimaced, but there was no anger in his voice. "Don't do that. You always sell yourself short. You have more passion in your little finger than most people have in their entire bodies." Jacob sensed her discomfort and changed the subject. "I see a few people with deep pockets I'm going to chat with. See if we can't get some additional funds for your sanctuary."

Jacob squeezed her hand and strode across the ballroom.

Lilly strolled to the bar, rejoining the elderly couple.

"Some excellent ideas, young lady. If you have plans to back up these dreams, we would be interested in perusing them." The gentleman toasted Lilly, their glasses clinking.

Lilly beamed. "I would be so grateful to get your thoughts on our long-term plans; perhaps you can identify areas of improvement."

"I believe as long as you have such powerful allies, your charity will do quite well." The gentleman's wife gazed at her, her eyes crinkling.

Lilly's brow furrowed, but the woman nodded, and Lilly followed her gaze to where Jacob was dazzling a group of women; their laughter rising like smoke above the crowd.

"Jacob's a remarkable help for our charity, and he's very charming."

"He is indeed charming, and handsome. And it's apparent he only has eyes for one woman."

Her heart beat wildly, but Lilly maintained a calm façade. "I'm sure I don't know what you mean."

The woman chuckled, patting Lilly's arm. "Dear, I'm sure you know exactly what I mean. He's quite enamored with you."

Lilly laughed off the comment. She desperately wanted to be Jacob's someone, but she read the magazine articles and saw the photographs—it appeared Victoria was still firmly entrenched in his heart.

"Jacob and I are just friends. He's like that with everyone. When you speak with him, he makes you feel as if you're the most important person in the world. It's intoxicating, but it's just who he is."

The elderly gentleman stroked his mustache, amused. "I'm an old man now, but I know what love looks like. I know how I looked at this woman next to me whenever she walked into a room, and fifty years later, I still see her the same way."

Lilly beamed at the couple. "That kind of adoration is rare."

"It is dear," the woman replied, "don't let it slip through your fingers. The heart wants what it wants." With that, they disappeared into the crowd.

Lilly watched them leave, the woman's words resonating through her head. *Such silliness*, she surmised, snapping from her reverie when Sabina and Ben motioned to her from across the ballroom.

She strolled over, wrapping one arm around each of her friends. "Where have you been all my life? How am I to survive without my darling comrades?"

151

Ben scoffed, twirling her playfully. "You're doing just fine, my dear. These donors are wrapped around your little finger."

"One in particular," Sabina interjected, a bemused smile on her lips.

Lilly shot her a questioning look. "You mean that couple? They're lovely, they've been married fifty years."

"I don't mean that couple, although congratulations for surviving that long without killing your spouse." Sabina motioned over Lilly's shoulder. "I'm referring to a gentleman who hasn't taken his eyes off you all evening. I overheard him speaking about you with some of the guests. He radiates when you're the topic of conversation."

"He's trying to get money out of them Sabina, it wouldn't do for him to down talk the charity, or me."

Ben and Sabina exchanged glances. "Whatever you say, dear heart. It's obvious you're in love with him, and the feeling is mutual."

"Jacob has a girlfriend, remember?" Lilly gritted out, hating how that statement felt in her mouth.

Sabina shook her head. "I told you, it's a public relations stunt. Apparently being the whore of Babylon has its consequences. In return for him escorting her to functions and restoring faith in her name, Victoria ensures Jacob gets the lead role in Milieu of Madness. It's a business arrangement."

Lilly rolled her eyes. "They're pretending to be together? If that's the case, why hasn't he told me about the situation? And if she's the whore of Babylon but he's acting as her suitor, then what does that make me, the whore of south London?"

Sabina offered up a smirk. "Hardly, Lilly. Despite her objections, he refused to attend with her tonight. Jacob wanted to escort you, and if that wasn't possible, he wasn't going with anyone. So, I think that makes you his love interest, wouldn't you say, Ben?"

Lilly scoffed, but Ben leveled with her, "I know men," eliciting a groan from Sabina, "save it peanut gallery. That man has fallen hard for you. If a man like that looked at me like he's looking at you…let's just say I would leave early tonight."

Lilly's throat tightened as the butterflies returned. Her gaze met Jacob's across the room, and he nodded towards the balcony, flashing a small smile. Sometimes, logic be damned.

"Excuse me," Lilly murmured to her friends, who responded with knowing smiles.

Lilly stepped outside, inhaling the crisp air. Jacob leaned against the railing, a glass of wine in his hands, his eyes raking over every inch of her body.

Lilly didn't know if it was the alcohol, Jacob's lustful stare, or her own undeniable desire, but at that moment, she didn't need a reason. She crossed the small space and without hesitation, reached up, pressing her lips to his. He fumbled to set the wine on the railing before wrapping his arms around her, his mouth opening to her kiss. She deepened the contact, pushing her body against him and he responded, lifting her onto the railing as her arms slid around his neck.

When they parted, his eyes were hungry, his breathing uneven. "I've been praying for that all evening. You certainly know how to keep a man waiting."

"Can't make it too easy." Lilly captured his lips again as his hand traced up her leg, pushing her dress out of the way. He pressed against her, and she felt him pulsating, knowing it echoed the pulsations of her own body.

"God, you're so beautiful. I want to spend hours kissing every inch of your delectable body," Jacob whispered, eliciting a low moan from Lilly. "Let me make love to you tonight. Say yes, angel."

Lilly met those deep sapphire pools and knew she couldn't resist him any longer. It was a miracle she'd held out this long. "Yes."

Jacob's mouth covered hers, his kisses telling her without words how deeply he cared. He broke the kiss, moving his mouth down her slender throat, his beard tickling the delicate skin.

There was a chill in the air, but Lilly was on fire as Jacob rained kisses down her neck and chest. She tossed her head back, allowing him greater access, and his mouth suckled the pulse point on her neck, releasing a soft cry from her lips.

Someone coughed behind them, and they broke apart, Jacob keeping his back to the intruder.

Lilly blushed. "Sabina, we needed some fresh air. We're coming back inside."

Sabina chortled. "Don't stop on my account but Jacob, someone is looking for you, and I don't know how much longer I can delay her. She's very persistent."

Jacob huffed, staring at the ground. "How long ago did Victoria arrive?"

"About fifteen minutes, there was quite the muckety-muck when she first got here, but that has since died down, and she wants to know where you're hiding."

Jacob's hand slid down Lilly's body before resting on the railing, looking at her with such longing it made her chest ache. "Her timing is, as ever, perfect.

I'll be right there. Thank you, Sabina." He gazed at Lilly as though desperate to say something but thought better of it and set her on the ground before returning to the ballroom.

"Are you kidding?" Lilly hissed at the sky. "I know what you're going to say, Sabina. It was rash and silly and stupid and amazing, and I feel like a complete fool." Lilly drew in a slow, ragged breath. "Worse, I look like a complete fool. I thought they weren't dating. I guess the joke's on me."

Sabina shrugged, examining her friend. "Jacob said they aren't dating. He didn't think Victoria would show when he refused to be her escort, but apparently, she had other ideas." She smoothed Lilly's gown. "Just because she's here doesn't mean anything. I saw you and Jacob together, and if you two got any hotter, the building would go up in flames." Sabina fanned herself with one hand.

Lilly scoffed in disgust. "And then Victoria arrives, and he rushes to her side."

"Luv, he might be doing damage control. He told me Victoria's a loose cannon and he wouldn't want her making a scene tonight. This night is about your charity. He doesn't want her to ruin it." Sabina tucked a strand of hair behind Lilly's ear and offered her a small smile.

Lilly groaned, hating it when her friend made an irrefutable point. "You're right. Actually, tonight isn't about her or him or me. What do you say we head inside and find the closest bar? I have a sudden hankering for a big glass of whiskey. Screw the champagne."

"Now you're speaking my language," Sabina quipped, linking arms with Lilly.

CHAPTER FOURTEEN

Jacob

J acob wasn't three steps into the banquet hall when he heard Victoria's shriek of excitement. *God, she sounds like a harpy.*

"There he is, the man of the hour." Victoria sidled up to him, her lips at his ear. "Did you really think I would let you get away with your little stunt?"

"I thought you weren't attending tonight. What were your exact words? I'd rather suffer ten hangnails than mingle with the lowlifes at this charity?" Jacob's voice held a veiled threat.

Victoria laughed so the crowd would assume they were sharing a private joke, but her green eyes pierced Jacob. "We have a deal, remember? And you aren't living up to your end of the bargain. Now pretend you adore me, and in a few weeks, you'll have your precious role, so you can go seduce whatever trollop stumbles across your path. I'm sure your little nurse will have outlived her usefulness by that point, and you'll be on to the next pitiful stand-in."

Jacob felt his temperature rising. He would like nothing more than to tell her off in front of the guests who were paying a bit too much attention to their exchange. Instead, he sighed, realizing that right now, he needed her as an ally.

He wished he could walk away from the movie role, tell Victoria to bugger off and never deal with her again. But reputations were built and destroyed daily in Hollywood, and the wrong word from the right person could send you to a blacklist of wannabes and has-beens. Victoria was cruel enough to pull that card if she didn't get what she wanted.

"Do we understand each other?"

Jacob forced a laugh. "Of course, darling; but remember, once the event ends, so does this charade. And you keep your hands to yourself."

Victoria smiled, showing straight white teeth—like a shark—and leaned into him. "I say when the charade ends, okay, darling?" She turned to the crowd. "Who would like an impromptu performance? Give me a few minutes to set up, and we'll have some fun!" She squeezed Jacob's ass, shooting him a seductive side eye before departing.

Jacob needed a shower. He felt dirty after their brief interlude and wondered how he would survive the next several weeks.

"Quite the performance, Mr. Edmonton," Sabina sneered, peering at him over her glass. "You may be in contention for an Oscar."

Jacob knew he deserved her scathing remarks. Their earlier conversation revolved around Lilly, and Sabina was candid. It was obvious he and Lilly were attracted to one another, but Sabina didn't want her friend played for a fool by a well-known playboy. "I told you, it's a public relations ploy. If I don't act as the doting escort, Victoria will ensure I'm blacklisted from the lead role in Milieu of Madness. Sabina, I explained all this." His last line resonated as a plea for understanding.

"You did, and I believe you, but Lilly has no clue what, if anything, you feel towards her. She's in the dark and feeling very small and stupid." Sabina's face softened at the stricken look on Jacob's face. "Lilly's the most understanding person in the world, but you've explained your situation to everyone, except the person who's directly affected.'"

"I hate that she feels that way. I'll speak with her, I promise."

"Tonight."

Jacob nodded. "Absolutely." He kissed Sabina on the cheek. "Thank you."

"Don't make me regret this. Don't make me regret not telling her to run as fast as she can in the opposite direction."

Jacob scanned the room for Lilly. He spotted her with Enrique and Ben, and suddenly his throat felt dry and his feet like lead. Her opinion was of the utmost importance to him, and he was terrified of her shutting him out.

Enrique's eyes narrowed at his approach, but he held out his hand, and Jacob shook it with a firm response. Jacob was no fool, he knew Enrique would like nothing more than to give him a good thrashing. In the surgeon's mind, Jacob was the only thing standing in the way of his relationship with Lilly, but Jacob would be damned if he allowed that to happen without one hell of a fight.

Ben nodded in Jacob's direction before pulling Enrique aside for a drink.

Lilly remained in the same position, shaking her head, and staring at the floor. "What do you want?"

"I want you to look at me."

After a moment, Lilly's gaze swung to meet his, and she remarked flatly, "I'm looking at you."

Every thought in his head went up in smoke when he saw her brown eyes darken with pent-up emotion. "I know how this looks, and it is ridiculous and stupid and—"

"How what looks? You and your girlfriend? Or what occurred between you and me on the balcony? Which part exactly is ridiculous and stupid?" Her eyes glistened, and he cringed at her biting words.

"What happened on the balcony was amazing—"

"I'm sorry I kissed you, I put you in an awkward position."

Jacob couldn't stand it. He grabbed Lilly's hand and dragged her to a hidden alcove, away from prying eyes. "Don't ever apologize for kissing me, or for anything that occurred between us. You don't know what you do to me, what touching you does to me. You're spellbinding. This whole thing between Victoria and me," he gestured in the general direction of the stage, "it's a ruse. She and I have an agreement. She's friends with the director of Milieu of Madness and if I don't play along, my chances of getting that role are nil." Jacob sighed as he leaned Lilly against the wall, one arm at each side of her head. "And it would have been fine—annoying, but fine—except I met you, and I don't want to pretend to want anyone. I just want you."

He could see Lilly considering his words, weighing the truth versus the appearance, and she softened. "That's horrible."

"Which part?"

"That someone would dangle your dream role over you, requiring you to make unrelated payments to be considered for something you have enough talent to play in your sleep." Lilly stared at her hands as if deciding whether to forgive him. "You're not together, even though she's here tonight? And I'm not some naive, idiotic homewrecker for what happened on the balcony?"

Jacob caressed her cheek, his lips touching her neck and softly tonguing circles there. *God, this must be what heaven tastes like.* "You're beautiful and what happened on that balcony was one of the most thrilling moments I've ever experienced. I could kiss you forever."

"Sabina told me about your situation, but after the way you ran to Victoria tonight, I thought you wanted to have your cake and eat it too." Lilly bit her bottom lip, her uncertainty evident.

"I'm sorry I took off so quickly, but I wanted to ensure Victoria toed the line. She was less than thrilled with me earlier tonight when I refused to escort her, and she is not beyond telling cruel lies in public. I had to protect you. You're too important to me." Jacob realized how true his words were, yet how unafraid he was of their connotation.

"You promise?" Her eyes glistened, and Jacob's heart sank at the pain in their depths. "I want to believe you, as ridiculous as your situation is, but I'm terrified I'll wind up the fool."

"I promise it's not real. I pretend I'm enchanted by Victoria while we're here and then she goes her way, and I go mine. The only woman I'm truly enchanted by is you. I'm asking a tremendous amount for you to understand this inane situation, but I have to ask."

Lilly shook her head, her laugh dry. "It wouldn't be the first time someone had to pretend to like someone to move ahead. It's the way of the world. I know what this role means to you. I won't get in the way of that." She paused, avoiding his gaze. "You'd better get back out there, she's about to perform. It wouldn't do for you to be skulking in the corner with me."

He pressed his lips to her forehead, unsure how he'd been lucky enough to come across the last true lady in England. "I promise this will be over soon. I want to see you later, after this…I need to see you tonight." He brought her fingers to his lips, sucking them gently. "Let me show you how much you mean to me. I'll beg if need be."

Lilly chuckled, but it rang hollow. "We'll see, one obstacle at a time."

Jacob trudged back to the central ballroom, listening to Victoria's pitch to the crowd about the charity. Victoria possessed a knack for public speaking, and so far, she was on point. She then belted out one of her hits, and the crowd went wild, but Jacob's focus was on Lilly. He caught sight of her across the room, leaning against a column, and it took everything in him to not cross that floor and sweep her into his arms.

He'd never experienced such a powerful desire, an almost insatiable need when he looked at her. Jacob had his pick of women, but Lilly captivated his mind and heart. She was the epitome of grace, complete with a wicked sense of humor and fierce loyalty to those she loved. However, Jacob was beginning to realize her outer layer was thin and underneath was a woman hiding brutal emotional wounds.

Victoria's song ended to thunderous applause, and Jacob clapped, smiling as partygoers commented on his talented girlfriend. Victoria coveted the mic—and the adoration—as she began personally identifying charity members responsible for the evening. She mentioned every board member, but never said a word about Lilly.

Jacob's jaw slackened, horrified that she failed to mention the person who spearheaded everything. She was provided a list of names, so her decision was deliberate and when Victoria's eyes found Jacob, her smile bordered on a sneer. She was no fool. She knew how important Lilly was to him and now, she would make them both pay.

"There's my wonderful man, the impeccably talented Jacob Edmonton. Come up here, darling."

Jacob shook his head, his fists clenched. He would take the microphone and bring Lilly the attention she deserved for her work. He smiled at the crowd as he climbed the stage, shocked when Victoria pulled him into a deep and public kiss.

Jacob startled at her tongue in his mouth, her hands holding his head in place. Jacob broke free but Victoria's appetite wasn't satiated, she pulled him back, throwing herself into his arms.

Finally, Victoria pulled away and kissed him on the neck, asking the crowd, "Isn't he wonderful? Anything you want to say, sweetheart?" Her eyes flashed a warning to play the game.

Jacob took the microphone as he tried to find his bearings. "Victoria saved the most important person for last. I want to bring your attention to Lilly Staver. Without her hard work and dedication, none of this would be possible." He searched the crowd, but Lilly was gone.

Patrons looked around the ballroom, their gazes questioning at Lilly's sudden disappearance.

"Perhaps she's on another rescue run. Let's get back to the music!" Victoria snatched the microphone from Jacob's hand. She went to kiss him again, but Jacob held her off as her lips drew into an angry snarl. "I want a kiss, sweetheart."

"Not in a million years, that was never part of our deal. You don't touch me again," Jacob seethed.

Suddenly she laughed. "You're quite fond of your little trollop, aren't you?" Her fingers hooked his belt loops and he flung her off, his fists clenching.

Their heated exchange was attracting attention, but Jacob didn't care. "Lilly's every inch a lady."

"She's a step down, if you ask me. But I suppose everyone is entitled to go slumming once in a while."

"Don't say another word about her. My relationship is none of your business."

Victoria's laugh made his skin crawl. "Your relationship? That's a laugh. Well, if your *relationship* with that skank is so important, I guess you won't have any issue walking away from your dream acting role, will you?"

And just like that, Victoria threw down the gauntlet. It was Jacob's ultimate test. And judging from her narrowed, scornful stare, she knew how Jacob would react to her ultimatum.

The only trouble was, she was dead wrong. "If that's what it takes to keep Lilly in my life and you out of it, then consider my interest in the role rescinded."

It would have been laughable—Victoria's green eyes widening in shock—if he hadn't thrown away the role of his dreams. He was grateful he

159

hadn't spoken with the director or read the script. It made this heart-wrenching decision a smidgen easier.

"Are you serious?" Victoria hissed.

Jacob leveled his blue gaze at her, his eyes afire with anger. "This is me walking away."

"This isn't over, Jacob. She can't win against me, neither can you; remember that. I always get what I want." Her voice sounded reedy and unsure, but her words held a viable threat.

Jacob strode off the stage and towards Sabina, whose eyes shot daggers at him.

"What the fuck was that fiasco onstage? Let's forget to mention the woman who organized the event and while we're at it, throw in some tongue play for good measure."

"Sabina, I had no idea Victoria was going to do that, you have to believe me. Where's Lilly?"

"She's gone. Apparently that fine display was more than she could stomach."

"I have to find her—"

"I think you've done enough damage, Jacob. I told you not to hurt her. You couldn't even make it through one night without tearing her heart apart!" Sabina's voice rose, and she snatched her arm away when Jacob grabbed it.

Something snapped in Jacob. Somewhere between Lilly's tears, Victoria's ultimatum, and Sabina's accusation. "I just walked away from the role in Milieu of Madness! I told Victoria to shove the role up her ass." He leaned into Sabina, his eyes bright. "So don't question how I feel about Lilly. I gave up everything for her just now."

Sabina's face paled, and her jaw slackened. "Holy shit, you did that for her?"

Jacob nodded. "And I'd do it again in a heartbeat. Now, will you tell me where Lilly went? Do you think she's still here at the fundraiser?"

"I'm assuming she went home. She doesn't have a car so she might be waiting for a taxi...or walking. She just left. She didn't say anything to me."

Jacob's eyes widened. "It's freezing outside, Sabina!"

Sabina's eyes held Jacob hostage. "Then don't waste any more time talking to me, go get her."

Jacob walked off, searching every nook and cranny of the facility, to no avail.

He shot a parting glance in Victoria's direction, surrounded by adoring fans, before heading for the valet station.

Lilly

L illy cursed not having a vehicle in the UK. The walk home from the banquet hall was over four kilometers and the night was bitter cold, her sheer shawl offering little protection against the wind.

She knew people would question her sudden departure, but it didn't matter. She had to get away, away from that building and Jacob's lips locked on his radiant, statuesque girlfriend.

A car approached, and she quickened her pace, aware she was an easy target on the darkened London streets. A knot formed in her stomach when the vehicle slowed, but she maintained a forward gaze.

The car parked on the street in front of her, and the driver hopped out. "Get in the car, Lilly."

Lilly shook her head, ignoring Jacob's request. "I'm fine, thank you."

Jacob moved in front of her and grabbed her shoulders, forcing her to stop. "You can be furious later. This isn't safe, and you're a long way from your house."

Lilly scoffed, her accent thickening. "You forget, I'm a New York Yank. I can take care of myself, and I can certainly make my own way home."

"Am I going to have to pick you up and put you in the car?"

Lilly gaped at Jacob's words. "You wouldn't dare."

In the next moment, Lilly was slung over Jacob's shoulder as he walked back to his car, tossing her into the passenger seat amidst a sea of curses.

Lilly's blood boiled when he switched on the childproof lock, preventing her exit. "Are you fucking serious right now?"

Jacob shot her a look before pulling back on the road.

Lilly flounced against the seat. She was grateful she didn't have to walk in the freezing cold, but she wasn't about to let him know that fact. Lilly shivered, and Jacob turned up the heat before resuming his white-knuckled drive. She felt his gaze on her at every light, but she focused out the window, unwilling to look in his direction.

She was acting petulant, but Lilly didn't care how childish she appeared. Her anger was the only thing keeping her from devolving into a puddle of tears, and she'd be damned if Jacob got to see those.

"Are you warmer?" He touched her arm, and she jerked it away, glaring at him. "At least now you're looking at me." He hit the steering wheel. "Dammit

Lilly, I'm sorry. I had no idea that was going to happen."

Lilly scoffed. "What kind of idiot do you take me for—oh wait, I am an idiot." With those words, the dam of emotions broke, and her tears won out.

Jacob pulled the car over, reaching over to cup her face. "I'm so sorry, please don't cry."

Lilly jerked her head away. "Don't touch me."

Jacob ignored the remark and pulled her to him, wrapping his arms around her until she rested her head on his chest. "I understand why you're angry. I'd be furious too. I *am* furious, for you. You should be celebrated for your hard work and dedication. Victoria was awful for denying you that."

Lilly jerked her head up, her eyes narrowing. "What in hell are you talking about?"

"Victoria ignoring your contribution to the charity, *your* charity, no less. Applauding everyone but you. I know how much work and time you've committed, and you deserved your moment to shine."

"I don't give a damn that she didn't give me credit." Jacob looked perplexed, so Lilly continued. "I don't perform charity work for accolades, that's the difference between you and me. One of many, obviously."

"Then, why are you crying?"

Lilly gaped at him. "I'm not having this conversation. Please take me home."

"Talk to me."

"You really don't know? Look, I know who you are, and I know who Victoria is, and I *definitely* know who I am…and I feel like an idiot, but I couldn't stay there and watch you kiss her."

"I didn't know how much you saw. When I looked for you in the crowd, you were gone. I prayed you didn't see it, it was awful, like kissing a cobra."

Lilly rolled her eyes. "Thanks for the visual. I saw everything. Why? Did you want to hide it from me?"

"Did you see me push her away?"

Lilly's jaw clenched. She left in such a tizzy that she hadn't watched the action play out. "No, as wonderful as I'm sure the ending was to that scene, I opted to depart early."

"Then you missed out on quite a public squabble—go ahead, ask Sabina. I think she had a right hook with my name on it until I threw Victoria off me. And damn, was Victoria livid when I mentioned you."

"You mentioned me to Victoria?"

"I mentioned you to everybody. I gave you the public accolades you deserve, but you had disappeared." Jacob sighed, leaning his head against the seat. "Trust me, angel, my feelings for you aren't news to Victoria. She already knew how important you are to me. That's why she failed to mention your contributions to the charity."

"She can't possibly think I'm a threat."

Jacob chuckled, grasping Lilly's hand. "You're far worse than that in her eyes. I'm not the same man I was a month ago, and you're the reason."

"I don't understand."

"Victoria gave me an ultimatum, you or the movie."

Lilly gasped. "Oh my God." Her brow furrowed in confusion. "Then what are you doing here?"

Jacob grasped her chin, bringing his lips next to hers. "What am I doing here, Lilly? I think you know the answer."

Lilly's heart beat a thousand miles a minute. Jacob sacrificed the role in his beloved movie…for her? She didn't know whether to kiss him or vomit. "I never wanted you to have to make that choice. I know what this movie means to you."

His lips pressed against her, his tongue flicking against her lips. "You mean more."

Lilly lost all hold on reason and grasped his face, slanting her mouth over his and unleashing every bit of passion within her body. Jacob returned the kiss, threading his fingers into her hair and trapping her in the embrace, not that Lilly was looking to escape.

"Come home with me," Jacob murmured against her mouth. "I need you with me tonight. You don't know how good it felt to sleep with you in my arms."

How could she deny him anything after the sacrifice he made this evening? Hell, she couldn't deny him regardless, her body vibrated at his touch. "Yes, I do. It was magic. Are you sure that's what you want?"

"I've never been more certain of anything in my life."

Lilly captured his thumb between her teeth as he traced her lip. *He'll likely break my heart, but if I say no, it will ache forever.* Lilly nodded, and Jacob gifted her with a smile before pulling back onto the road.

They reached his home within five minutes, and Jacob escorted her inside, turning on the fireplace in the living room. The touch of his hands on her back startled her, her breathing increasing as he pulled the zipper down, his lips kissing the back of her neck. "Let me help."

Lilly spun around, clutching the gown to her body. Every cell of her being reacted to his touch, but she needed to ensure they were on the same page. Even though she hadn't asked Jacob to make a choice, she knew all about remorse. It was its own kind of death—one that ate away at your soul. "I don't want you to do anything you'll regret tomorrow…any decisions you made in haste."

Jacob kissed her firmly, his tongue playing along her lips. "I stand by my decisions. And there's only one regret I could have for this evening."

"What is that?"

Jacob's lips caressed her clavicle, his tongue dancing along her skin. "Not being able to hold your body against mine tonight."

His admission floored Lilly, and she stopped asking questions. Instead, she stood on tiptoe, pulling his mouth to hers. She deepened the kiss when he shivered, a low moan rising from his throat. Jacob's arms pulled her close as he freed her hair from the clip, her waves tumbling over her shoulders.

His gaze was dark with desire when he pulled away. "If you keep kissing me like that, I'm going to lay you down and make love to you for the next three days."

"Is that a promise?" Lilly stepped back, her body warm as his eyes raked over her form. Her hold on reason flew out the window when she saw the raw lust on his face—that insatiable wanting—all aimed at her. She released her grip on the gown and watched his eyes grow large as it pooled around her feet. "I have three days."

Jacob groaned as he scooped her into his arms and laid her down on the plush rug by the fire. His tongue and teeth wasted no time unclasping her bra, his hands cupping her full breasts while his tongue suckled her nipples.

Lilly melted against his welcome onslaught. "It's not fair, I need you naked too."

Jacob unbuttoned his shirt, cursing about the number of buttons before jerking it over his head. Lilly reached up, her hands running over his chest and shoulders, her teeth nipping his neck.

Jacob claimed her lips again, his mouth possessing hers as his fingers traced down her abdomen to tease her clit. Lilly moaned into his mouth as his hand slid between her legs and his fingers sank into her, stroking her slow and deep.

Lilly bucked her hips against him, riding his hand with a slow rhythmic pace. "Oh, Jacob."

Jacob's lips broke from her mouth and attacked her neck, his tongue sucking the delicate skin. "You're so tight, Lilly."

Lilly arched into his caress, moaning at the feel of his mouth on her body. Jacob was working her into a frenzy of erotic sensations.

When his lips broke from her neck, Lilly grabbed his shoulders, willing him to return to her mouth. But Jacob had other ideas. He tongued down the length of her stomach, trailing kisses to the inside of her thighs. His fingers slid from within her and Lilly balked at the sudden emptiness. "No, no, please don't stop."

Jacob shot her a sultry, hooded gaze as his fingers hooked her g-string and pulled it off, his eyes reflecting back all the desire Lilly felt coursing through her body. "I'm just getting started." He nuzzled her mound, his hands sliding under her ass and bringing her even closer to his mouth. "You have no idea how much I've wanted to taste you again." He lowered his head between her legs and parted her folds with his tongue, his hands wrapping around her thighs.

Lilly bit back a whimper, her hips grinding against him. Jacob emitted a low growl, his tongue sinking inside her, and Lilly's body clenched. She couldn't think, all she could do was feel how his tongue teased every inch of her until her entire body was aflame with desire.

"I need you inside me."

Jacob nipped her inner thigh, his deep blue gaze molten. "I'm not finished with you yet. I want to make you scream."

His fingers slid inside her again as his tongue circled her clit, sucking gently. Everything went white as Lilly dug her nails into his shoulder and her body shattered underneath him.

Jacob eased her down from her orgasm, his lips nipping at her stomach and breasts before capturing her lips again. "You taste incredible, Lilly."

Lilly's hands slid down his abdomen and after some initial fumbling, she pushed his pants down, feeling the exquisite thrust of his erection pressed against her.

She fixed her gaze on him and saw a new emotion in his eyes, a deep-seated need emanating from their depths. They kissed, their lips fluttering against each other.

"Angel, what have you done to me?"

Lilly's lips were against his when the doorbell rang. They both started, the sound blasting through their veil of emotions like a shotgun.

"Who the fuck could be here now?" Jacob muttered, but Lilly had a sinking sensation she knew the answer. "Ignore them, they'll go away." Jacob's lips nuzzled her neck, but she pushed against his chest, eliciting a groan. "Lilly, please ignore it."

"You know exactly who's on the other side of that door, and we both know she isn't going to leave."

Jacob pushed himself up with a grunt, pulling on his underwear. "That

165

fucking wanker, I swear to God, her timing, her fucking timing." He threw on a t-shirt before turning to Lilly. "Do not put on a stitch of clothing. I'm coming right back, and we will continue where we left off—ugh. I'm coming!" He yelled as the bell pinged out again.

Lilly sat motionless, looking at the reddened areas on her body where Jacob's beard and kisses had traveled. She heard people conversing, but their words were garbled.

Without a sound, Lilly pulled on her bra and panties.

"What are you doing?" Jacob's voice sounded annoyed. "I told you not to get dressed."

Lilly bit her lower lip. "Does Victoria plan on staying here tonight?"

Jacob guffawed. "Lord no, she was with Albert, the director of Milieu of Madness. They wanted to discuss the role at his office."

"The director wants to discuss the movie? Now?" Lilly's eyes widened; this news was huge. "You need to get dressed. I'll grab a cab." Lilly moved quickly, picking up her scattered clothes.

Jacob stilled her. "Lilly, stop. I told Victoria no. It's fine."

Lilly's heart swelled at his words. "It's not fine. Tell her you'll meet them at his office. This opportunity is too big to pass up. Besides, she pretty much killed the moment anyway." Jacob groaned, slumping into a chair. Lilly knelt beside him. "Go, I'm serious. I can find a ride home."

He met her gaze, his chin resting on his hand. Lilly knew he was weighing his options. He was torn between losing her or the movie role. "Lilly—"

"You thought you threw away your big chance, and you did it for me. Now you can have both. I'm not mad. I love you for choosing me over her tonight."

His expression softened. "I—I lo—" but Lilly silenced him with a finger to his lips.

"Get dressed. Don't let her win. You've worked too hard for this opportunity."

Jacob stared at the carpet as if searching for answers. "I was exactly where I wanted to be. I was making love to you."

Lilly kissed him hard on the mouth but pulled away before his arms enveloped her. If she didn't force him to leave now, they would be naked within moments, and as much as her body ached for his touch, it would be suicide for his sought-after role. "I'm going to head home; let me know how the meeting turns out."

"No, please stay. I won't be gone long and knowing you're here when I get back—"

"I don't think—"

Jacob cut her off, shaking his head. "I'll go, but only if you'll stay. Give me something to look forward to when I get home."

Lilly hesitated before nodding in agreement. Jacob led her to his bedroom, her eyes widening at the four-poster bed and antique furniture decorating the room. He showed her the television and bathroom, then pulled her into a deep kiss, his eyes sparkling as they parted. "You do sleep in the nude, don't you?"

Lilly giggled. "I can put a shirt on to retain some modesty, if you prefer."

"Like hell, you will," Jacob replied, unfastening her bra and tossing it on the floor. His eyes blazed again, and he pushed her onto the bed, his mouth suckling her breast. He finally pulled away at her insistent nudging. "You're killing me, Lilly."

"Sex with me is not going to be the reason you don't get that part, now go. And don't forget, you deserve this role. It's as good as yours." She scooted under the covers, Charlie greeting her with a sloppy kiss. She snatched the remote from Jacob's hand with a playful grab and shooed him out of the room.

She leaned against the pillow, hearing the door close downstairs a few minutes later. She petted Charlie's head, wondering if she was a fool for insisting Jacob leave her and return to Victoria's side. "I'm in real trouble, Charlie. I've fallen completely in love with him."

CHAPTER FIFTEEN

Jacob

Jacob wasn't sure which he hated more—leaving Lilly's side or Victoria's mocking tone when he agreed to meet them at the director's office. Her voice dripped saccharine when she remarked how she "knew he would come around."

The director's name was Albert, a man of about sixty whose decadent lifestyle was evidenced by his portly silhouette. He had a firm handshake and honest eyes. Jacob liked him immediately.

Albert looked surprised when Victoria introduced Jacob as her significant other, but he played it off well. His focus was on the brass tacks of the script—his vision and the adaptation from the novel. Jacob listened with intent, but for the first time questioned if he was the best choice for the lead role.

Jacob's phone buzzed, and he excused himself to answer. It was Sabina. Jacob and Lilly departed in such a hurry she wanted to ensure neither was lying dead in a ditch. Jacob guessed Sabina cared little about his well-being but was grateful for her effort. He reassured her Lilly was safe, then spent the next few minutes wrangling Lilly's phone number out of her best friend. He thought it odd that he and Lilly almost made love, but he didn't have her phone number. *Nothing about our relationship has followed a traditional path.*

Jacob sent Lilly a text, along with a follow-up message disclosing his identity. He recalled his discussion with Lilly that night after the karaoke pub and her thoughts about his acting roles and choices. Her opinions kept replaying in his mind as he returned to the meeting, spilling out when Albert asked about Jacob's thoughts on the film.

"I think the lead character in the graphic novel is a bit two-dimensional, even as an antihero, he fails to connect at a human level. I believe it will translate better if he has something that humanizes him, be it a dog or a love interest, something brings vulnerability to his character." Jacob realized he could be talking about himself, his rise to fame, his sardonic views on love and his tendency to keep everyone at a distance—he was, himself, somewhat two-dimensional.

Victoria threw back her head with a mocking laugh. "I'm sorry, Albert, it's so amusing to see Jacob embracing sentimentality."

Jacob's face remained neutral as he looked at Victoria, but his eyes burned with hostile fire.

Albert scratched his chin, considering Jacob's words. "I thought the exact same thing. It's refreshing to hear someone agree with my take on the role. Sentimentality is a dying artform."

The director's barb hit its intended target and Jacob damn near guffawed at Victoria's shocked expression. *First person in history to ever shut Victoria up—the man deserves a medal.*

After an hour, the conversation wrapped, and Albert promised to update Jacob on any developments.

Jacob realized as he departed Albert's office that Victoria didn't have a car; lucky for all other motorists considering the copious amounts of champagne she imbibed throughout the evening.

With a resigned sigh, he drove her to The Lanesborough, extricating himself from her embrace and ignoring her pleas for a nightcap. "Don't get too big for your britches and think you get to call all the shots here. Remember who set up this meeting for you. You owe me, especially after that stunt you pulled earlier. You're lucky I'm even considering helping you after that debacle."

"I stand by my every action tonight."

"A little graciousness can go a long way, Mr. Edmonton." Her hand reached across his lap, but Jacob caught it mid-air. "You might enjoy my form of gratitude."

"I said no."

Her eyes flashed, a mercurial storm was brewing. "Let me guess. Is your little woman waiting at home? How long until playing house becomes cliché?"

Jacob sighed, shaking his head with a tired laugh. He knew it was pointless to answer her accusatory questions—why poke the bear. "I'm not coming inside with you."

Victoria surrendered, leaving with a parting shot. "Fine, but if you create one more scene like you did tonight, I'll make your career disappear."

"Goodnight Victoria." Jacob's jaw clenched as she slammed the door.

Jacob was shocked by how drained he felt being in Victoria's presence for two hours. She took the wind out of his sails, and he wondered what he ever saw in the woman. He walked into his house, eager to curl up next to Lilly and recharge his batteries. He paused halfway up the stairs, realizing that Lilly energized him, she made life look new again.

When he walked in the room his bed was empty, save for Charlie, who had taken up residence at the foot. Jacob feared Lilly had left.

His sigh of relief was audible when the bathroom door opened. "You're still here; I thought you'd gone."

Lilly smiled, looking a bit embarrassed. "I was going to leave, I felt strange staying, but then I got your text message. I didn't realize you had my phone number."

Jacob chuckled, pulling his shirt over his head. "I didn't. I got it from Sabina and trust me when I say, it cost me."

"You're going to owe that woman your soul soon," Lilly joked, sitting on the edge of the bed.

"Too late, that was my first bargaining chip." He paused, raking his eyes over her petite form. His gaze settled on a gift box lying on the nightstand. It was the necklace he purchased for Lilly but hadn't had the opportunity to give her. Nodding in the direction of the box, he asked, "Did you open it?"

Lilly shook her head. "Of course not."

"It's addressed to you, it's yours to open."

"You didn't mention it, and I'm not one to go snooping. Besides it could be meant for another Lilly."

Jacob guffawed. "Right, I have people named Lilly lined up outside the door, so please hurry." He placed the box in her hands.

Lilly hesitated before opening the gift. Her eyes widened at the necklace, her hands moving to her chest as though she feared touching the item.

"It won't bite, although I actually didn't ask the jeweler about that."

Lilly rewarded him with a sarcastic smirk. "That should have been your first question. Jacob, this is breathtaking."

Jacob smiled, thrilled by her words. He never wanted to please someone so badly, and despite his reputed prowess with the opposite sex, he felt like a bumbling fool around Lilly. "You're breathtaking."

"I can't accept this."

"Why not?"

Lilly sighed. "It's too much. I can never repay you for something like this. Have you seen how much nurses make?"

He removed the necklace from the box, fastening it around Lilly's neck. "I have no idea what nurses make, although I doubt it's anywhere near what they deserve. The jeweler said this is the evil eye, it protects the wearer. It's rose gold with diamonds and sapphires…and you absolutely will accept this gift. You gave Janie your talisman when she needed it, and I wanted to give you a new one." Jacob admired the pendant against her porcelain skin. "Besides, it looks beautiful on you."

"A piece this gorgeous would look beautiful on anyone!" Lilly's hand rested on the pendant around her neck. "I don't need expensive gifts. The one

I gave Janie didn't have diamonds or sapphires. I don't have anything to give you in return."

Jacob kissed her shoulder. "You have no idea how much you've given me. This is a tiny token of appreciation. It will protect you. That's what's important to me."

Lilly's smile lit her up from inside, and she captured his lips in a tender kiss. "I'll have to be worthy of such a gift, then. Thank you."

Jacob had given expensive gifts before, but they were expected within the Hollywood set. This was the best four thousand pounds he ever spent, and he knew Lilly appreciated the gesture more than the price tag. "You are more than worthy. I'm jumping in the shower. Join me?"

Lilly bit her bottom lip and giggled. "We both know how that will turn out."

"Is that so bad?" Jacob's eyes stared at her intently.

Lilly looked at the rug, her nervousness evident. "It's late, and we're both exhausted."

"If I promise not to touch you, will you join me?"

"Do I smell or something?" Lilly asked, a bit indignant.

"Yes, you smell wonderful; I just want to be near you."

Lilly considered his statement. Then with a click of her tongue, she shrugged, slipping off her bra and panties. "Let's go."

Jacob inhaled sharply as his body responded to her naked form. "You can't just do that."

"Would you prefer I shower with my clothes on?" She brushed past him, strolling into the bathroom. The dim light played off the curves of her hips and breasts, and Jacob knew there was no way in hell he was keeping his hands to himself.

He turned the radio to some slow R&B, then followed her into the bathroom. She stood there, a smirk on her face.

"Something amusing?"

Lilly shrugged nonchalantly. "Just the sheer amount of clothing you're wearing for someone taking a shower."

Jacob smiled at her sarcasm and pulled her to him, his lips devouring hers as her hands pushed his pants down over his hips. He backed her into the grotto-style shower and pressed her up against the wall, water streaming over their bodies. Lilly's eyes drank him in before claiming his lips again.

Jacob grabbed the soap, massaging the lather over her body. He could push her back against the wall and take her in the shower, but he wanted their first time to be beautiful, it didn't matter that his body was screaming for release. Lilly's pleasure was more important.

Lilly took the sponge from his hands, massaging his back and shoulders, first with her hands and then with her lips. Jacob feared he'd explode from the sheer intimacy.

"Let's go to bed," Lilly whispered, turning off the water.

Her body glistened with water droplets, and he admired her form, his breath coming in ragged gasps. She had to be aware of her beauty, but she didn't flaunt it like the women in Hollywood. She maintained an understated sensuality that Jacob found irresistible.

"Do we have to sleep?"

Her lips tickled his, an impish grin on her face. "I'm sure you can think of ways to keep me awake. You've yet to show me your final superpower."

He carried her to the bed, lowering himself on top of her and capturing her lips with his own. His tongue swept into her mouth as he tried to convey all the feelings coursing through his body. "I love coming home to you. I'm so glad you stayed," Jacob murmured into Lilly's neck.

"I couldn't leave after your text message." Lilly's giggle resonated in the bedroom, and Jacob smiled.

"I'm glad you're amused." Feigning anger, he held her wrists with one hand and began tickling her, eliciting squeals when he found the right spot.

"I give, I give!" Lilly cried as he released her hands and she claimed his mouth again. "I'm glad I'm your biggest weakness." Her words were a direct quote from his text, but she added her own embellishment. "You're my biggest weakness as well." Their lips were almost touching when his phone rang. Lilly rolled her eyes, laughing. "I think the Gods are trying to tell us something."

"That electronic devices are tools of Satan? At this moment, I agree with them. It'll stop in a minute." The phone went quiet as the voicemail picked up, only to start ringing again.

Lilly pushed against his chest. "You should answer it, it might be Janie."

"It's not Janie."

"It might be—she only went home yesterday—and you just returned from being with Victoria…that, and your ringtone is driving me insane!" Lilly shaped her hand into a mock gun and fired.

Jacob groaned as he rolled off her and grabbed his phone. He expected an inane message from Victoria, but it actually *was* Janie. His heart skipped a beat when he listened to her message.

"Hi Jakey, I know it's late, but I needed to call. I feel like I'm starting life over again. I wanted to make sure I told the people I love that I love them because second chances are never guaranteed. I hope you realize that, dear brother and I hope you attended Lilly's fundraiser. I like her, and more than that, you like her; she's right for you."

Lilly perched on the bed, her eyes studying him. "It was Janie, wasn't it?"

Jacob nodded. "She's fine, getting her feet back under her again." Jacob considered his sister's words; her opinion of Lilly echoed his own sentiment. He was getting too involved, or was he? For the first time, the idea of getting serious was a welcome idea.

"It can be hard for patients for the first few months; their bodies recover, but their spirits are forever changed by the experience. It's a second chance at life, and they want to make sure they're worthy of that opportunity."

"Did you overhear her message?"

Lilly smiled. "No, I've been a nurse for a long time; I've seen how it affects patients. But Janie is already such a sweetheart, I can't imagine her getting any sweeter."

He became solemn after his sister's message. She was right, life moved at warp speed and he didn't want to miss out on the most important aspects. Namely, he didn't want to miss out on a future with Lilly.

Lilly seemed to pick up on the change in mood and smiled, patting the bed. "It's late; you'll be asleep in five minutes."

"I have chronic insomnia. I rarely sleep."

Lilly considered his words as she slid under the covers. "Did you sleep the other night at my house?"

Jacob smiled. "I did."

"So, do you want to try again? See if it wasn't a one off?"

Jacob's eyes warmed as he climbed into bed, pulling her tight against him. "I do." Lilly turned on her side, and he spooned her, breathing in the scent of her hair, his hand clasping hers. "You feel like home, Lilly." He kissed her neck softly and closed his eyes, falling asleep within minutes.

The sun streamed through the curtains as he opened his eyes. *Damn, I haven't slept that well for years.* He reached over to the other side of the bed to stroke Lilly's body, jerking his hand back when it instead touched Victoria's thigh. His ex-girlfriend lounged against the pillow next to him, a sultry smile on her lips.

Sitting up, he blinked, clearing the fog of sleep. "What the—what are you doing here?"

"Good morning to you too, handsome." She dangled a key from her hand. "I still have my key, remember?"

Where is Lilly? Likely hiding from Victoria, which is exactly what I want to do right now.

Jacob grunted, realizing he was naked under the sheet. "I'm going to have to ask for that back." He muttered a thank you when she grudgingly released her grip on the fob. "You still haven't told me what you're doing here."

"I have a photoshoot for Vogue. I think it would benefit us if you participated."

"You mean benefit you, right?" Jacob scrubbed his face with his hands, willing his temper down. It appeared Victoria had forgotten the events at the ball and still assumed their facade was a go. "So our original deal still stands, is that what you're telling me?"

"Only if you want it to. If you still want that role. It's not that big a deal—a few photoshoots, a couple press releases, acting the way we used to act together—a few weeks and you get everything you want."

Jacob chewed his lip as he considered her offer. He craved this role, it had been a dream for a decade, and his relationship with Victoria would be no different than any other romantic role onscreen. It would mean nothing to him, but to the public, it would mean everything. But how would Lilly accept this proposal? She had been on board with it, but that was before last night.

"If you're worried about your nurse friend, look at it this way. If she really cares about you, she'll understand. If she doesn't, then I suppose she never had your best intentions at heart. Besides, it's only in public, she can still be your private whore." Victoria practically spit out the last words and Jacob's eyes narrowed in anger. "Save your self-righteous act. You know as well as I do this is a good deal. Little Ms. Nurse will simply have to endure."

"You are the most conniving human being I've ever met, you know that?"

Victoria shrugged, picking up the empty jewelry box. "What happened to the necklace?"

"None of your damn business. Look, have you seen—" Jacob stopped short. If he admitted Lilly was in the house it would open up a whole new can of worms. "Hannah, have you seen Hannah?"

"There was no one here when I arrived." She held up the box again. "Where did the necklace go? I assumed it was for me."

Jacob snorted. "Your ego is astonishing. Go downstairs, and I'll get dressed so we can get done with this charade." Victoria obliged, leaving Jacob alone in the room. He grabbed his phone, but there were no messages, no texts.

Lilly just gets up and leaves? No call, no note? What the hell? He felt his anger rising but let it simmer. She would contact him soon. For now, he had to dance with the devil on the pages of a Rolling Stone.

Lilly

"Come to Roger's house tonight." Janie and Lilly were eating lunch at a pub near Janie's flat, braving the chill on the patio to take advantage of the rare sunny afternoon.

"What's at Roger's house?" Lilly inquired, marveling at her friend's recovery. Less than three weeks ago Janie was undergoing open heart surgery, and now she was scarfing down a hamburger.

"Poker, of course, and the requisite scotch and whiskey—not that I'm imbibing any," Janie retorted when Lilly raised an eyebrow in her direction. "You must come along, it'll be fun."

Lilly smiled, shaking her head. "I don't think Roger would appreciate someone he barely knows invading his private space."

Janie snorted. "It's a party, you aren't going to the loo with him."

Lilly burst out laughing. "A valid point, although you never know what will happen with too much whiskey." She paused, reaching into her bag and pulling out the necklace Jacob gave her the week before.

"And what's that?"

"I was hoping you might return this to your brother, or you wear it. I don't feel right keeping it." Lilly paused, blinking back tears. "And I don't feel right coming tonight in case Jacob is there. I don't want to interfere in his life."

Janie leaned forward, admiring the necklace. "He showed this to me when he bought it. You can't give it back to him. But what the fuck happened with you two?"

Her words caught Lilly by surprise. She surmised Janie knew the whole story—she had hoped to find out details from her. "I actually don't know. We had this amazing night together…at least *I* thought it was amazing. I wrote him a note before I left—a sappy, love note actually—and haven't heard from him since."

"You left a note?" Janie continued when she saw Lilly nod. "I don't think he ever found that note, in fact I know he didn't. Jacob was upset when he woke up, and you were gone. He didn't know why you left so suddenly. Then as the days went by and he didn't hear from you, he became more distraught, and my brother shuts down emotionally when he feels threatened."

"I had to leave early. I got called into work. I figured when I didn't hear from Jacob, he was either busy or back together with Victoria. I decided to leave him alone. I almost texted him a few times, but I didn't want to appear desperate."

Janie groaned. "Oh hell, it's complete miscommunication. My brother is such a stubborn ass! He was waiting for you to call him since he didn't know why you left without saying goodbye and he thought—oh never mind, just come tonight, okay?"

"Are you sure that's a good idea? Jacob may not want to see me."

"He definitely wants to see you."

Lilly considered the situation. "And what about Victoria? What's it going to look like if she shows up?" *And how will I handle it if she accompanies Jacob?*

Janie grabbed Lilly's hand. "It's going to look like I brought my friend to play poker, but Victoria's not going to be there. Roger despises her. He has a hard enough time appearing civil during public events, he would never invite her to his home." She sent Lilly a reassuring smile. "Besides, chances are Jacob won't even be there."

"Are you lying?"

"Perhaps," Janie smirked.

"This is ridiculous. I have no idea where I stand with your brother. He walks out on me that first night, then gives me this gorgeous gift, then falls off the map again. It's maddening," Lilly huffed.

"Well, come tonight, and if he's there, you can tell him *all* this. Come on, be the third wheel for Audrey and me."

Lilly sighed. "Fine, I'll go. I hope I don't end up looking like a total idiot."

Janie laughed heartily. "Well damn, here I thought we would have some entertainment for the evening!" She handed the necklace back to Lilly. "And wear that, please. Jacob put a lot of thought into this gift. It would break his heart if you gave it back to him."

Lilly's fingers trembled as she fastened the chain around her neck. Warmth spread throughout her body as if Jacob's fingers were caressing her. "He puts a lot of thought into everything."

Janie nodded. "That he does, but he's terribly scared right now."

"I can't imagine why. Jacob has the world at his feet. He can have anything he wants."

"He's afraid of how he feels about you and you not reciprocating. In that department, he's an idiot."

Lilly laughed. "He's a man." She pushed her food around her plate, delaying her next question. "What's the situation with him and Victoria?"

"As far as I know, he's still posing as her public escort, but he sure as hell isn't happy about it."

"Are you sure it's only a public arrangement?"

"He hasn't intimated otherwise."

That's reassuring, Lilly considered, swigging her beer.

"Hey, chin up. The rumor on the street is that my brother is head over heels for some Yank."

Lilly's heart pounded like a drum. It wasn't possible, was it? "Never trust a rumor unless you know the source."

Janie winked. "I *do* know the source, we share a bloodline." She squeezed Lilly's arm. "We're going to have fun tonight. Pick you up at six?"

"I've got the rental car remember? I'm still terrified of driving on the wrong side of the road, but it feels good to have my independence back."

"Wrong side of the road? You mean the side you Yanks drive on in America?"

"We drive on the right side, literally. Everything else may be upside down in my country, but we've got the driving thing locked down."

Janie giggled. "Good to know."

The women finished their lunch in leisurely conversation and parted an hour later. Lilly returned to her cottage, proud she only white-knuckled it half a dozen times in the five-kilometer drive, a definite improvement over her former ventures.

She walked into her cottage and looked at her phone, plugging Jacob's name into a text.

'I don't know if it matters, but I left a note, I didn't realize you never saw it. It must have fallen behind the bed. It was such a beautiful night, and I hate that it looked like I left without a word. Perhaps, though, you were glad that I made myself scarce. Regardless, it was lovely, and I've missed you.'

She stared at the words, wondering if she should send the text or forget the whole thing.

Huffing, she tossed her phone on the table. If Jacob wanted to speak to her, he would have called. She went to her closet to select an outfit, deliberating over a dozen before settling on a light blue shift dress and a pair of gray knee-high boots. The dress hugged her curves yet provided the right amount of warmth against London's evening chill, and if Jacob was there, she didn't look like she had just rolled out of bed.

A couple hours later, Lilly grabbed her phone on the way out the door, her finger hitting the send button on the text she had composed to Jacob. She stared in horror at the screen, wishing the world would swallow her. "Oh shit, shit, shit."

She considered faking her own abduction, never to be seen again, but even she chuckled at that ridiculous notion. "I was afraid to look like an idiot at the party, but I get to look like one before I even arrive."

Screw it, there's a chance he won't even look at his phone. Hell, he might not even be there.

Lilly sighed, punching in directions on her GPS and backing out of the drive.

CHAPTER SIXTEEN

Jacob

"Whiskey?" Roger asked, handing Jacob a glass.

Jacob nodded, mumbling thanks under his breath.

"You really shouldn't look so thrilled to be here. Try and keep your enthusiasm under control."

Jacob's laugh was dry and hollow. "Sorry mate, just tired."

Roger regarded him soberly. "I know a load of bollocks when I hear it. Bad news about that role?"

"No, that's moving along quite nicely. I spoke with Albert earlier this week. Of course, I have to spend time with Victoria and pretend I'm enamored with her which is more than I can stomach."

"Then stop pretending. No one told you to play this farce with Victoria. You've got enough merit as an actor to earn that role without having to be her pool boy."

"You know as well as I do it's not that easy. People talk, and rumors—true or not—can destroy your career. And that woman—" Jacob hissed, "—is a bloody rumor mill."

"Enough about the succubus, how was the fundraising ball? It was for Lilly's charity, right?"

"It was a huge success, they were able to raise a large sum of money."

Roger shot Jacob a side-eye. "Let me guess, Lilly is a money-grubbing python too, and won't leave you alone?"

Jacob guffawed. "Hardly. She's perfect, actually." His expression softened, recalling their nights together. "She understands me, and she's so kind...but I haven't heard from since the night of the fundraiser, so, it's obvious she doesn't feel the same way about me."

Roger set his whiskey down with a triumphant flourish. "A-ha, I knew it! I knew this poor-me bullshit had nothing to do with Victoria."

"Lay off."

"You know, Lilly is coming tonight with Janie."

Jacob straightened, trying not to appear too interested. "She's coming here?"

"Unless you want me to uninvite her. I thought you'd be happy to see her. Speaking of which, there's Janie and Audrey now."

Jacob's eyes flew to the door, where Janie and Audrey had entered, but

Lilly wasn't with them. "I guess she opted not to come after all. Excuse me."

Jacob walked over to his sister, offering a tight smile. "Hello Janie, Audrey. Good to see you both."

Janie wrapped her arms around Jacob, an amused smirk on her face. "If your face got any longer, you'd trip over it."

"Funny." Jacob ran a hand through his curls. "I heard Lilly was coming with you tonight."

Another smirk, God his sister was maddening when she behaved in this manner. "Change of plans."

"Of course. Sounds about right."

"I get the distinct impression that your brother misses Lilly. What's your take on the situation, Janie?" Audrey inquired, wrapping her arm around her wife's shoulder.

"Sod off, both of you." Jacob growled. They spoke the truth, but he didn't need to be reminded of how the woman had left him high and dry. *And this is why you don't fall for anyone. You wind up looking like a foolish git.*

"Who is this Lilly you're all referring to?" Edward, a friend of Roger's, popped into the conversation.

"Lilly is the woman my brother is so crazy over—"

"I am not, Janie," Jacob lied, turning to Edward. "She's the nurse who took care of Janie while she was in the hospital. We all became friends."

"Is that what you're calling it these days?" Audrey was enjoying this ribbing far too much, and it was touching on Jacob's last nerve.

"Yes," he hissed. "Considering she up and vanished on me. What would you prefer I call it?"

Janie patted Jacob's cheek. "You, being a stubborn ass. Admit it, you're in love with her."

Jacob had heard enough. He muttered an excuse about retrieving his phone from his car, but in truth, he needed some air. He missed Lilly so much he felt like he was suffocating.

Jacob paced the patio, willing himself to calm down and relax when he saw Lilly walking up the driveway. His breath quickened. *Why was she here? If she wasn't interested in pursuing a relationship, then why show up at his bloody best friend's house?*

"Lilly, this is a surprise." His voice was calm, but his heart hammered in his chest; he hoped she couldn't hear it. Damn, she looked beautiful. He wanted to peel off her dress and lick every inch of her porcelain skin. *Focus man, focus. This woman doesn't want you. Remember that.*

Lilly shifted, looking uncomfortable. "Janie invited me. I hope you don't mind. I'm an awful poker player but…" her voice trailed off as she looked away, biting her lip in that sexy manner that drove him crazy.

"It's fine," Jacob snapped, "I'd walk you inside, but I have to make a phone call. The housekeeper can show you the way. If you'll excuse me."

"Of course, thanks. It's so wonderful to see you, Jacob. I really missed you."

"Right. I'll see you later." The words were clipped and harsh, and they hit their mark as Lilly's face fell. All he wanted to do was grab her to him and tell her how empty his life was without her, but his heart was wounded and his haughty facade firmly in place. It was his only protection against this woman and his overpowering feelings.

Lilly nodded, looking wounded as she turned toward the house.

Jacob sighed, running his hand through his hair and turning his phone on. The battery had died again. It booted up after what seemed an eternity, and he was about to dial his voicemail when the message alert sounded. It was a message from Lilly.

'I don't know if it matters, but I left a note, I didn't realize you never saw it. It must have fallen behind the bed. It was such a beautiful night, and I hate that it looked like I left without a word. Perhaps, though, you were glad that I made myself scarce. Regardless, it was lovely, and I've missed you.'

"Shit," Jacob hissed under his breath as he reread the message. He thrust his phone in his pocket and ran into the house to find Lilly.

Lilly

This was an epic mistake, Lilly thought as she followed the housekeeper through the mansion. She figured Jacob might not be thrilled to see her, but he was downright biting at her presence. She needed a few moments to collect her emotions.

"I'm sorry, is there a bathroom I could use?"

The housekeeper directed her to a bathroom, giving her the last few directions to the rec room where Roger's friends were gathered.

Lilly mumbled her thanks as she closed the door. She moved to the sink, taking a few deep breaths. She was out of her element, unwelcome, and didn't know what the hell to do next. Should she leave without a word? Invent an excuse and make a hasty exit? Hide in the bathroom until everyone forgot she was there?

Realizing she couldn't spend the evening in the loo, she gathered herself together and opened the door.

Jacob stood on the other side of the door, his hand impatiently tapping the jamb.

"H—hi." Lilly stammered.

His blue eyes were searching. "You left a note?"

Lilly nodded, her eyes glassy. "Do you want me to leave?"

Jacob didn't answer with words. His arms wrapped around her, lifting her off the ground and enveloping her in a blistering kiss. He kicked the bathroom door shut and placed her on the vanity, his tongue searching and needy, his hands hiking up her skirt to caress her thighs.

Lilly pushed away from him, her brown eyes confused. "I don't understand, do you hate me or do you love me?"

Jacob caressed her jaw. "I never saw the note, I thought you just left, that *you* regretted the entire evening and—"

"Are you kidding? I've been waiting all week for you to call me, I thought you regretted the whole thing."

Jacob smiled and nuzzled Lilly's neck. "That night with you was perfect." His eyes fell upon the necklace as he nipped her collarbone. "You're wearing it."

Lilly returned his smile, recapturing his lips with her own. "Do you mean it? No regrets regarding our evening together?" He deepened the kiss, his tongue ravishing every corner of her mouth, and Lilly had her answer. She wrapped her arms around his neck and pressed herself against him, relishing his scent and the feel of his hard shoulders beneath her hands.

She lost track of time as they caressed each other, their mouths insatiable. A knock on the door snapped them from their reverie, and they separated with a guilty smile.

"Lilly? It's Janie, are you okay in there?"

Lilly giggled as Jacob opened the door. "Yeah, she's fine."

Janie's eyes widened. "I see, here I was about to send out a search party; meanwhile you're holed up in here together." Her words were sarcastic, but her smile belied her happiness.

"We needed to have a little talk." Jacob smiled, ruffling his sister's hair.

Janie's eyes scanned Jacob and Lilly, taking in their swollen lips and mussed hair. "Talking, obviously. A ton of talking happening here. Do you two have more to discuss or would you like to join us for a game?"

As much as Lilly would love to stay locked in the bathroom with Jacob the rest of the night, she hopped off the sink, kissing Janie on the cheek. "Let the poker games begin."

Roger greeted Lilly and Jacob with bemusement, stating how glad he was Jacob was no longer such an angry pickle.

It was a fantastic evening. Lilly won the last three hands, and Janie jokingly accused her of being a hustler, but it was Jacob's hand on her thigh and his adoring gaze that made her night.

At first, she was uncertain how to behave around Jacob, considering how many of his friends were present. She opted to let his behavior guide her own and realized he had every intention of showering her with affection. He seized any opportunity to touch her, whether it was a kiss on her nape while refilling her whiskey or a caress of her shoulder when he got up to change the radio station.

Roger smiled at Lilly over his cards. "I, for one, am bloody thrilled. Thank you, Lilly."

Lilly gazed at him, perplexed. "You're very welcome. What did I do?"

Roger gazed in Jacob's direction. "You have managed the impossible, you have tamed the elusive Edmonton. Bravo."

Lilly's cheeks flamed. "I wouldn't quite go that far. I doubt he'll be tamed by anyone, least of all me."

A fellow actor named Edward spoke up, he had remained silent up to this point, but Lilly noticed him observing her interactions with Jacob. "I didn't realize the two of you were dating." Lilly couldn't determine if he was curious or voicing disapproval.

Lilly's jaw slackened at his pointed statement. "We're—we're not—"

"I suppose she's the woman you were speaking about earlier?"

Jacob nodded. "It's a new relationship, Edward. She's upended my world, and I couldn't be more grateful." His arm slid around Lilly, his hand caressing her back.

Lilly shot Jacob a questioning look. Were they officially dating? Feeling the need to collect her thoughts and quiet her hammering heart—she excused herself to the bathroom.

Jacob offered to escort her, and Roger snickered. "About time you two tended to that electricity sparking between you. It's lighting up the damn room."

Lilly flushed, stopping outside the door to wait for Jacob. He slipped his hand in hers and walked her down the hall, pointing out various paintings in the hallway he jokingly dubbed 'Roger's Millions.'

Stopping at the bathroom, Lilly offered him a shy smile. "Thank you, you don't have to wait for me."

Jacob caressed her cheek, his lips capturing hers in a soft kiss. A flush crept over his cheeks. "Are you okay with what I said in there?"

"With what, specifically?" Lilly knew the answer, but she needed him to repeat the words.

"That we're dating. That is if you want to date me."

"Is this we're casually dating and seeing other people and all that jazz?"

Jacob's eyes widened. "Is that what you want?"

Lilly shook her head. "I don't share very well."

Her statement earned a slow grin from Jacob and another sensual kiss, his tongue sliding along the roof of her mouth. "Neither do I."

Lilly smiled at his remark, it was obvious he wanted to be a one-woman man, and she was that one woman. Lilly's arms went around his neck, and he pushed her against the wall, wrapping her leg around him. "Christ, I'm craving your body. I don't think I can hold out much longer." Jacob murmured his mouth at her ear.

Lilly's voice purred with emotion. "Then don't."

He hoisted her up, pushing her into a dressing area. He locked the door behind him and pushed her against a wall, their lips never breaking contact.

Jacob wasted no time pulling her dress overhead, his hands unclasping her bra and his mouth finding her breasts. Lilly closed her eyes at the rising

185

passion and tugged at his shirt, helping him jerk it over his head.

His mouth found hers again, pulling off her boots and thong while she unclasped his belt. Despite the speed with which he removed her clothing, he loved her slowly, his tongue working over her entire body. Lilly reciprocated, eager to explore every inch of him. Her lips trailed down his stomach as her fingers closed over his hard flesh, and his breath hitched as she took him in her mouth.

"Fuck. Lilly." He released a heated gasp, his hand tangling in her hair as he guided her rhythm.

Lilly's mouth moved up and down his shaft, sucking gently at the tip and smiling when he groaned.

"I need to be inside you," Jacob murmured, pulling her back to standing and capturing her lips. His eyes held hers, his fingers tracing her jaw. "I need to feel every inch of you." He laid her back on the couch, his body moving over her.

Lilly nipped his bottom lip, lifting her hips when his fingers slid between her folds, diving deep inside her. "I need that too."

Jacob's lips captured hers as he slid inside her, igniting a firestorm of tingles throughout her body.

He stilled, his forehead pressed against hers, his breathing shallow and rapid. His entire body emanated emotion as his lips trembled against her mouth. "Lilly. My God, you feel so good, how do you feel so good?"

Lilly moved against him in an unspoken answer, lost in the moment, their moment, where anything beyond their bodies ceased to matter. Jacob lifted her hips, plunging inside her and she arched her back to deepen the movement, her entire body clenching around him.

His eyes never left her face, desire and longing written in their depths. Lilly saw her own heart reflected in his gaze, and she knew intrinsically that this man held the other half of her soul.

"Jacob," Lilly murmured, her hands running over his chest, her nails scratching along his skin. "It feels so perfect." She felt the fire spreading through her body, the flames licking her insides.

"*You're* perfect, angel. Come for me, Lilly."

She moaned, tilting her hips against him. "Make me."

His thrusts deepened as a growl rose up from his chest, and Lilly tumbled over the edge, her nails digging into his back as erotic delirium overcame her senses.

"Fuck Lilly…fuck, you're incredible." Jacob hissed the words in her ear as his own body released, his hands gripping her hips tight enough to leave marks.

Their breathing mingled and eased as their lips nuzzled. Jacob propped on his elbows, a strange smile playing on his face. "You've changed everything."

"What do you mean?"

His fingers caressed her jaw, his eyes traveling over her face. "Everything I wanted in life, all the things that meant so much now seem unimportant."

"And the things that were unimportant?"

Jacob's gaze locked on hers. "Impossible to live without. You've shown me heaven, angel."

Lilly's heart leapt at his confession. She wound her hands in his curls and pulled him to her, her tongue dipping into his mouth. They were still connected, and she felt him hardening again as he continued to move inside her. Her heart wanted to burst, the flood of endorphins was overpowering. Before her mind could rein the words back, they tumbled from her lips. "You're making my reality better than any dream. My heart knows what it wants. It wants you. I just really hope you want it."

"I do, Lilly. I want every part of you."

His smile melted any last holdout in her heart and Lilly let her heart go. It didn't belong to her anymore anyway, it was always meant for Jacob.

A rapt knock jerked them both to reality, and Jacob choked out, "What?"

It was Roger. "Listen, mate, I hate to bother you two since it's obvious you really like bathrooms, but you have a visitor."

Jacob huffed with exasperation. "Give me a fucking break! Can't you handle it, Roger?" His lips kissed Lilly's forehead, mouthing an apology.

"Yeah, that's just it. She's very insistent. I don't know how she knew you were here, she's got fucking radar on you or something. You know what? I'll tell her to fuck off. You're here with your girlfriend, and she needs to leave." The disgust in Roger's voice left no question to the identity of the mystery visitor.

"No, don't say anything. I'll be right there, give me a minute." Jacob sighed, his face pained. "I'm sorry Lilly, I have no idea how Victoria knew I was here."

Lilly sat frozen, mortified by Jacob's response to Victoria's sudden arrival. "You're leaving? You're going to Victoria? After what just happened? I thought you were her public escort, why do you care what she thinks tonight?" The questions were choked, her throat struggling to find enough air.

Jacob pulled out of her and stood. "She's going to make everyone's life hell if I don't get out there. I'm so sorry."

Lilly's cheeks flamed. She played right into Jacob's hand. He got what he wanted and now, he was done. She stood up and began pulling on her clothes, refusing to meet Jacob's gaze. "You're sorry? That's your response? You're sorry?"

He stayed her movements, pulling her to him. "Being inside you, making love to you, it's the most incredible feeling in the world. I've never felt this way before either—"

Lilly's anger flared, and she pushed out of his grip. "You could have fooled me as you're running out the goddamn door back to your ex-girlfriend! Or is it current girlfriend? Was that another convenient lie you spouted?" She ignored the look of pain that crossed his face. "Fool me once, shame on you. Fool me twice, shame on me. Fool me three times, I'm a fucking idiot!" Jacob reached for her, but Lilly was in no mood to be coddled. "You won't even admit to Victoria you're here with me, will you? You fuck me and then run out the door to her."

"I didn't fuck you, I made love to you."

He also didn't answer her question, which meant Lilly had her answer.

Tears spilled from her eyes as she fought to maintain any vestiges of her dignity. "That wasn't love, that was a mistake. The biggest mistake of my life."

Jacob cleaned up and pulled on his clothing, but Lilly could see his hands trembling. He paused at the door, his ever-present prose failing him. Finally, he sputtered, "You're the most amazing woman I've ever met, and what we experienced was *not* a mistake. How I feel is not a mistake. My situation is so complicated—"

"Stop. I've heard enough of your lies."

"They're not lies, Lilly."

"You have to make a choice, right? Life is full of choices—"

"Lilly, please."

"I'll make it easy on you. I'll make the choice for you. You got what you wanted—another checkmark in your black book. There's no need to continue. You got what you came for." Her words were no more than a whispered garble as her heart shattered in her chest. "Goodbye, Jacob."

His blue eyes were unusually bright as he drew in a shaky breath. "Lilly, that is *not* true. You are everything to me! Don't do this—"

"Go."

Jacob shook his head, sniffling as he opened the door. "I didn't know life could feel this way, that *I* could feel this way. You're the best moments I've ever had."

"If I was, then you wouldn't be leaving. Go. Leave. Now." Even she was surprised by the strength in her voice, in those few words. Conversation over.

Lilly waited until the door closed to release the dam of emotions, utter humiliation rushing through every pore. *You're an idiot, you fell for it, hook line and sinker. You believed every lie he told and gave him exactly what he wanted...another notch on his goddamn bedpost.*

Sucking in her breath, she wiped her face. She wanted to sneak out but realized her purse and jacket were still in the other room. She'd have to face the music, so she donned her strongest armor before opening the bathroom door.

CHAPTER SEVENTEEN

Jacob

Jacob paused outside the bathroom in a futile attempt to squash his emotions before confronting his ex-girlfriend. *Get a grip, mate. Go in there and tell Victoria to leave. Then get down on your knees and beg Lilly to forgive you.*

After a few moments, he realized the anger he felt towards Victoria would never simmer down and stalked to the rec room.

Victoria perched on a chair, resplendent in a black dress, downing a glass of whiskey like it was milk. Her loving smile was all prepared for Jacob's entrance, but it faded when she noted his stony expression. She slipped over to him, wrapping her arms around his neck. "Hi, baby."

Jacob disentangled her hands from his body and grabbed her by the arm, muttering, "What in bloody hell are you doing here?"

Victoria feigned surprise at his words. "I'm here to see you. I'm going back to America in a couple days, and I didn't want to leave without seeing you again."

"Don't give me that crap, how did you even know I was here?"

Her smile resembled a snake, ready to sink her fangs into flesh. Her hand grasped Jacob's chin, as she whispered, "I always know where you are, remember? Now, we can do this the easy way or the hard way. It's your decision. But don't forget, Albert has yet to finalize his casting choice."

"That wasn't part of our deal; I'm your escort in public only."

Victoria's lips found his ear, sucking the lobe into her mouth. "I changed my mind. I want you back as my lover—both publicly and privately. And since this is my game, we're playing by my rules. Your choice, my way or you kiss your movie role goodbye."

"I'm beginning to think no role is worth the hell I'm living with you."

"Sweetie," Victoria hissed, kissing his neck, "that role means more to you than anything, you said so yourself. Now be a good boy and play along, the walls have ears, and you wouldn't want something unfortunate turning up in a tabloid."

"You're a twisted maggot." Jacob stalked over to the bar where Roger stood, shooting him a look of reproach. "Save it, Roger, give me a damn drink." He grabbed the whiskey and swallowed it down, the burn of the alcohol nothing compared to the burning in his heart. "Who the hell told her I was here?"

Roger shrugged and motioned to Edward. "Edward would be my best guess. They became friends when he was in her last video. I didn't think he knew your history with her though."

Jacob scoffed. "The world knows our bloody history."

Roger gripped the edges of the bar, apparently aggravated by the situation. "I'm going to say this once, because you're my friend. No role is worth selling your soul, and it certainly isn't worth hurting an amazing woman."

"You think I don't know that?" Jacob sputtered, pouring himself another glass.

"No, I don't think you do know, or you wouldn't have deserted Lilly to run back to *that* woman. You're my mate, but I thought you were better than that."

"It's a fucking business arrangement—"

"What a load of bollocks! You're no fool, Jacob. You know damn well that Victoria is setting you up. And you're falling for it…just like the last time. I thought you finally grew up, grew past your selfish ways—"

"What would you have me do, Roger, since you're so bloody perfect?"

Roger took a deep breath, his voice low but firm. "Show Victoria's ass the door, tell her to stay the hell out of your life and then spend the next several months making this up to Lilly." He downed his shot, shaking his head. "But you won't do any of that, because you think you deserve it all."

Jacob snickered, his temper flaring. "Don't you know? I'm a shallow piece of shit that only cares about my acting. Nothing to do with the fact I've waited for this part for the last decade. I've sacrificed everything for this chance, now you want me to walk away when I'm at the finish line?"

"For the love of a good woman, I thought maybe you would; but I was mistaken. My apologies. If you'll excuse me, I'm going to check on Lilly, who is undoubtedly humiliated right now. Well done, Jacob." Roger moved towards the doorway, where Lilly stood, Janie already at her side.

Jacob stared at his glass, tempted to hurl it against the wall. Victoria slipped up next to him, laying a possessive arm around his shoulders. "Who is that? Wait, isn't that the…nurse? What the hell is she doing here? Oh wait, you mean you're still in a *relationship?*"

"Not now, Victoria," Jacob whispered.

"Yes now. I want that woman out of *your* life, or I'll make certain you never act in anything better than a community theater in bumfuck."

"You would ruin my career because I'm with someone else?"

Her teeth sank into his shoulder, more possessive than seductive. "In a fucking heartbeat. But it wouldn't be just your career I'd ruin…"

The threat hung there like a noose and Jacob felt his blood boiling. She didn't admit outright that Lilly would be a target, but it wasn't much of a stretch. "You fucking—"

"Save it. Remember what I told you? You can't win against me, no one can." She ran her hand down his back, caressing his hip. "Are we on the same page, darling?"

Jacob gritted his teeth before giving a curt nod. He'd seen her wield her power before and he had no doubt she would turn both barrels on him if he didn't agree. Worse, she would turn both barrels on Lilly.

Victoria strained to see something and then walked straight up to Lilly, pointing at the necklace. "Of course, now I see what happened to the necklace. You gave a five thousand dollar necklace to the fucking help?"

Roger flew in Victoria's face. "This woman is my friend, she's not the help, you insensitive bitch."

Lilly unclasped the necklace and tossed it at Victoria. "You want it? Take it. I never wanted anything from Jacob but his love."

Her words pierced Jacob's heart like an arrow. Her love was the only thing he wanted too.

Jacob rushed over to the group as Victoria leaned into Lilly's face. "Aww, how cute. You're the one who left him the sweet note. I'll bet you thought he actually cared about you, didn't you? You thought you were different than all the other women he's had. You were more than a notch on his bedpost, right?" She laughed. "How charmingly naive."

Lilly swallowed, but her voice was steady. "I am different than those women. I'm not using him to salvage my career."

Fury flashed in Victoria's eyes. "You've stooped to a new low, Jacob. How drunk do you have to be to fuck someone like this?"

Lilly looked as if she had been punched and Jacob grabbed Victoria, dragging her away. "That's enough Victoria! She's a better woman than you'll ever be."

"If she's so wonderful, then why did you choose me over her? Go on, tell her. Tell her what we discussed not two minutes ago." Victoria turned back to Lilly. "I hope you enjoyed being fucked by the A-list, sweetie, because he always returns to me. You were just a way to pass the time and get a rise out of me. It worked, I'm back and you're done."

"Get her out of here," Roger snarled, as he wrapped his arm around Lilly to shield her from Victoria's verbal onslaught.

Jacob wanted to dropkick Victoria out the window when he caught sight of Lilly's stricken face and the tears in her eyes.

Victoria shot Lilly one last scathing glance. "I warned you to stay away from Jacob. Now, you've learned the hard way."

Jacob couldn't handle the verbal onslaught slamming Lilly any longer. He moved towards her, but Roger blocked his movements. "I mean it, Jacob. Get the fuck out."

Feeling as if he'd been kicked in the gut, Jacob grabbed Victoria's bag and dragged her by the arm out to his vehicle.

He started the car and screeched out of the driveway, hitting the dash with such force it rattled. "What the fuck is wrong with you, Victoria? Why do you hate me so much?"

Victoria's green eyes widened, and for once she looked contrite. "I don't hate you; I love you."

Jacob sputtered with rage. "You love me? What a load of bullshit!"

"I know I screwed up and I shouldn't have been so awful to that woman, but have you considered how I feel?"

"How you feel? Why the fuck should I care how you feel? You cheated on me, remember?" Jacob's voice boomed in the interior.

"I know, but I want another chance. We were good together," Victoria pleaded.

"We weren't a couple, we were a publicity field day. It was a nightmare."

Tears slid down Victoria's cheeks in a ploy for sympathy, but Jacob had witnessed her ability to turn on the waterworks on numerous occasions. "How could you really care about that woman? She's not like us, Jacob. She doesn't understand our life."

"And she's a better person for it. I adore that woman, but you have ruined any future I have with her. You won, there's no coming back from this disaster. Go ahead and do your victory dance."

Victoria's hand slid down to his crotch, her lips curving into a seductive pout. "I can make it better. Let me show you one of the many perks of our reconciliation. I'll make you forget about your little nurse."

Jacob looked at her, his blood boiling, tossing her hand off him. "You'll never make me forget about her, no one can."

But Victoria wasn't going to give up so easily. She unzipped his pants, gripping the base of his cock and lowering her head to him. "I can make it better though. I know you're angry right now, but soon you'll realize how much better we are together. Until then, take all your anger out on me. Show me how much you hate me."

"Get your hands off me, Victoria," Jacob barked.

Victoria sent a sly glance, her lips curling in an evil smile. "That isn't

193

how this is going to work, Jacob. Either you play along completely, or you lose…completely." She released a low, wicked chuckle. "You might as well comply. You've already lost Lilly. She knows what you are now, where your priorities lie. She'll never take you back."

Jacob's body shook with the anger building inside him like a volcano. The worst part? Victoria was right. He'd blown his chance with Lilly. The future that he saw with his petite beauty went up in smoke as Victoria continued her erotic assault.

"So, what's it going to be, Jacob?" Her tongue licked along his shaft, and Jacob groaned, pulling over to the side of the road so she could finish him off. If he couldn't make love to the woman he cherished, he would fuck the woman who wouldn't let him go.

Lilly

I want to go home," Lilly sniffled, wiping her eyes. "I've never had anyone make me feel so insignificant, and Jacob didn't say a word. He didn't even try to defend me."

A fresh batch of tears started, and Audrey wrapped her arms around Lilly. "I'm going to kill him." She looked at her wife, and Janie nodded in agreement. "What a tosser."

Janie knelt in front of Lilly, wiping her tears with a tissue. "There's no excuse for what Jacob did, I'm sorry I even know him right now. And there's certainly no excuse for what that harlot said to you. It isn't true, not a word of it."

Lilly smirked. "But it *is* the truth. I don't fit into his world, and after seeing how people treat each other, I don't want to. I'm fine being a nobody who cares about others and treats people with respect."

Roger popped his head into the dressing room, a fresh glass of whiskey in his hand. "I can't fix what my wanker friend and his she-devil did, but I can numb it for a while."

"I think I'll go home, thanks anyway," Lilly said, refusing the glass.

Roger pressed it into her hand. "Like hell, you will. You're our friend too, and I'll be damned if he ruins that. Now come on, drink up, we can play some poker and talk trash about the blonde bimbo. She thinks she's so gorgeous, but she looks like a damn piranha, has the teeth and everything." He made a gnawing face, and Lilly laughed through her tears.

"He's right, fuck 'em both. Being happy is the greatest revenge," Janie stated.

"Jacob is definitely not happy right now," Roger interjected.

"Sure," Lilly stated, sipping the whiskey. "He's so unhappy that he dropped me like a bad habit and left with Victoria. Hell, he's probably fucking her right now." Janie and Roger exchanged a glance. "I know how men can be, no offense Roger, and I have enough male friends to know your libido doesn't require love, especially when alcohol's involved. I'm just another faceless name in his little black book now. I may be insignificant, but I'm not stupid." Lilly looked down at her glass and whispered, "Actually, I guess I am stupid."

Audrey scoffed. "You're neither, and I don't want to hear that kind of talk again. Come on girl, I'll do a shot with you, and we can talk all kinds of trash."

Lilly laughed, hugging Audrey. "Janie, your wife is amazing. How many people would bash their brother-in-law just to make someone feel better?" Her words brought much-needed laughter to the group as they walked back to the rec room.

Although Lilly was still heartbroken and humiliated, things had improved in the last ninety minutes. It might have been the whiskey or the camaraderie of the folks around the poker table, but Lilly realized she might remain a member of the human race after all.

Edward turned out to be charming, appalled with what transpired. "I've never seen Victoria behave in such a manner. You didn't deserve any of it. You behaved like a true lady."

Lilly thanked him, opting to change the subject. "Could we not talk about either one of them for the rest of the evening and focus on the beautiful souls who are present?"

Roger raised his glass and toasted to her 'brilliant idea' when his phone started ringing. Looking down, he muttered, "His ears must be burning," and excused himself.

"So much for that idea," Lilly commented.

"Look, I know we agreed not to speak of—" Janie began.

"Those we will not mention?" Lilly filled in, eliciting a laugh from Edward.

"Exactly," Janie commiserated, "but I know my brother and Lilly, I've never seen him look at a woman like he looks at you."

Lilly swallowed around the lump in her throat, the tears threatening to fall once again. "It doesn't matter. He made his choice, and it's quite clear what my role is in his life. As Victoria stated, I was a temporary distraction until she was ready to return."

"He doesn't want to be with her—"

Lilly released a guffaw. "Sure as hell looked like he did when they left together." She wiped her eyes, there seemed to be an endless supply of tears. "Thank you, all of you."

"For what?" Audrey murmured.

"For not judging me after what happened earlier."

"Why in the world would we judge *you* in any negative light?" Edward asked, patting Lilly's hand.

Lilly flushed, mortified at her impetuous, emotion-driven actions.

"I believed he cared about me the way I care about him, and I behaved accordingly."

Edward's eyebrows knitted. Men could be so clueless.

"Luv, you're not an idiot for believing him. We *all* believed he was falling for you. He's a git for treating you in that manner." Audrey clinked her glass against Lilly's and offered a small smile.

"I'm still not understanding," Edward interjected, his poor face so perplexed.

Lilly exchanged a glance with Audrey and Janie, a small giggle escaping the trio. Sometimes ignorance was bliss—or confusion, as was the case with Edward.

Roger returned from the other room, squatting next to Lilly. "Before you say anything, I promised I would repeat this information to you." He cleared his throat. "Jacob knows he's an asshole, and he knows damn well you have every right to hate him. But he also wanted you to know—and this part I didn't understand—that he definitely doesn't hate you."

"Well, that's kind of him," Audrey gritted. "He treats her like shit, yet he doesn't hate her? Brilliant."

Roger placed his hand on Lilly's shoulder. "Does that make any sense to you?"

Her question from earlier—'do you hate me or do you love me?' bounced into her thoughts, but Lilly shook her head, biting back tears. "It doesn't ring a bell."

Roger nodded. He knew Lilly was lying but opted not to push the issue. "Jacob is still on the line, and he would like to speak with you."

Lilly shook her head vigorously. "No, Roger, I can't speak to him."

"I told him that's what you were going to say, but he made me promise to ask. Back in a second." He left the room again, and Edward patted her arm.

"Men like that, they always think the grass is greener. They wind up old and alone."

Janie stiffened at Edward's words. "You barely know him."

Edward snorted. "Am I wrong? You saw what happened here today."

"You know, Edward, how did Victoria know Jacob was here? I know I didn't tell her, and Roger didn't tell her. That leaves you, doesn't it?" Janie's eyes narrowed in Edward's direction.

"I'm not denying I told her, Janie. She texted me, and I told Victoria where I was. She asked if Jacob was here and I said yes. That doesn't make me responsible for how either of them behaved this evening." Edward hit the table. "I never would have told her if I knew this was going to happen and Lilly was going to get hurt."

Lilly had heard enough. "Stop, no one in this room behaved maliciously, and it's over now. We certainly can't blame Edward for Victoria's bad behavior. I can't change what happened, I can only learn from it, and never be that foolish again."

Janie embraced Lilly. "You're amazing. I'm so glad you're my friend."

Audrey concurred, before adding, "I'm still kicking his ass."

Lilly laughed and nodded. "You have my full consent."

"It's a good thing he's leaving for Greece," Janie mused.

Lilly's mind agreed with Janie's statement, her heart, not so much. It cracked a bit more at the mention of the place where Jacob planned to take her on an extended holiday. It was supposed to be their beginning, now it was relegated to the past. "He leaves in a couple days."

Janie nodded. "He'll be gone for the next few months. Some thriller-type script that will make a fortune at the box office with all the car chases and sex scenes." She stopped, shooting Lilly a sympathetic look. "I'm sorry, they're not real, the sex scenes."

"It's Victoria's problem now, not mine." And for a while, Lilly believed her words. She may not be a worldwide celebrity, but she was a decent person, and she deserved to be treated decently.

CHAPTER EIGHTEEN

Jacob

Jacob's morning run usually meandered once around the park, but he had circled twice already and had no intention of stopping. He needed to keep moving until the events of the other night stopped playing in his head.

Even when Victoria hurled atrocities at Lilly, she hadn't retaliated. She didn't have it in her to be cruel, even when deserved. Jacob's heart ached as he recalled the taste of Lilly's skin and the feel of her body beneath his hands. He had never felt this way about another human being and yet he allowed someone to tear her down while he watched.

All for a fucking movie role. A role that no longer held any meaning for him because of what he'd lost in its pursuit.

He glanced at the time. He had a lunch meeting with Albert, and it was already past nine. He returned to his house an hour later and headed straight for the shower. Victoria was in the bathroom, a smug smile on her lips.

"Hello, darling." She kissed him, and he recoiled, nauseated by her touch.

"Are you finished?"

"There's plenty of room in here for us both, and we have some time before our meeting with Albert." She grabbed his shaft, massaging him into an erection.

Jacob felt no different than a two-bit whore, sleeping with the enemy in the hopes of scoring the big payday, and Victoria took full advantage of her position of power.

Jacob relented to her sexual demands, but his mind always drifted to Lilly's porcelain skin and the way she moaned when he was inside her. He couldn't come any other way. Victoria, despite her outer beauty, reeked of self-importance and egoism. Sex with her was a dreaded chore.

Victoria knelt in front of him, and he clenched his fists against the shower wall. "Relax, baby. Enjoy it." Her falsetto voice sent him over the edge, and he backed away.

"Get up, Victoria," Jacob snapped.

"What's wrong? You weren't complaining yesterday, or the day before."

"Would it have mattered? You told me if I didn't give you exactly what you wanted, you would feed rumors to the tabloids and tank my career. And let's not forget your threats against Lilly."

Victoria expelled a low growl. "I am so tired of hearing that bitch's name."

Jacob got in her face, his jaw twitching. "Don't you ever say another word against Lilly. Do you understand?"

Victoria tried to embrace him, but he shrugged her off. "I love you."

Jacob guffawed. "You don't love me, you don't know the meaning of the word."

"And you do? I didn't see you defending your little nurse the other night, so how much do you really love her? You never put anyone ahead of your precious career. You know it, I know it...and Lilly definitely knows it." Her shrill voice cut through his mind like nails on a chalkboard. "You and I are the same that way. We both understand what's important."

Jacob shook his head, images of Lilly's face floating through his mind. "We're not alike in any way...and I do know what love is...and what it's not. We're going to be late, please leave me alone."

Victoria grimaced but obliged, leaving the bathroom. As soon as the door shut, Jacob rested his head against the shower wall, wondering how in hell to fix this mess.

◦◦◦

The meeting was, by all accounts, a huge success. However, Albert hadn't made any final decisions about his casting choice. The director seemed aggravated by Victoria's presence, although he didn't mention it outright. Jacob surmised Victoria could annoy anyone who had too much contact with her, she was the only one who thought she was infallible.

Thankfully, she had to return Stateside that afternoon. Media gathered by her private jet, ensuring photos of her locked in Jacob's passionate kiss were published in every tabloid. Jacob wanted to gargle with boiling water after she stuck her tongue down his throat.

Driving away from the private airstrip, he realized Janie had left a voicemail. She ignored his phone calls the last few days, but her message asked him to stop by before he left for Greece.

He was relieved his baby sister might forgive him, although he was far from forgiving himself.

Returning home, he finished packing, catching a glimpse of himself in the mirror. The beard and long hair would soon be a thing of the past. His character was cleanly shaven with a crewcut. He recalled Lilly mentioning her preference for long hair and beards.

"Fucking perfect," Jacob muttered.

He grabbed his phone and dialed Lilly's number, but it went to voicemail—no surprise there. He started to leave a message but hung up when he realized he had no excuse for what she endured at Roger's house.

"Bugger," he muttered and poured a glass of whiskey, dialing Roger's number. He was surprised when his friend answered.

"You packed and ready for Greece?"

"Yeah," Jacob replied, "I leave tomorrow night. It's probably a good thing I'll be more than three thousand kilometers away."

Roger was silent for a moment. "What do you want me to say, Jacob? You want me to placate you and tell you what happened the other night was fine? Nothing about it was fine, and the way you and Victoria treated Lilly was abominable."

Jacob's breathing became ragged. "I know, it was unforgivable, and I hate myself for it."

"Has she called you?"

Jacob scoffed. "Sure, she's been blowing up my phone. Oh, you mean the woman I actually want to speak to? No, Lilly is far too good for me."

Now it was Roger's turn to scoff. "That's a load of bollocks, and you know it. You two would have been great together. I hope that damn role is worth it in the end because women like Lilly don't come along every day. In fact, they often don't come along at all. Take care in Greece, mate."

Jacob stared at his phone, knowing that Roger's words were right and feeling an ache in his gut unlike any he'd experienced before.

He dialed Janie, and she picked up on the first ring. "Hello, are you still coming over?"

"Janie, can you get Lilly to your house tomorrow?"

Janie groaned. "Come on Jacob, don't ask me to do that."

"Please," Jacob pleaded. "I know I don't deserve it, but I can't leave and not see her one more time."

The silence lasted forever, and Jacob realized he was holding his breath as he awaited his sister's reply.

Janie sighed loudly. "You're lucky, on more than one count, that Audrey won't be here tomorrow. If she found out I helped arrange a meeting with you and Lilly after what you did to her, you wouldn't survive long enough to see Greece."

"I know," Jacob mumbled.

"Why do you want to see Lilly? Is it to mend your ego, so you don't feel like the bad guy?"

Jacob's emotional dam broke at that moment, and he knew his sister had never heard him cry before. "I'm in love with her. Totally and completely in love with her, and I don't know how I'm supposed to live without her now."

"Really? You love her? Jacob, your actions the other night were reprehensible. How can you say you love Lilly when you allowed Victoria to treat her in such a manner? When you treated her in such a manner?"

Jacob raked his hand through his hair, tugging hard enough to feel discomfort. He deserved worse than that—far worse than that. He let out a low, mirthless laugh. "I thought...I thought I could balance everything—"

"You thought you could have your cake and eat it too."

"I guess—"

"Jacob, you've always been that way. Your gift is acting in your own best interest. You've never put another person's needs in front of your own. It's no different with Lilly." Janie's words echoed an eerie similarity to Victoria's earlier that day, and it made Jacob nauseous with shame.

"I *did* turn down the role, the night of the fundraiser. Victoria gave me an ultimatum, and I told her to shove it up her ass. I chose Lilly."

"Then what happened the other night? You had sex with Lilly and then ran out the door to another woman. You barely had time to put your pants on! Badly done, Jacob!"

He fell back against the couch, the truth of the situation sinking in. God, he really did only think of himself.

"Jacob, are you there?"

"I'm a selfish bastard. Once I saw the quality of the script and the talent of the director, I knew it would make my career. I wanted it so badly that I was willing to put it before everything—and everyone—else. Victoria knows that, that's how she played me. The final straw was when she threatened Lilly—"

"She did what?" Janie exclaimed, her voice rising in volume.

"It wasn't a direct threat, but it didn't take a rocket scientist to figure out to whom she was referring."

"That fucking bitch. That alone should have been enough for you to send Victoria crawling back to whatever hole she crawled out of. But instead, you allowed it. I don't understand you or the moral code you live by. Lilly is one of the greatest women I've ever met. Any man would be lucky to have her love, but you threw it away. Tell me again why I'm supposed to feel sorry for you?"

He sniffed loudly into the phone, his head pounding as the severity of what he'd done came into sharp focus. "You're right, I don't deserve Lilly."

"I think you *do* deserve Lilly. I think you two are wonderful together. I can see your future with her—complete with babies and animals and

202

laughter—but only if you find the courage to love her completely."

"I don't know how to do that. I've never loved anyone like this. The truth is, I'm a fucking coward, Janie. I'm terrified if I give Lilly my heart—my whole heart—she won't want it." God, the truth hurt. It felt like a dagger in his soul.

"She wanted it, Jacob." Janie remained silent a few moments. "I'll do my best to get Lilly here tomorrow, but I can't guarantee anything. But remember, big brother, on the off chance she does forgive you, don't make it a habit of shattering her heart."

"Thank you. Should I bring her flowers?"

"Definitely not, Lilly is not going to be buttered up by roses. In fact, I have the necklace here. She gave it to me the other night after Victoria left in laying on the ground."

Jacob sighed, hurt yet unsurprised. "I bought her the necklace to protect her."

"Forgive me for saying this, but I don't think she feels safe in any way around you."

Jacob mumbled his agreement and hung up, unsure what he could say to salvage his relationship with Lilly. The only thing he knew for certain was that he had to try.

Lilly

illy knew something was amiss the minute Janie opened the door. Her friend was flighty and nervous, and Lilly wondered if it was due to the events the other night. But when she walked into Janie's kitchen, the ruse was revealed.

"No way, I'm out of here." Lilly walked back toward the door, but Janie blocked her path.

"Please Lilly, he begged me to set this up. Give him five minutes. It's your opportunity to nail him square in the balls."

Lilly's jaw twitched. "I don't want to touch any part of him, even to inflict pain. Why would you do this to me?"

"I begged her to do it," Jacob's voice stated behind her, but Lilly kept her back to him.

Her body reacted on a visceral level to his voice, but Lilly inhaled deeply, willing herself to remain calm. It worked, for about three seconds, before the intense anger bubbled to the surface again.

"Haven't you done enough damage, Jacob? Do you hate me so much you want to keep twisting the knife?" Lilly whirled around, her brown eyes blazing. "What kind of sick joy are you getting from this situation?"

Jacob reached out to touch her, but Lilly leapt backward, and his hands fell by his sides. "I hate myself for what I allowed to happen to you. I didn't stand up for you, I didn't fight for you—"

"I don't need you to fight for me, I can take care of myself. I've practically mastered the art form so you can save your apologies, I'm good." Despite her harsh words, Lilly felt tears springing to her eyes. "Shit!"

Jacob's voice was low and shaky. "Can you look at me please?"

Lilly kept her head down for a few moments before meeting his gaze. There were tears in his eyes. Lilly felt something kick in her heart but pushed it aside. He was an award-winning actor and could cry at the drop of a hat. She could not fall for his lines again. "I'm looking, what?" she snapped.

Jacob raked his hand through his curls. "I'm leaving tonight for Greece. I'll be gone for three months."

"Have fun in Greece. Can I go now?" Lilly turned toward the door, praying there was a pub next door to Janie's flat. She needed a drink. No, she needed a bottle.

Jacob blocked her path. "I want to make this right. I'll do whatever I have to do to make it right."

"How do you expect to do that? I saw photos of you with your precious Victoria at the airport. You two belong together."

She needed to escape, her heart couldn't handle any more of this torture. She loved him, and he didn't love her back. She chose him, and he chose someone else. Now he stood there asking her to forgive him? Fuck that.

"I'll call and issue a retraction. I'll say the photos were staged."

Lilly rolled her eyes. "I don't give a shit! Let people believe you two are the happy couple, just leave me out of it."

"Please don't believe what the tabloids print," Jacob begged.

"Why not? According to you, they generally have the real scoop."

Jacob sank into a chair, his head in his hands. "I don't know how to fix this. Just tell me how to fix this mess. I'll do anything. I'll issue a retraction, I'll rescind interest in Milieu of Madness, I'll do anything."

Lilly surprised herself with the strength of her words. "It's too late. The damage is done, all we can do is move forward with our lives."

"I've destroyed the most important thing that's ever come into my life. The greatest woman I've ever known despises me, and I deserve every ounce of her hatred."

His stricken appearance broke Lilly, and she sighed, sitting down opposite him. She was too tired to keep fighting. "I don't hate you. I want to hate you, but I believe hatred is a terrible emotion. It's a waste of time and energy."

"You should hate me."

Lilly let out a harsh laugh. "Yes, I should. But I don't." She neglected to mention how it's impossible to hate someone you adore—she'd keep that fact tucked safely away. She made the mistake of opening the door to her heart once with Jacob Edmonton, she wouldn't let it happen again. "I won't lie. I'm not a terribly big fan of either you or your girlfriend at the moment. You two deserve each other, I suppose."

Jacob wiped his eyes. "I know I never deserved you, angel."

"Please don't call me that—"

His eyes were so bright it looked like the tears would win at any moment. "I can't help it. From the moment we met, you've been my angel. It's not going to change, no matter how you feel about me or the time we spent together."

Lilly released a deep sigh. Damn this man and his ability to penetrate to her very core with his words. Apparently, love replaces brain cells with fuzzy hearts.

She blinked back tears. "If I'm your angel, why couldn't you have been mine?"

He shook his head, not meeting her gaze. He seemed too overcome to speak.

She hesitated before placing her hand on his. "I don't think your goal was to make me feel so insignificant and foolish—"

"Never," Jacob murmured. "I would never do that intentionally, especially not to you. Things got so buggered."

"I know how much you have on your plate right now. You've worked your entire career for this movie role. I threw a cog in the wheel, I messed up the order of things—"

"You didn't do anything wrong. You're perfect."

"I know I didn't do anything wrong, but I still threw off the order of things. You and Victoria had a plan sorted out before you met me, and while I understand why you need this role and why you need to stay with Victoria to get this role, I need more than that in my life. I deserve more than that."

"You deserve the world. God, I want to give the world, I want to give you Paris. I want us to build our own world."

Lilly was shocked by the strength in her reply—her heart hammered in her chest, but externally she was calm and collected. "But you can't. You can't do any of those things, and if you care about me at all, you'll realize that too."

Jacob's eyes met hers, grabbing her hand and kissing her fingertips. "I need you in my life. I don't think I can live without you, Lilly."

Lilly's fingers tingled where he kissed them, but she squelched the feeling, forcing herself to remain on topic. "You'd be amazed what you can learn to live without."

"Fuck..."

Her words were gutting him, but it wasn't bringing Lilly any joy to cause him pain. Jacob seemed to be inflicting enough torture on himself already. "I'm not going anywhere...perhaps we can try to be friends. I won't promise anything, and I'll need time before I can even consider that as an option."

His face crumpled at her statement, but she stuck to her guns. She couldn't risk her heart being trampled again.

"Now, I'm going to bid you adieu and wish you a safe journey. I hope you get that part, and I hope your life is grander than you ever imagined."

"Please don't tell me this is the end," Jacob begged.

Lilly shook her head, tears sliding down her cheeks. "If you ever really need me, I'm here." She stood to leave, but Jacob clung to her hands.

"I'll make this up to you, Lilly. I'll spend the rest of my life protecting you. Protecting your heart."

Lilly pulled her hand away. "I didn't want your protection, Jacob. I wanted your love."

Jacob chewed his lip, his face a turbulent sea of emotion. Finally, he whispered, "I'm terrified of losing you."

"I was never *yours*. You didn't want me."

Jacob stood suddenly, pulling Lilly against him. "I want you, Lilly. In a hundred lifetimes, I will always choose you." His mouth found hers, begging entrance, pleading for one more chance.

It was a chance Lilly wasn't willing to take.

Lilly pulled out of his embrace and wiped away her tears, her heart splintering. "You promise me lifetimes…I only wanted one." She turned and slipped out the door, leaving him staring after her.

"He's still an asshole," Sabina muttered, swigging her beer and shooting Lilly a defiant look. "And I'm not the only one who thinks that, right Ben?"

The three friends huddled in a booth, commiserating over recent events. Lilly realized she wasn't the only one to experience a miserable few days. Ben had been on a promising date only to be stood up the next night, and Sabina's ex-husband missed another child support payment.

The answer to all those problems? Friendship and liquor, not necessarily in that order.

Ben shrugged. "Men can be dogs, I don't deny that, but it sounds like Jacob's destroyed over the situation. I can't imagine the pressure with his level of fame."

Sabina shot him a dirty look, but Lilly agreed. "I can't either, it's like our lives on steroids. Everything is much, much better or it's way worse." She sipped her whiskey. "He's essentially her puppet. If he doesn't do everything she wants, Victoria will ruin his career."

"Why does everyone assume Victoria has that much power?" Sabina asked, receiving looks of surprise from her friends. "Oh fuck, you're right. She's basically the queen of the world. She could shit in a cup and people would line up to buy it."

Lilly cast her a side eye. "Exactly, and she's used to getting everything she wants. I think Jacob not reciprocating that desire made him her greatest challenge."

"He really did seem to be into you, Lilly. The way he looked at you." Ben pretended to swoon, earning a swat from both women. "I'm serious, you can't fake that level of admiration."

"I hate to admit that Ben's right, but he is. It's obvious that Jacob is head-over-heels for you," Sabina murmured, finishing off her drink.

Lilly shrugged. "I don't know how he felt about me, but if Victoria thought he felt something, I would be a bug she had to squash." She imitated smooshing a bug under her thumb.

"Are you Victoria's cock-a-roach?" Sabina asked, giggling.

Lilly giggled at the idiocy of the situation. "I suppose I am. Some people toil their whole lives to be her cock-a-roach, I accomplished it in mere weeks."

The friends collapsed in a fit of laughter and downed the shots that arrived at their table.

"I love you ladies, and I wish I loved ladies in that way because I would scoop up both of you and have my own private harem," Ben proclaimed, waving his empty glass above his head.

Lilly put her hand on her heart, laughing. "I would so be your concubine. In fact, that's the best proposal I've gotten this year."

Sabina held up her glass, demanding silence. "I do have to know, as an inquiring mind, how was sex with the infamous actor?"

Lilly rolled her eyes. "Could we not discuss that?"

Ben and Sabina exchanged horrified looks. "Absolutely not!" They exclaimed in unison.

"Come on, spill. Was it worth it?" Sabina nudged Lilly in the arm.

Lilly teared up but blinked them away. "He was incredible. It was incredible. I made such a fool of myself—"

"No, you didn't, Lilly," Ben interjected, tugging her close.

"Yes, I did," Lilly spat. "I told him I was falling for him...right before he rushed out the door to Victoria."

"Shit," Sabina breathed. "I'm so sorry, luv."

Lilly took a deep, fortifying breath. "Don't be. I got schooled in my own preaching. Just because you care about someone doesn't mean they return your affection, lesson learned." She wiped the remaining tears from her eyes. "That's absolutely the last time I sleep with a Hollywood actor."

"I don't think Mr. Edmonton is going to let you go that easily. Judging from his reaction this evening after you told him goodbye, I think he'll fight tooth and nail to have you in his arms again."

Don't I wish, Lilly thought wistfully before her mind pushed aside the thought. She deserved better than Jacob Edmonton, her heart simply had to get with the program. "I'm pretty sure Jacob will forget all about me within a few weeks. He's not exactly hard up for lovers. Not that it matters. We would never reconcile regardless. Hell, I only dated him for an hour. I think that's a short relationship even by his standards."

"*No* chance of reconciliation?"

Lilly shook her head. "For what reason? To be tossed aside again? He and I come from vastly different worlds—they're like oil and water—they don't blend."

"Looks like you two blended pretty well to me," Ben ducked, avoiding the balled-up napkin Lilly lobbed at his head. "Time will tell how the saga of Lilly and Jacob plays out, but my money is on an autumn wedding. Sabina, do you care to place a wager?"

Lilly shot Ben a scathing glare. "You mean Jacob and Victoria's wedding?"

"Funny."

"Not at all, actually. But I suppose I have to get used to the idea."

"Bollocks. He won't marry that bitch. No way in hell." Sabina downed the rest of her drink. "He might have to pretend to care about her until his role in the movie is solidified, but he would *never* marry her."

"How would you know that, Sabina?" *Do I even want to know the answer to that question?*

Sabina toyed with the ice cubes in the bottom of her glass. "I shouldn't say anything. I don't want to make it any worse."

"Worse?" Lilly wailed. "How much worse can it get?" She placed her head on the table, emitting a low groan. "Just tell me. Put me out of my misery."

"Jacob and I spoke about a week ago on the phone. He told me that since he met you, all he wants is to be worthy of you…he wants to be the kind of man you would want to marry. He knew it would take time to prove himself, but he said you were worth every moment."

That did it. The dam burst and the tears spilled from Lilly's eyes, and Sabina held her friend, rocking her gently. After a few minutes, Lilly settled, blowing her nose into a napkin and wiping her eyes. "He said in a hundred lifetimes, he'd always choose me." Hot tears welled again behind Lilly's eyes. "But he didn't."

Ben and Sabina wrapped their arms around Lilly, sandwiching her in the middle. "Wait and see, darling. That man will realize he can't live without you. Then you'd better be prepared because he'll stop at nothing to make you his."

"I won't hold my breath," Lilly muttered.

"Enough tears for one evening. Let's change topics to something more fun. We need to get Lilly laid," Sabina remarked, smoothing Lilly's hair.

"Hard pass," Lilly grumbled.

"They say the quickest way to get over someone is to get under someone new," Ben added. What a helpful friend.

"Whose side are you on?" Lilly barked.

"*Your* side, darling. I won't let you go into another self-imposed yearlong celibacy. It's harmful to your health."

Lilly sputtered her drink, blowing her nose again. "I'm so glad you're not a doctor, Ben."

"He's right. You need to focus on having a good damn time. Let your hair down and live a little. I know it's too soon, but Enrique is a hell of a catch, and I don't think he would do what Jacob did."

"*Way* too soon. I'm going to grow old alone, surrounded by a hundred cats." Lilly smirked at her friend's expressions. "Fine, I'll see how I feel in a couple weeks. Give me until then to enjoy my pity party, huh?"

The friends fell out laughing, opting to table any further talk about Jacob and Lilly's sexual debacle.

They departed the bar an hour or so later, and Ben lagged behind. "Lilly, what Jacob did is inexcusable, but as a man, I really do think he's in love with you."

Lilly snorted in disbelief. "Are you insane?"

"Technically or literally?"

"Either. Why in the world would you think Jacob is in love with me?"

"You didn't see the way he watched you, the way he lit up when you were around; he looked at you as if you were the most precious creature in the world."

"What am I supposed to do with that information, Ben?"

Leaning down to kiss her cheek, he whispered. "Anything you want, my love."

Lilly walked to her car, releasing a resigned sigh as she fell back against the seat. Her mind and heart were a jumbled mess. Various accounts of the situation, Jacob's perspective, and her own emotions tumbled about in her head until she couldn't think or feel straight.

Her phone buzzed. It was Enrique. He was supposed to join them for their communal pity party, but a last-minute consult kept him late at the hospital.

"Hello, Dr. Torres."

"Good evening, Ms. Staver. Are the shenanigans still in full swing? I just got to the pub, and I don't see you."

"We left a few minutes ago. I didn't think you were going to make it. Give me a sec, and I'll come in for one more drink."

"Are you sure? If you want to head home, I understand."

His voice was soothing to her ears and her ego needed bolstering. "I'm positive."

Lilly walked back into the pub and found Enrique at a corner booth. Even in scrubs, he caught the attention of all the female patrons, but he was charmingly oblivious. She slid across from him, forcing a smile.

"I ordered you another whiskey."

Now her smile was genuine. "You know me too well."

Enrique shook his head, leaning against the seat, his dark eyes probing. "No, I don't know you well enough. So? Are you going to fill me in?"

Lilly huffed, slumping her shoulders. "I'm sure Ben already filled you in on the debacle that is my life. But please don't say 'I told you so', I realize I was an utter idiot."

"You're not an idiot, far from it. You look for the best in people and sometimes that compassion is taken advantage of by unscrupulous people." Enrique took a sip of his whiskey, shooting the waitress a dimpled smile.

"You have dimples," Lilly noted.

His smile—and dimples—widened. "I do."

"I don't know why I never noticed, perhaps you should smile more."

"Perhaps you shouldn't change the subject." Enrique swirled the whiskey in his glass, clearing his throat. "Are you in love with him?"

Lilly released a sound somewhere between a laugh and a strangled cry. How the fuck was she supposed to answer that question? "No, I was in love with the idea of him."

Enrique raised his brows but stayed silent.

"The idea of a talented, handsome, intelligent man choosing me over anyone else when he has thousands of more appealing options. I thought I was special, but I see now that it wouldn't have worked out. His sole focus is his career. My career is important, but love will always win that hand for me." Lilly scratched her thumbnail into the veneered surface of the table. "I'm a silly, romantic sap that should have known better."

Lilly gasped when Enrique clasped her hands, his thumbs moving in small circles over her skin. "He should have known better. He was an idiot to let go of a woman like you. I hate that this happened—"

Lilly rolled her eyes, letting out a chuckle. "Sure, you do. You couldn't stand him."

"Lilly, I saw through his nice guy facade. Now there is a chance he's a decent person, but his priorities are beyond screwed. He's a climber on the ladder of success, and he'll walk over anyone who gets in his way. I don't think he loves Victoria, but she can bring him the success he craves. It's like a drug for some people."

"How do you know so much?" Lilly leaned forward on her hands. She hungered for the knowledge her friend possessed.

Enrique chuckled. "That woman you met? Emma?" Lilly nodded, and he continued. "She's the female version of Jacob. I was always second-best to her job or her coworkers or her networking, and I finally said enough and left."

"Wow, she seemed so interested in you that evening, desperate to spend time with you."

Enrique ran his hand through his dark hair. "I became far more enticing when I was no longer available."

"You said she was your fuck buddy, but that isn't the case, is it?" Lilly took another sip, intrigued by Enrique's revelation. "Did you love her?"

"That's where you're lucky—you didn't love Jacob—or at least you're not telling me that you did. I did love Emma. But, as you eloquently stated, I see now I was in love with the idea of Emma; the real Emma has a lot of growing up to do."

"And if she were to grow up?"

"I don't see that happening, at least not anytime soon."

Lilly knew she should drop the subject, but she needed to understand this man's mentality. It so closely mirrored her own. "But if she did? What then?"

Enrique shot her a sad smile, taking another sip of his drink. "Only time will tell, but I'm not waiting around to see if she grows up and figures out what she needs in life…and whether I'm part of that equation."

It was a rash move, but Lilly stood and slid into Enrique's seat, wrapping her arms around the muscled surgeon. He was so different from Jacob; so honest and real. He wasn't ashamed of having feelings or letting people into his heart, even if they'd only break it. In that regard, they were two peas in a pod. "You're an incredible man, and you will find an amazing woman who doesn't have to grow up to realize what she has right in front of her. I think sometimes, we have to go through the hardships so that we realize how grand the good times truly are. Is that a silly sentiment?"

"It's a lovely sentiment, from a lovely soul." His arms tightened around her, and she found solace in his embrace. There were no fireworks, but after Jacob, she realized that fireworks may be beautiful, but they were also fleeting. "I know my happiness is out there and so is yours. Don't close off that beautiful heart. Don't let him win."

Lilly cupped his face, pressing a kiss to his lips. "Ditto for you, sir." She hesitated before pulling away, watching as Enrique's gaze moved from her eyes to her mouth.

His lips settled on hers a moment later, kind and gentle. Although Lilly knew she should stop him, her loneliness won out as his tongue slid forward to taste her. It wasn't a demanding kiss, it was soft and lovely, but she wasn't Emma, and he wasn't Jacob.

Lilly pulled back, licking her lips. "Enrique—"

"Fuck, I should not have done that. I'm sorry. I don't know what came over me. Please don't think I'm trying to take advantage of your situation. I would never do that to you."

Lilly placed her hand on his cheek, offering a small smile. "Don't apologize. Perhaps we're both lonely."

Enrique's gaze hardened at her words. "You think I still want Emma?"

"I know you still want Emma. It's written all over your face. You long for her."

Enrique grasped her hands again, squeezing her fingers. "That's where you're wrong Lilly. I don't long for Emma, not anymore. But the woman I long for has her heart tangled up with another man, one who doesn't deserve her affection."

His words turned her world sideways, and she faltered for something to say—anything meaningful, hell, anything in English at this point. Thankfully, his phone rang; it was the hospital.

"I need to return to the hospital."

"I hope you're not performing surgery after whiskey," Lilly half-joked, grateful for the interruption. She needed time to consider his statement, and her heart wasn't up to the task tonight.

Enrique laid a twenty pound note on the table and showed her his full glass. "I've only had two sips, but I'm not performing surgery." He stood up but hesitated. "Can I walk you to your car?"

Lilly nodded, and they strolled to her vehicle, a strange feeling settling over her after Enrique's admission. "This is me. Thank you for everything tonight."

"I know the bastard broke your heart and destroyed your confidence, but please bear in mind some men would walk to the ends of the earth for you."

Lilly wanted to believe that, believe him even, but her gut told her he was still nursing a broken heart himself. "Perhaps one day I'll find him."

Enrique leaned in, kissing her on the cheek. "Stop looking so hard. If someone loves you, nothing will keep them from your side. They'll break through any barriers, traverse all obstacles and wait for as long as necessary to prove their devotion. If they walk away, then they never loved you the way you deserve to be loved."

Tears sprang to Lilly's eyes as he departed, and she began the short drive to her cottage. What if Enrique was right? What if she was so busy looking for fireworks and butterflies, she missed the real and determined love of a good man? Did she have to cling to some impossible dream, or could she finally put both feet back on the ground?

All she knew for sure was when she fell for Jacob, he wasn't there to catch her, and she'd be damned if she made the same mistake again.

Janie's car sat in her driveway when Lilly arrived home. Her friend huddled on the front stoop.

Lilly sat beside her, hugging her around the shoulder. "It's chilly out here, you want to come inside?"

Janie shook her head. "I hope you're not angry with me."

"I was, initially, but a few hours and a few drinks have mellowed my stance."

"He's a mess, Lilly. I've never seen him like this, not once in my life. Jacob's always held people at arm's length or had such high standards that he bored of people within weeks. Then he met you. I knew it the first time I saw him look at you in the hospital. He never looked at anyone like that. He's never been like this with any other woman."

Lilly threw up her hands in an exasperated gesture. "Why are you telling me this, Janie? What do you want me to do?"

Janie shrugged. "I don't know! I understand why you can't give him another chance, I just hate seeing Jacob hurt." She squeezed Lilly's hand. "And seeing you hurt. It's obvious how much you two care for each other."

Lilly scoffed. "I beg to differ. It's not obvious at all from my end. He didn't choose me, Janie, he chose Victoria."

"He's trapped by Victoria, he didn't choose her. I just hope that one day he'll be free of her for good."

"I guess that decision is up to him. At least it will be easier with him being so far away, for so long."

Janie smiled sadly. "I don't think it will be easier for either of you. He calls you his angel, Lilly. I tried to fight him for the title, said you were *my* angel, but he refused to share you. He said you walking away from him was the hardest thing he's ever had to endure."

"He still let me go," Lilly choked out, tears rolling down her cheeks.

"I don't think he's let you go, not by a long shot." She pushed Lilly's hair out of her eyes. "I love you, my beautiful friend."

Lilly stood and hugged Janie. "I love you back. Lunch with Elizabeth next week?"

Janie nodded, heading to the car.

Lilly watched her friend pull away before entering her cottage, feeling numb inside. It was back to life as she knew it if that was even possible.

Her life before Jacob Edmonton was predictable and safe. Life after that man was as intoxicating and deadly as oleander. You were drawn to its beauty even when you knew it would only end in despair. But Lilly didn't regret one moment with Jacob, despite her broken heart. With Jacob, she opened the door to her soul, and in those unguarded moments, he awakened feelings in her that she didn't believe possible.

Perhaps soon, she might move on with someone capable of loving her without restriction. But for now, she needed to forget Jacob Edmonton. Problem was, Lilly's heart didn't want to forget him, and her head didn't know how.

* * *

A SERIES OF MOMENTS

From the Moment We Met

M.L. BROOME

About the Author

M.L. Broome is a bohemian spirit, but she carries her love of New York, her sarcasm and New England spirit wherever she travels. She's been writing since she was a child, but only recently garnered the courage to publish any of her works—with the assistance of her wonderfully supportive family and friends—and she is eternally grateful for the kick in the ass.

When she isn't nurturing nature, rescuing fur babies or communing with faeries, she loves spending hours by the ocean. An island native, she knows there is nothing more soothing than the sound of the waves and the salt on her skin.

She's a teller of stories, a believer in love and a lover of life. ***"You'll climb as high as you dare believe you are capable. The stars are only as far as we imagine them to be, and time is neither friend nor foe. Magic is everywhere. Life is a thing of beauty."***

www.ingramcontent.com/pod-product-compliance
Lightning Source LLC
Chambersburg PA
CBHW020942180626
46814CB00003B/898